"*The Wonder of Us* is an epic journey of love and friendship, forgiveness and possibility. And hope. So much hope. The novel itself is a beautiful wonder, and I would follow Riya and Abby anywhere."

Jennifer Niven, *New York Times* bestselling author of *All the Bright Places* and *Holding Up the Universe*

"The witty, sensitive story – with strongly drawn characters and a fun, vividly described tour – will capture and celebrate BFFs."

Booklist

"A classic case of opposites attracting, both Abby and Riya are well-drawn and dynamic characters. A nuanced, positive vision of an evolving friendship."

Kirkus

"A giddy travelogue … that should please any reader nursing dreams of European getaways."

Publishers Weekly

"Rich descriptions of European cities paired with highly emotional settings … offer readers a mature exploration of the importance and fluidity of life-long friendship."

VOYA

the Wonder of Us

KIM CULBERTSON

WALKER
BOOKS

This is a work of fiction. Names, characters, places and incidents are either the product of the author's imagination or, if real, used fictitiously. All statements, activities, stunts, descriptions, information and material of any other kind contained herein are included for entertainment purposes only and should not be relied on for accuracy or replicated as they may result in injury.

First published in Great Britain 2018 by Walker Books Ltd
87 Vauxhall Walk, London SE11 5HJ

2 4 6 8 10 9 7 5 3 1

This book has been typeset in Perpetua

Printed and bound by CPI Group (UK) Ltd, Croydon CR0 4YY

British Library Cataloguing in Publication Data:
a catalogue record for this book is available from the British Library

ISBN 978-1-4063-7717-0

www.walker.co.uk

for Peter

the first Wonder

FLORENCE, ITALY

Abby

I have a history of getting stuck in bathrooms. Back home in Yuba Ridge, I've been trapped in at least eleven different bathrooms around town. Sierra Theaters. The Gas & Shop. Dave's Deli. I got stuck six times in the Blue Market employee bathroom before Dan, my manager, made a special sign for me to hang on the doorknob so I don't have to lock it. It says, *Abby occupied, stay back!* Dan thinks he's hilarious. But it's not like I panic about it. I've grown up knowing I have a tendency to lock myself into places. A latch gets stuck. My hair gets caught on the towel hook on the back of the door (long story). The door swells and sticks. The lock spins and spins but won't open. "Ha-ha," I say when I finally emerge. "Got myself stuck in a bathroom again."

But this is the first time I've been caught in an airplane bathroom miles up in the sky. And this time, I might have panicked slightly. I might have banged too loudly on the unmoving accordion door, the metal latch not clicking back to Vacant. The poor flight attendant on the other side of the door clearly read it as panic, because she keeps saying, "Don't panic," every minute or so. "Don't panic, honey," she murmurs through the door. "I'm getting someone to help. The little lever thingy must be jammed." Jammed airplane lever thingy. Add that to the list of reasons Abby's been stuck in a bathroom. "So weird," I hear her say to someone who has come to assist her, someone who is now jiggling the door. As if I hadn't tried just jiggling it myself. "This never happens," she adds.

Figures. I can practically hear Riya saying, "Because this airplane isn't Abby-proof."

Riya.

My best friend.

Can I still call her that? I haven't seen her in person since last August, almost ten months ago. And I haven't talked to her for longer than five minutes since the end of April. Is someone still your best friend if there's a chance you don't know her anymore?

The door folds open with a whoosh. "Oof, there." The flight attendant blows a lock of black hair from her sweaty face. "Wow. You really got jammed in there. That took some effort." I'm not sure if she means the actual getting-trapped part or her work to free me. My face flames as the people sitting nearby burst into applause. Mumbling an embarrassed thank-you, I slink back to my seat.

Several hours later, the plane hums with landing noises: people waking and shifting around, wadding up their thin blankets, snapping open the airplane window blinds to let in sheets of eye-stabbing light. I sit up, tug off my glasses, and rub my eyes with my free hand. When did I doze off? I couldn't sleep for hours after getting on the plane in San Francisco, restless in my seat, so it must have only been in the last hour. Which is worse than getting no sleep at all. Groggy, I swallow thickly, and for about the tenth time since getting on the plane, read Riya's letter again:

Ab,

Yes! That other thing in your hand right now is a ticket to Florence, Italy – for you!!! Surprise! My nani is sending us on an incredible multi-city trip this summer. She's giving me my eighteenth birthday trip four months early. Two and a half weeks of European fun! I know this year has been the worst for you, and when I was telling her about it, she said we need this trip because "travel cures all ills" (sounds like her, huh?). And she will not take no for an answer. You're coming. No excuses – no: "I've got SAT classes" or "I'm working at the Blue

Market" or "I'm so mad at you right now." I know you're mad at me - I can feel the Abby-chill all the way across the Atlantic. We're both mad. And we have a million things to talk about. So don't tell me you don't have time and blah, blah, blah. If you want to fix things, you'll get on that plane! Courtesy of Bharti Nani.

Because we need this, Abby.

You have your Seven Ancient Wonders. And we have the wonders from being best friends since preschool, but here's what we need right now: We need NEW wonders. And we need to find them together. In Europe. This summer.

See what I'm doing here?!

Aren't you impressed with me?!

So pack your bags and meet me in Florence.

(Wow, I really like the sound of that, don't you?)

xoxoxoxoxox R

I fold the letter back into a square, its edges soft like tissue, thinking about the moment last summer when Riya told me she was moving to Berlin for a year with her parents. It had been an ordinary evening – could have been any one of our days spent by the river that cut through the back of Riya's property where her dad built his family a cedar-planked cabin.

I guess everything is ordinary until it's not.

We were sitting on our favorite flat rock that juts out into the water. "You don't even speak German," I said to her, the river moving its green ink around us. "You can't move to Berlin. They speak German there." I rolled onto my back, watching as the Northern California sky grew a mockingly cheerful shade of pink.

Riya sat up, crossing her legs and flipping her thick black braid down the length of her back. "Abby, they speak English, too. It's an English-speaking school. And I can learn some German." As if that explained it. As if that was enough to explain a move across the world to a German place with German buildings and German food and new German friends. "It's just a year," she said.

"Did you know the Gregorian calendar we use today was named after a pope? In 1582. Pope Gregory XIII."

"Fascinating." She shooed away a dragonfly hovering nearby. "This history tidbit brought to you by Abby Byrd, Wikipedia addict." Pawing through her ancient blue-and-white cooler, she said, "See, I'll miss that. You'll have to send me tidbits when I'm in Berlin. It can be one of our things while I'm gone." It was Riya who'd named my random history facts "tidbits" in fourth grade. That year

I'd had a borderline unhealthy obsession with Greek mythology, and, for reasons I can't remember, the crested porcupine. And the Seven Wonders of the Ancient World. That hasn't changed.

I remember Riya pulling the silver foil from the top of an organic strawberry yogurt. She licked it, folded it delicately in half, and tossed it back into the cooler. She'd been doing that exact move for years, but seeing it follow her Berlin news made me want to dive into the river's depths and pile the gray-blue stones on my back to fasten me to the bottom. There was a good chance the tiny silvery fish that darted around down there wouldn't move to Germany on me, right?

But I tried to appear cool that day. I was sixteen then, not eight. I knew I was supposed to say something like "you'll have a great time" or "how exciting" or "I wish I could take my junior year abroad," but I only wondered how you say "this sucks rocks" in German, and I didn't say anything at all. Riya didn't mind, though. My silences were as familiar to her as the river she'd grown up by.

We studied the water growing silver as the sun dipped behind the pines. Finally, she said, "If the whole world can go on after some pope changed the calendar, we can be fine for a year."

Sometimes my history tidbits backfire on me.

We haven't been fine, though. Nothing about this year has been fine.

But I can't turn back now even if I wanted to. The plane is landing. The man next to me, who still looks crisp in his black suit and white shirt, pulls a plastic bottle from his seat-back pocket and swishes water around his mouth. I do the same with my bottle, giving him a look that I hope says, *Yeah, here we are. Done this before.* Only I haven't ever done this before. I've taken two flights in my whole life: Sacramento to LA for a cousin's seaside wedding, and Sacramento to Portland, Oregon, to check out colleges for my older sister, Kate. Until today, Europe had been a multicolored blotch on my world map and the background for countless History Channel documentaries.

I stuff the worse-for-wear bottle into the seat back. I bought the Vittel water in Frankfurt, where I nearly missed my connection to Florence. Now I'm pretty sure I resemble the bottle – crumpled, drained. My jeans and black T-shirt look like I pulled them from the depths of a laundry hamper before flying in them. Funny how eighteen hours of travel can make hours feel like weeks. Still, less than a day to fly from San Francisco to Italy amazes me. In the 1600s, it took months to make this kind of crossing, maybe even a year. I resist the urge to text Riya this particular history tidbit. I'd stopped sending her much of anything these last few months.

"Il Duomo," the man murmurs, motioning at Brunelleschi's looming burnt-orange icon as the plane settles lower into

the Tuscan sky. I've seen pictures of the famous Santa Maria del Fiore, but to be suddenly *flying by it*... I must make some sort of awed noise, because the man asks, "First time in Florence?" Somehow he smells like citrus and cinnamon, which is impressive after such a long flight. I'm pretty sure I can smell my own feet.

"Yes, I'm meeting a friend." The plane bumps down. Italy. My head spins. I've crossed an ocean to meet Riya in Florence, where she'll be waiting for me after customs. Customs! I've never been off the West Coast and soon I'll be clearing customs in Italy. Maybe it was better when it took months to get here. Made you feel like you'd earned it.

When I peel my eyes away from the window, the man waits in the aisle, his black bag smartly tucked under his arm. *"Ciao."* He winks as the line begins to move sluggishly toward the exits. I bet he never gets trapped in airplane bathrooms. I tug my bag from the overhead bin (*pack light,* Riya had said, *some layers, we'll shop!*) and follow the other weary passengers off the plane.

I don't recognize Riya at first. She's cut her waist-length hair and it's not just her usual trim. It's half a foot shorter and has actual layers, touseled but purposely so. She wears a plum-colored tank dress with a chunky belt, dangly silver earrings, and aviator glasses.

Apparently, Europe looks good on Riya.

"Abby!" she squeals, spotting me, and hurries to engulf

me in a floral-scented hug. After a year, after this stupid, harsh year, I thought I might be too angry to hug her, to pretend we aren't furious with each other, to act like we never said all those things the last time we talked, but it's Riya and she's hugging me, and I've missed her so much and I'm exhausted from the travel and from this year, so I melt into her. After a moment, she steps back, takes my bag, and slings it over her shoulder. "How was the flight?"

Exhausted, I babble random history thoughts at her. "I couldn't stop thinking about how a hundred years ago, people were just starting to consider that a transatlantic flight was possible. Weird, right?" Nodding, Riya tries to follow my line of thought as she leads me toward the airport exit. "I mean, I couldn't stop thinking about Charles Lindbergh and the *Spirit of St. Louis* and how he was just alone up there in the sky above all that dark water."

As we walk into the hot Italian air, Riya takes my hand. "I missed you."

"Missed you more."

Riya

In the back of the taxi, I study Abby as we speed toward the city center. She looks exhausted, and I know it's not just the long day of travel etched in those dark smudges beneath her eyes. It's worse than I thought. I poke her. "Try to stay awake. We'll hit the hotel so you can change into something cooler, and then we'll go to dinner. Seriously, you have never tasted pasta like this – try not to sleep until at least ten."

Abby slouches into the worn leather of the taxi seat, fighting her heavy lids. "Does jet lag feel like the stomach flu?"

"It can." As Abby's eyes slip shut, I jostle her again. "Don't sleep!"

She jolts, eyes wide, and tugs at her black T-shirt. "Ugh, it's humid." She motions to the driver. "Can he turn on the air?"

I shake my head. "Get used to no air-conditioning. It's actually better. Just let your body acclimatize to the heat."

"How is sweating like a farm animal better?"

I grin – there's my Abby. As she paws through her bag, I notice an entire box of full-size Reese's Peanut Butter Cups. "What you got there?" I motion to the box.

"Oh, that sounds good, actually." She tears open the box and grabs an orange package. "Maybe the sugar will wake me up."

I watch her unwrap the candy. "Did you think they wouldn't have sugar in Italy?"

She unpeels a cup and takes a bite. "It was a gift. From Dan. He said when he went to Europe, it was super hard to find peanut butter anything."

"Yet somehow I survived."

She ignores this. "Want one?"

I take the other cup. "Glad to see Dan's still encouraging healthy eating habits in his employees."

"Don't start on Dan."

Abby's been weirdly protective of her boss since she started working at the Blue Market in her freshman year, so I don't say anything more. "Here." I hand her a bottle of water. "Stay hydrated."

"Thanks." She takes a drink, her eyes tracking the road ahead of us. "So, why Florence?"

I hesitate. She made it clear when we fought in April that she was sick of my Europe stories. So I keep it short. "I came here last year with my parents and just couldn't wait to come back." Then I sweeten the deal. "You're going to love all the history stuff. And the gelato."

This gets the flicker of a smile. "And after Florence?"

"It's a surprise. I'll tell you when we're about to head to the next stop."

"Seriously? You're still not going to tell me where we're going?"

"It's more fun this way!"

"For who?" She frowns out the window. I knew this would bother her, not knowing our full itinerary, but it's good for her to be surprised. Abby always takes too much on with planning things. She's usually the one helping Dan sort out the Blue Market schedule or making sure her dad books camping reservations for our favorite Lake Tahoe spot six months in advance. It's time for her to just sit back and relax. Not an easy task. A funny look steals across her face as she glances back at me. "Do my parents know where our next stop is going to be?"

I know what she's doing. "My mom sent them our itinerary, but don't ask your dad to tell you. That's cheating."

She turns back to the window, the dark look lowering her lids again. "I wasn't going to do that." Yes, she was.

"Speaking of your parents, did you let them know you landed?"

Abby caps the water, tucking it into her backpack. "Both of them. I have to do everything twice now because they can't handle being on a group text together."

My stomach twists. “I’m really sorry, Abby. We were so shocked. My parents didn’t even believe me when I told them.” I glance down at the text my mom just sent. “They say hi, by the way.”

“Hi, Anju and Dean,” Abby sighs. She looks hollowed out like a pumpkin. I’ve heard traces of it in her voice since January, but seeing her now makes me wish I’d flown home last spring instead of just letting her tell me that she was fine. That things were fine. They clearly weren’t.

I follow her gaze. The outskirts of Florence slip by: plain apartment buildings with clothes flung over railings, squat storefronts, the giant Coop sign with the clock announcing 18:24. A few more hours and then I’ll let Abby sleep. “I wish you’d told me how bad things were.”

Abby’s eyes slide to mine. Even as hot as it is, she gives off her trademark chill, what my dad calls her “Abby Armor.” She shrugs. “It is what it is.”

Typical Abby. She doesn’t like to dredge things up. But we haven’t talked about our fight, or about the silence since, and we’ll need to before this trip is over. Such a stupid fight. I’ve gone over it in my head a million times. I Skyped at the end of April, just to say hi, and she was red-eyed, distracted, so I tried for overly upbeat, hoping to coax a smile out of her, telling her how I’d tagged along with Mom on a business trip to London, how much I’d loved the city, but before I could finish,

Abby snapped, "You know what, Riya? You'll excuse me if I'm not really in the mood to hear you brag about your jet-setting lifestyle right now. I'm busy living in the sucky real world."

Her words shot through me, and I blinked into the screen, stung by her hard stare. In all of our years as best friends, in all of our school years and sleepovers and vacations and summer camps, she never snapped at me like that. Before I could stop them, my own terrible words spilled out. "You're not the only one in the world whose parents are getting a divorce, you know? You're acting like you invented it." She ended the Skype call, and I imagined her slamming the laptop screen shut. The next day, I sent three texts. Unanswered. I tried FaceTime. Nothing. Skype. Nothing. Forget it, I thought. I'm busy, too. My life wasn't all trips to London this year. I'd dealt with tough things, too. She was acting like her problems were the only ones in the entire universe.

After three days of silence, I texted: you're being so immature. grow up!

Not the best thing to say. But it got her attention.

She immediately texted back: i hope you stay in germany.

I threw my phone across my bedroom, where it hit the wall, the screen cracking. I've been carrying around that visible crack ever since.

After that terrible text, we didn't have any form of

communication for three weeks. It was the longest I'd ever gone without talking to her. Finally, I express-mailed her the package for our trip and waited.

A week later, she called to say she would meet me in Florence the last week of June. "Thanks for the drawing," she added, her voice quiet, hard to read. "It's hanging on my board." Along with the letter and a printout of her ticket, I'd sent a picture I sketched of the Lighthouse of Alexandria, her favorite wonder, only I'd drawn it looming over our own river back in Yuba Ridge. I pictured her tacking it to the layers of pictures and concert ticket stubs and other paraphernalia Abby keeps on an enormous, messy bulletin board in her room.

We've texted off and on again since, but nothing real. Just trip stuff. What to pack. What the weather might be like in Florence. Little pebbles to rebuild the crumbled bridge between us.

Now Abby watches the modern buildings move past us. "This isn't how I imagined Florence."

"Just wait."

Soon, the scenery shifts from the more modern outskirts to the historic center of the city, the buildings going back in time, turning into towers and arches and wide stone, the colors muted with sepia tones. Abby perks up, sitting forward, practically pressing her nose flat to the glass. Abby's history addiction spans *much* wider than Wikipedia and history tidbits. Sitting here, I can sense her excitement for the history passing by us, but I feel something else there, too, the faint trace of the invisible ribbon that has always connected us. I can't help but smile. This is exactly what we need. This will fix us.

The taxi driver stops at the corner of Via del Proconsolo and Via del Corso. "We're going to the Albergo Firenze," I tell him, frowning.

"You walk from here." He motions vaguely in the direction of the hotel. "Is close."

We step out onto the buzzing street corner, hauling Abby's duffel and backpack out with us. I'd checked in earlier and it's not *that* close, our hotel. As we start walking, a group of young Italian guys wave to us, offering to help carry our bags, but I wave them off: *"No grazie."* They mime being seriously wounded by our rejection. Abby's eyes go wide at their exaggerated pouts, and I laugh. "Get used to it."

We trudge through the hot sun. I turn to point out the hotel awning up ahead, but Abby's fallen behind, kneeling next to a scruffy beige dog, scratching him affectionately behind his fanlike ears. His owner, an old man in trousers, a matching vest, and long-sleeved white shirt beams down at them. She sees me waiting, gives the dog a final scratch, and catches up. "Cute dog."

"You're here ten minutes and you find a dog to cuddle."

"They find me."

"Of course." I tug her toward the awning. Almost there.

At the hotel entrance, she pauses, turning to me. "I can't believe this, Riya. I can't believe we're in Italy. I will never be able to thank your grandma enough." She looks more stunned than happy.

"You can thank her by loving it here, by seeing the sights and shopping and eating great food, okay?" I usher her through the front door. "Come on. This hotel is next to the Torre dei Donati, where Dante's wife was born. Just one of the soon-to-be-many fabulous history tidbits you will learn on this trip."

My promise draws a smile to Abby's face, even if it looks like a ghost there.

Abby

"Riya, slow down. It's too hot to walk this fast." The whine in my voice seems directly linked to the amount of sweat running down my back. "Are we in a hurry?"

Riya looks distracted, stops short, and then pulls me across the street, barely missing a shirtless man on a Vespa. "We're almost at the café."

I catch a quick flash of a dramatic-looking arch up ahead, but then we duck down a side street and it's gone. "It doesn't seem very Italian. All this hurrying," I grumble, glad I changed into the yellow sundress of Kate's she'd told me to take because I'd "live in it" while I was in Italy. Kate spent a month in Rome after her sophomore year of college so I guess she knows.

"Neel is a little fussy about punctuality."

"Neel?" I stop, grabbing Riya's elbow. "Wait, your cousin Neel? British Neel? *Percy?*"

Riya chews her lip, her liquid eyes darting to the side. "Okay, so it's not going to be just us on this trip."

I squint at her, my eyes feeling almost sticky with exhaustion. "Right, your grandma is going to be with us."

"Not exactly."

She tugs me into a café, its windows a rainbow of stained glass. We blink into the dim light inside, Riya searching the room until she spots her cousin. Riya has long described Neel as an Indian Percy Weasley, that bossy redhead from the Harry Potter series. Even though Riya has spent time with Neel in London and India, he's never been to California, so I've never met him. In my mind he's drawn from Riya's stories about her know-it-all cousin and the pictures of the skinny, sullen kid in glasses always toting a show-offy leather-bound book or cricket bat or some other prop you might see on a PBS period drama. Now Riya waves to a cute, preppy guy across the café. "Wait," I whisper. "*That's* Neel?"

"Ugh, I'll explain later."

"Hello, ladies," he says when we arrive at his table in the back corner. "How nice of you to finally make it."

"We're fashionably late." Riya smiles in an overly sweet way and settles into a chair next to him.

"I ordered," he says, snapping a napkin into his lap.

"For all of us?"

"Of course not."

Riya rolls her eyes. "Neel, this is Abby. Abby, Neel Sharma."

Flashing white, even teeth, he leans across the table to shake my hand (who does that?) and says, "A pleasure," like he's forty instead of nineteen.

I mumble something sleep-deprived and unintelligible as Riya gets the waiter's attention and orders something for the two of us. I sink into my chair, the soft light and savory smells infusing the air adding to the dizzy sensation of needing sleep. Maybe I can just nap under the table until the food comes. I reach for some bread, hoping that chewing might keep me awake.

"So, I thought we'd set up some ground rules for the trip," Neel says crisply, scooting his chair back and folding his hands in his lap. He's wearing slim pants and loafers and doesn't seem warm at all, even as I can feel sweat beading on my upper lip.

Riya grimaces. "No way, that's not how this works. It's my grand tour and you're not the cruise director."

This wakes me up. "Your what?"

"My grand tour," she says mysteriously. Then she narrows her eyes at Neel. "A gift from Nani *to me* as an early birthday present. You had yours already."

"Except I had to actually turn eighteen to get mine," Neel points out.

My sleep-deprived brain tries to catch up. "Wait, where is your grandma? I thought she was taking us?" A waiter sets what looks like half a pan of lasagna in front of Neel.

He picks up his fork. "Our grandmother is traveling in

Scotland for a month," Neel explains. "So I have the honor of being your tour guide for this trip."

Riya shakes her head. "Not guide. Chaperone. That's it. No guiding, no telling us a schedule, no dictating the restaurants or sights we choose. You follow us around and make sure no one kills us. That is all."

"So I'm kind of like Batman." Neel winks at me over his lasagna, and I can't help but smile back. Riya has called him many things over the years. She left out charming.

Only Riya doesn't seem to find him charming. "You are nothing like Batman. You are, at best, Batman's butler guy. What's his name?"

"Alfred," Neel and I say in unison, and he grins at me.

Riya glances between us. "Don't encourage him," she tells me.

Neel raises his glass of red wine at me. "Cheers."

"No cheers." Riya waves off his glass. "Are you perfectly clear on your job description?"

Neel sets down his glass and looks at me. "You'll excuse my cousin for being rude. She's never gotten over my win at the sack race at my sister's wedding five years ago."

Riya makes room for the waiter to set down a plate of steaming pasta. She points her fork at Neel. "Because you cheated?"

"Did you cheat?" I ask Neel. "Tell the truth."

"I most certainly did not."

Riya groans and digs violently into her pasta. I take a bite of mine and am grateful for the delicious burst of flavor because I'm trying to ignore the buzz in my stomach that started when Neel first smiled at me and hasn't gone away since.

After dinner, we walk to the Arno, the lights wriggling across the night water of the river, and I try to stay awake, to take in the hum of this new city pulsing around me. When I first hear the distant ping of bells, I think my ears must be ringing. Some sort of by-product from the jet lag. But then the jingling intensifies behind me, and I have a flash of Santa bearing down behind me in his sleigh.

It's not Santa.

I step aside to allow a jangling gaggle of people clad in masks and vibrant costumes to hurry by us. "What the—"

Her eyes bright, Riya watches them shuffle down the street. She grins at me. "You should see your face right now."

"Did I just dream that?"

"No. That was real. Probably commedia dell'arte actors. Off to do a show in a square somewhere. We can try to find them later if you want."

"Commedia dell – what?" I peer at the space where they disappeared down a side street, their ringing growing faint before dissipating entirely.

"It's an old form of Italian theater," Riya says. "With stock characters. They improv a loose script based on the reactions of their audience."

I squint at her. "Why do you know that?"

"Who wants gelato?" Neel cuts in, motioning to a small *gelateria* nearby.

A few minutes later, we stand at the glass case, staring at the dozens of bright rectangular mounds of gelato. The colors swirl in front of me, my tired eyes trying to decipher the names. *Fragola. Cocco. Stracciatella. Amarena.*

I frown into the case. "I'm not sure I can eat anything else after that dinner."

But I'm wrong.

We find a bench where we can sit and see the water. From my first bite, I know that I have found love in Italy. And its name is gelato.

"What is in this? This is the most delicious thing I've ever eaten in my entire life," I say, between mouthfuls of my chocolate-and-cream mix.

Riya grins. "Try the coconut." She holds out her cone, and I take a lick. Neel makes a face from where he stands a few feet away. "What?" she asks him.

He takes a careful bite of his hazelnut. "Nothing."

"You are such a germophobe." Riya tries mine and laughs at Neel's grimace. "Seriously, it bothers you?"

He shakes his head, clearly disgusted. "All very hygienic, I'm sure."

“She’s like my sister.” Riya catches a drip before it lands on my dress.

“Glad I stand firmly in the cousin position, then.”

Riya jumps up and pretends to descend on his cone. “Aw, come on, Neel, let me try yours.”

We both giggle at his discomfort as he turns in circles, attempting to keep it away from her. “Just stop.” He holds it up over his head. Changes hands. “Stop it, Riya.”

“Aw, come on.” Riya takes more swipes at it. “It looks yummy. Let me try it.”

“Fine, try it.” And before she can react, he has planted it straight into her face. He looks almost as shocked as she does. When he pulls it back, her nose and mouth are covered with sticky cream, her mouth a wide O of disbelief.

Her eyes narrow to slits. “You did not just do that.”

“You wanted to try it.” He glances at me. “Right?”

Waving him off, I say, “I’m not getting involved.” Then I add, “But it doesn’t seem like a very chaperone-y thing to do. Are you sure you’re up for this?”

He takes in Riya’s livid face, her coiled body ready to spring, but he’s too quick; he manages to dodge her just in time as she hurls herself at him, and they take off down the sidewalk, Riya chasing him with her own cone poised and ready.

He moves surprisingly fast for a guy in loafers.

Riya

It's after ten when I half carry Abby back to the hotel so she can get some sleep. When we finally reach the Via del Corso, she's moving like an extra from a zombie movie, nearly colliding with other people or a streetlamp, tripping over her own feet, her glasses askew. I resist the urge to laugh. We must be quite the pair: Zombie Girl and Gelato Face.

Upstairs, I wash off the remaining sticky mess. We brush our teeth and change into pajamas. Abby falls into the narrow bed near the bathroom. I watch her for a minute, her breathing evening out into a steady rhythm. Abby has slept like this for as long as I can remember, on her side in a curl like a comma. I pull the duvet over her, envying how quickly she's out. There's no way I'm sleeping before midnight tonight. Stupid Neel and his *you wanted to try it, Riya*. Tour guide. More like tour dictator. The fascist kind. Every muscle in my body is a clenched fist. Even worse, I missed Neel when I chucked my cone at him before. That's a miss *and* a loss of delicious gelato. Double fail. On the walk back, I texted my dad to complain and he said not to let Neel get to me. Easier texted than actually done. Trying to relax, I pull a wooden chair next to the open window as quietly as possible. Outside, warm lights dot the rows of buildings along the Via del Corso and snippets of conversation float up through the air. Italian. French. A man bellows in German, *was geht*, which I recognize as *what's up?* I've learned a few things this year.

Like, a year can be terribly long and aggressively quick at the same time.

When we left for Berlin in late August, Abby's dad, Geoff, had driven us to the airport in Sacramento. We'd shipped most of our things ahead of us, so we only had a few carry-on bags. Abby and I stood hugging on the sidewalk by the passenger drop-off, the Sacramento air hot around us. At the time we promised to check in every day, and for the first month or so, we did. She kept me updated on school and work and, sometimes, things happening with kids we knew at Yuba Ridge High. I texted pictures of the intense new city I'd landed in: of the vibrant, ubiquitous graffiti; of massive buildings where modern new ones were built towering over historic ones; of food vendors selling fresh pretzels and currywurst; of the dark swirl of the Spree River at night.

Then it stopped being every day. It would be every two or three days. It would be once a week. At first, we tried to Skype at least twice a week. Then it was once. We sent gifts at Christmas. On New Year's Eve, we'd Skyped at midnight, both for my New Year's Eve and then again for hers. But a few days later, she called to tell me about her parents, her voice like a shadow. My family was sitting at our table in the Berlin apartment, the sky outside like steel in the winter light. Mom was slicing a loaf of sweet bread Dad had bought from a nearby bakery. As she listened to my end of the conversation, her brow knitted in concern, and she set down the knife. "What?" she mouthed. I held the phone against my chest. "Abby's parents are splitting up."

Now Abby's phone beeps, glowing on the floor next to her bed. A picture of her German shepherd, Henry, fills the screen. I tiptoe over to see who sent the text. It's her dad wanting to know how things are going.

I text: geoff, it's riya. abby's crashed out.

I take a picture of her and send it to him.

He texts back: Sleep is good! Just wondered about your first day in Florence?

Me: fabulous. pasta. gelato. a walk by the arno.

Geoff: Rough life.

Me: sure is.

Geoff: Yuba Ridge misses you, kid.

I pause at this, opting for a smiling heart-eyed face and an off to bed! text. A ribbon of guilt moves through me at what an honest reply would have been.

Because I don't really miss Yuba Ridge.

I set Abby's phone back down and breathe in the warm Italian night – just not too deeply since the Florence air seems to smell slightly like pee. Which I guess is like most cities in the summer. Still, the air also has something sweet in it. Something like a promise. From the moment Nani offered this trip, I instantly suggested we start in Florence, with its buttery light and gelato and the entire city bursting with shopping and beauty and something new around every twisting street. When I came with my parents last fall, it struck me as a city I would want to return to time after time in my life, with its magical ability to feel both brand-new and familiar. Its dreamy hold is the perfect place to spend the first few days of our trip while Abby shakes her jet lag. She doesn't know it yet, but in the next two and a half weeks, we'll tour six cities, exploring the nightlife and history and art and food across the constellation of places I've mapped out for us.

Now it's my phone buzzing with a text, and I hurry to grab it from the dresser.

Neel: Uffizi tomorrow morning.

I send back: you're not in charge!

Neel: I booked us a tour. You can thank me later.

Me: turning my phone off!

Too bad I can't turn off the sour twist in my stomach when I think about having to share this trip with Neel. When Mom told me he'd be coming along as our chaperone, I'd begged for her or Dad to come instead, but Nani had already asked Neel, and Mom insisted we'd have more fun with him along. "No one has *ever* had more fun with Neel along," I said, sulking, silently pleased at the belly laugh I elicited from Dad in the next room. He knows Neel is worse than having a grown-up with us. Which is probably part of their evil plan.

As Abby snores in her thin, even rhythm, my theatrical thoughts send a second, smaller flicker of guilt through me. There is no evil plan. Just Nani sending me and my best friend on a fabulous trip. And I'm sitting here like an ingrate thinking murderous thoughts about my annoying cousin. So what if he has to come as part of the deal? We'll have an incredible time – a *grand* time on our grand tour. How many people get this kind of opportunity? Not many. I sit up straighter in the chair. Nothing will ruin it, especially not Neel and all his Neel-ness. I won't let him.

A sheet of paper whooshes under the door.

UFFIZI TOUR 9 A.M. SHARP.
8 A.M. IN THE LOBBY.
DON'T BE LATE.

Annoyance returns like a geyser, and I shred the paper into a pile of tiny confetti pieces on the floor.

Abby

The rumbling sound of what can only be the second coming of Pompeii jolts me awake. I sit up in the gray early-morning light of the hotel room, the duvet a tangle at the foot of the bed, and try to locate the source of the horrible noise. If jet lag has a noise, it sounds like this.

Of course, Riya sleeps through it in her bed near the window. A truck could drive across her head and she wouldn't wake up. She's always been like that. Whenever we'd camp in Tahoe over the years, every snap of a twig would leave me wide-eyed, pulling my sleeping bag to my chin, but Riya would snore on next to me, her black hair a bramble across the pillow. This trip will prove no different, I'm sure.

I pad across the room and peer out in time to see a street sweeper make its way down the empty street. We appear to be the only souls awake. Then it hits me. I'm in Florence. *Italy*. It sends an eager shiver through me. I check my phone and notice Dad's texts with Riya last night. Wow, I must have really been out. I do a quick calculation of the time change. Florence is nine hours ahead and it's 4:10 a.m. here so it must be 7:10 p.m. at home. Dad would be just finishing dinner.

I text him: just woke up to a street sweeper that sounds like you snoring only like fifty times louder.

A minute later he writes: Must feel homey. I just heated up one of your frozen enchilada trays!

Me: don't eat the whole thing.

Dad: I just might. You made me too much food!

I suddenly ache for my own bed and a street without sweepers and enchiladas that have black *and* pinto beans and the guacamole I make from scratch. I probably won't be able to find a single enchilada in all of Italy.

Me: make sure you take the foil off before you put it in the microwave.

Dad: Not my first enchilada!

Me: okay. i'm going to try to sleep again.

Dad: Good luck! I'm going to turn in early tonight. Your exciting old dad will be out by eight...

Me: bye, love you.

Dad: Love you back.

He's not joking about the sleeping thing. Ever since Mom left last January, he sleeps a lot. Like maybe he'll wake up one day and she won't be dating our dentist and acting like we should all just be happy to go to family therapy together, be happy she's "found" herself.

We hadn't known she was lost.

I try to go back to sleep, but a couple of hours later, I can't stand it anymore, so I slip on my glasses, the yellow sundress, and my Tevas, and head downstairs. Neel is drinking coffee in the small breakfast area of the hotel. He reads a newspaper, his brow knitted.

"You're up early," I say, checking my phone. 6:42.

"Some monstrous machine woke me at four. It was touch and go after that."

"Same." I browse the breakfast table – a selection of breads and pastries, some baskets of butters and jams – but mostly use it as an excuse to study Neel. For someone who couldn't sleep, he seems fresh and alert in a pale green polo shirt and the pants and loafers from last night. Maybe it's the espresso. "Where'd you get that?" I point to his cup.

He flags a woman in a crisp white shirt and motions to his coffee and then to me. She nods and hurries from the room.

I slip into a seat next to him. "Thanks." He returns to his paper, the *Guardian*. "Anything interesting?"

"Probably not to you." He sips his espresso.

"Wow, big assumption for so early in the morning." The woman sets down my own steaming cup and the smell of it makes my eyes cross. "Um, do you have milk?" She motions to the breakfast station. After pouring as much milk as the tiny cup will hold and sipping it down (strong!) to pour in some more, I return to the table.

Neel is watching me, his paper folded in half. "I'm reading about the economic impact of refugees in the UK. I'm studying economics at uni. I'm sure Riya's mentioned it."

"Riya doesn't really talk about you." I enjoy telling him this more than I probably should. "Are you interested in the refugees themselves or just their economic impact? Your country has an interesting history on that front, as you know."

He blinks. "As does yours."

"Fair enough." I stir sugar into my coffee with a tiny spoon and then go in search of some pastries, bringing a full plate back to our table. "It seems like it's a constant balancing act between the human rights issue and the economic one, don't you think? And I always lean toward the human rights side of things, but that's just me." I take a big bite of a croissant. He blinks again, not bothering to hide his surprise, and I grin at him through the pastry. I actually wrote a paper on this exact topic for AP History last year, but he doesn't have to know that. He can think I just pulled that one right out of the Italian air.

He leans forward in his seat. "Riya tells me you're quite the history aficionado."

"I like older things." A heated flush follows the words out of my mouth. What did I just say? What if he thinks I meant *him*?

He considers me for a moment, and I try to focus on

eating enough croissant to offset the thick coffee. That and not making eye contact. Finally, he snaps his paper back open. "Well, today will be full of older things, I should think." Just when I might be in the clear, he leans in, adding, "At the minimum, I'll be along for the ride."

As we hurry left on Via del Corso, Neel points out the arch in Piazza della Repubblica, but Riya just grumbles something about how he could have woken her up sooner. "I texted you," he tells her. "But you turned off your mobile."

Glowering, she marches on, mumbling about espresso. She didn't have time for coffee, and the lack of it fuels her sour mood. We turn left again onto Via dei Calzaiuoli, passing a string of shops I don't recognize. Furla. Wolford. Coin. When Riya slows in front of Coin, her face full of longing, I hang back to wait for her.

"It's not going anywhere," Neel says over his shoulder. "We're late."

"I didn't book this tour," she tells me.

"We can shop soon," I insist. "And I can't wait to see the Uffizi."

Her expression softens until Neel shouts at us to hurry again.

As we follow him toward the Piazza della Signoria, I try to drink in every detail of Florence around me, even at this fast-forward speed. After a few more minutes,

Riya calls, "I need coffee. There's a shop right—"

"You should have gotten up earlier," Neel cuts her off, and picks up the pace.

She motions as if she's strangling him. "If I wanted this much cardio," she grumbles, "I would find an Italian spin class!"

"What's the big deal?" I hang back with her. "You barely used to drink a mocha."

"Well, now I drink double espressos," she snaps.

Grouchy much? I keep silent and trudge on after Neel. Soon we're facing the Palazzo Vecchio, the Uffizi looming next to us. The line already snakes along the massive columned building, but Neel hurries past it. "Private tour," he tells one of the museum staff near the entrance, and she points him in the right direction.

I nudge Riya. "Private tour, swanky-swanky."

She exaggerates wiping the sweat from her forehead. "Is sweaty the new swanky? Seriously, next time you guys have to come wake me up. It's bad enough Neel hijacked our day with a nine o'clock tour, but now I'm all sweaty and gross."

"So, just the sweat is out of the ordinary, then?" Neel quips before moving off to find our guide.

She glares after him. "I swear I will throw him in the Arno and not feel remorse. Him and his old-man pants."

"You're fun this morning. But you don't look gross," I assure her. Actually, she's adorable in her purple dress and belt from yesterday. I take a deep breath and look around the piazza. I feel better today, fresher, even with the early wake-up, and I have the buzz I get in my stomach when I'm about to go to a museum. And not just any museum. The Uffizi in Florence! Home of pieces by Michelangelo, Caravaggio, Botticelli, and so many other mega-famous artists.

Riya rubs her temples. "Would it have been so hard to stop for a coffee?"

Let it go about the coffee. I tuck a loose strand of hair from my ponytail behind my ear, sweat already forming at my hairline. "I don't feel sorry for you. I've been up since the crack of street cleaner."

She eyes me. "And you think *I'm* fun in the morning?" When I shrug, her voice softens. "This is Neel's fault. He's driving me crazy."

"Really? I couldn't tell."

"I promise Neel won't get to run our whole schedule. This trip is for us." She drops her gaze, a pained look creeping across her features. "I know we need to talk."

"I know, too." My phone rings, the name *Stephanie Byrd* emerging on the screen.

Riya notices. "You can pick up. We have time."

I shake my head, slipping the unanswered phone into my backpack. "I'm really looking forward to this tour."

Riya holds my gaze. "You know what would be cute? You should change the caller ID for your parents to Papa

Byrd and Mama Byrd. Then you could be Baby Byrd."

"Do you remember that book we used to read in preschool?" I ask her. "That one where the baby bird wanders around looking for its mom?"

"*Are You My Mother?* I loved that book."

"Right. It sees the dog and the cow and stuff and keeps asking, 'Are you my mother?'"

Riya laughs. "I think it even asks a plane."

I nod. "I've been feeling like that baby bird for months."

Riya glances toward the hidden phone in my backpack. "Abby—"

"Okay, ladies. Tour time." Neel returns with our guide in tow. Matteo – a squat, middle-aged Italian man with a wild amount of reddish-brown hair. He's like a suit-wearing grown-up version of one of Rafael's little cherubs. We start our tour through the lavish space of the Uffizi, the hours melting into the past as we roam the different rooms – international Gothic, the light and dark of the early Renaissance, Filippo Lippi, Leonardo da Vinci – one recognizable name after the next. Seeing them all in one place catches my breath in my chest. Matteo is a patient and informative guide and doesn't seem to mind the dozens of questions I ask, even random ones like, "Filippo Lippi married a nun, right?"

Studying another painting commissioned by the Medici family, Neel comments, "The concept of patronage is so interesting; I mean, how many of these works would exist without the elite class financing them?"

Riya groans and wanders off into the next room. I hurry to catch her. "You okay?"

"Sure, just kind of want to take it all in." That's not what she's doing. I know she has always preferred the osmosis approach to any experience, to soak it all in instead of focusing on facts, but she's visibly annoyed at Neel's presence and clearly letting it get to her.

We continue on, finally stopping in front of *The Birth of Venus*. Matteo motions to the famous curves of her body as she stands demurely on her shell. When he finishes talking, he steps aside so we can study the painting. Neel leans into me. "You must be especially interested in the role of antiquity in Renaissance art."

I try to see the brushstrokes Matteo just mentioned. "I am, yes."

He peers at the Botticelli. "It's impressive when a young person values history. Usually, teenagers are too self-absorbed to see the importance."

"*You're* a teenager," I remind him, but he's moved away to ask Matteo another question about the meaning of the Zephyrs in the painting, so I drift over to where Riya stands studying a smaller painting on a far wall. Adopting a fake British accent, I murmur, "Speaking of patronage, your cousin can be quite the patronizing arse." We break into the sort of giggle fit that prompts Matteo to hurry us into the next room.

Eventually, we make our way out of the Uffizi through the Vasarian Corridor, and Matteo's voice lowers into a dramatic hush. "We're now truly walking in the footsteps of the Medici family. This corridor linked them to their private palace, the Palazzo Pitti," he explains. My skin tingles as I study the portraits lining the walls, their faces stern and powerful. This place feels haunted, though I don't say so to Riya. I tease her about her fierce belief in ghosts, but in places like these I start believing in them, too. These people were powerful and greedy and rich. And some of them, if you believe Matteo's tour info, died in pretty sketchy ways. Those kinds of spirits hang around. I stop, closing my eyes for a moment, waiting for that history shiver I sometimes get in places like this one.

"Boo!" Riya jumps at me from behind. I start, letting out a little yelp. "Gotcha. This place is totally haunted."

"Oh, yes," Matteo murmurs solemnly, coming up alongside us. "It is haunted."

Outside, Matteo helps us skip another line before we step into the green expanse of the Boboli Gardens. He gives us a quick history of the gardens and I hear, just in the edges of it, the rehearsed quality of his speech. Mopping his brow with a white handkerchief, he smiles. "Please, enjoy the gardens at your leisure." He waves us on, tucking the cloth back into his suit pocket. We take a few uncertain steps, used to being pulled in his wake the last few hours, but he is checking his watch, off to his next tour, and we're suddenly alone.

The Boboli Gardens spread out around me, and I can't help but feel like I've just stepped back in time into the Hanging Gardens of Babylon, one of the Seven Wonders of the Ancient World. It's hard not to. Once, Riya tried to help me make a replica of the hanging gardens in my backyard, but we accidentally flooded the deck when we tried to re-create the various waterfalls the gardens supposedly had. Dad wasn't too happy when he came out to read a book in his gravity chair only to find it partly submerged in a pool of muddy water.

Riya reads my mind. "Remember when we flooded the deck?"

"Dad turned three different shades of red."

She grimaces. "Yeah, he wasn't a happy daddy that day."

He's not a happy daddy now.

I almost didn't come on this trip it's been so bad. When Mom first left, he wore the same jeans and flannel shirt for two weeks until I forced him to change. Then he got a haircut and went back to his job as a city planner. At night, though, he sat in front of the TV watching documentaries and golf. And he doesn't even play golf. I did all the laundry and cooking for two months before he started to realize we needed things like groceries and toilet paper. With my bagging job at the Blue Market, it was easy for me to bring that stuff home, but it was like he didn't even *notice*. He's been better the last couple of months, but I hope he's okay with me gone.

I shake the thought from my head. I'm in Italy, I remind myself. I need to focus on these beautiful gardens. After about five minutes of taking it all in, I break our wandering silence. "The Hanging Gardens of Babylon are the only one of the ancient wonders whose location can't be proven. Some people doubt they existed at all."

Riya points out a beautiful urn, dripping with green vines. "I know. You may have mentioned it once or twice. Or a thousand times."

I give her a playful shove. "Well, I'm mentioning it again and pleading relevance. Look at this place. You did this on purpose. This is our first wonder, right? This garden."

She pulls me to a nearby bench. "Okay, I know how your mind works, so I'm going to say this now. I didn't *plan* any wonders. Part of this trip was so we could create new wonders, but I want them to happen naturally in each of the cities we go to. Maybe it will be this garden, or maybe it will be something else."

I pull off a sandal and rub the ball of my foot. Even my supposed walking sandals aren't holding up on all these cobblestones and uneven ground. "Well, this heat will not be one of my wonders."

Neel appears on the path near us. "Let's go, ladies. No time for sitting around."

I whisper in Riya's ear. "Your cousin will definitely *not* be one, either."

She nods. "I told you. The Arno. Splash."

Later that evening, Neel continues to prove this. "Seriously, he's trying to kill us." I lean heavily on the stone edge of the bridge, watching the sunset turn the water of the Arno into the blue-purple of a bruise. Every cell in my body throbs with our day – the Uffizi, the gardens, a walking tour of Florence, the heat a constant press around us. And I'm pretty sure I'm still sticky with jet lag. At one point in the late afternoon, Riya just plopped down in the middle of a cobbled street and refused to get up until Neel found us some shade and a plate of actual food.

"Don't bridges often have evil trolls lurking beneath them?" She stretches her arms over her head. "Where's ours?"

I scan the crowd around us on the bridge, pointing out Neel across the way, talking intensely on his cell phone, his voice raised. "Ugh. That call looks pleasant."

Riya perks up, her eyes following mine. "I bet it's Moira. She wasn't thrilled when she didn't get a grand tour invite." Speaking of evil, Riya's expression has a shade of fairy-tale witch as she delivers this choice bit of news.

"Who's Moira?"

"Misery with a lab coat and a handbag. Neel's girlfriend.

Well, sort of depends on the day you ask him, but I think today she's his girlfriend."

I try to ignore the quick twist in my stomach at the word *girlfriend*. "You've met her?"

"A few times. She's two years older than he is. And you'll think I'm exaggerating, but I'm not: She's the worst. Rude, entitled. Leave it to Neel to find someone bossier and more of a know-it-all than he is. She's not on this grand tour because she's a grand pain in the—"

"I get it." With Riya, the descriptions of Moira will be endless if I don't call a stop to it right away. I lean against the bridge, staring out at the water. "This place is even more incredible than its pictures."

"It's beautiful," Riya agrees, turning back to the light-drenched river, now shot through with ribbons of pink. She holds her hair away from her neck. "Do you feel that breeze? That's what heaven feels like."

"Truth." My eyes slip back to Neel, who has drifted to this side of the bridge a few yards away, his back to the river view, a hand clamped over one ear, his forehead creased. When he catches me looking, he walks away.

"Earth to Abby Byrd! Did you hear what I said?" Riya elbows me.

"Ow – what? Yes."

She narrows her eyes at me. "Yes to ditching the dud tomorrow? Were you even listening?" I wasn't. She repeats her idea to ditch Neel tomorrow. "I'm over his sprinting tour of Florence. It's too hot. And he's not taking a hint." If by hint, Riya means he's not listening to Riya yelling at him, she's right. He's not. She tucks her hair behind her ears and ticks off options on her fingers. "We could rent Vespas and drive out to Fiesole. I hear it's pretty. Or sit by the Arno and eat gelato all day. Or whatever we want to do. It's *our* trip."

I take a deep breath, wanting to say something but not knowing how. I have so many questions swirling through my head that I'm not even sure where to start.

She notices. "Just ask me, Abby. I know that look."

"I don't have a look." She mimics my expression. I have to admit, she does a good Abby-wants-to-ask-something face. Since I got her letter in May, questions keep multiplying in my brain. Can we fix this? Can we stay the friends we've always been? Can we patch the rips we've made in each other so the ragged seams stop showing? Or worse: Is there something terrible she's not telling me? But as she blinks back at me expectantly, her liquid eyes waiting, I chicken out, and instead ask one of my more practical questions. "How are you paying for all this?"

She frowns, clearly disappointed. It's not a surprising question from me. Money has always been a source of weirdness between us. Our whole lives. But I know she doesn't want to talk about money. She wants to talk about us. "I told you. My nani is paying." Since I can remember, Riya's family has just operated on a different level with money than the practical, budget-driven Byrds. Dad says that Riya has "family money," but I don't really know what that means because doesn't every family just have the money they have? But when he says it, he hints at hidden wells of it. Still, this trip feels lavish even for the Sharma-Collinses.

She fiddles with her purse. "Was that really the question you wanted to ask me?" she presses, eyeing me from under her lashes.

I swallow. She has already read my face better than anyone. "I know this is an early birthday present for you, but … are you sure it's not more than that?"

Again, the pained expression, and she turns back to the water, the breeze fluttering the hem of her dress. "Can't I just bring my best friend to Europe for a once-in-a-lifetime trip?"

That does it. The tiny, sharp seed of worry that her letter planted in my gut finally sprouts. "Listen, Rye – be straight with me. This is the kind of trip someone takes when she's sick … or maybe" – I swallow hard – "dying?" My body goes weak with her possible answer. "Out with it. Are you dying? Just tell me. I can't stand it anymore."

"What?!" Riya pushes back away from the ledge, eyes wide, nearly colliding with a family of tourists trying to take a group picture, sputtering, "No! Geez, Abby!" She apologizes to the family and pulls me by the arm farther down the bridge.

I follow her, untangling myself as relief floods through me. "It's not so far-fetched. This seems like a trip you might take because something awful like that has happened!" I stop walking, forcing her to look at me. "And you should've known I'd think that and not make me think it for so long! It's really disrespectful to people who are actually dying!"

She shakes her head, but a smile starts to bend the corners of her mouth. "You're a crazy person, you realize that, right? I should have written in the letter: 'Come to Florence. P.S. I'm not dying'? What is wrong with you?"

"I was scared, you jerk. It has been that kind of year, okay?"

Riya's smile fades. "Oh, Abby, I'm sorry. I'm sorry your year—"

"Let's go," Neel interrupts, pocketing his phone, striding by us. Maybe he's too soaked in his own drama, but he doesn't read the tension between us, doesn't notice the troubled looks on either of our faces.

Riya and I lock eyes, and she bursts out laughing. "Well, at least I'm not *that* clueless." She shouts after him, "You are a rude man, sir, and it is not an attractive quality!"

I lean into her as we follow him off the bridge. "Okay, so we are most definitely ditching him tomorrow." After a moment, I add, "And I'm glad you're not dying."

She puts her arm around me. "Well, that's a step in the right direction."

The next morning, I make it all the way to five a.m. before the gray light seeps in through my eyelids. No street cleaner today? Maybe I actually slept through it. The heat hits me first. Not that sticky-dust feel of midday, but hotter than it should be at five in the morning. Ugh. I sit up. At some point in the night, I kicked off the duvet. Riya has hers pulled to her chin, but her feet stick out the bottom, her toenails painted a bright lime green. Her toes make me smile. Riya is really vain about her feet. Once, in Tahoe during a summer camping trip, a guy at the Safeway there told her she could be a "foot model" with her "pretty" feet. I thought that was mega creepy. Who tells a twelve-year-old girl in the graham cracker aisle that she has pretty feet? A creepy guy is who. But she got a big head about it for a while. At Christmas that year, we got in a fight about … something stupid … I can't even remember now, but I finally got fed up and snapped, "Well, not all of us can be foot models!" We laughed for days, and it became one of the things we always say to help us end silly fights.

Or used to always say.

I run my fingers through my tangled hair. I could use a shower, but I don't want to wake Riya up. Or maybe I do. Maybe we can sneak out this morning before Neel gets up? Over dinner last night, he read us his proposed itinerary for today and Riya rejected each suggestion as he read it. She had a point. I love history more than most other humans, but after page two of Neel's schedule, it started to feel more like a sentencing than a vacation. Riya raised more than a few eyebrows in the restaurant when she leapt from her chair to threaten him with a pasta spoon.

I grab my toiletry bag, the one with the plasticized image of the Great Pyramid of Giza on it, and head into the small bathroom. Five minutes later, I stand over Riya's bed, letting my hair drip onto her face. "Mmmmmmf, whaaaa?" She buries herself under her pillow.

"If we leave now, Neel won't stand a chance," I tell her, poking her one exposed shoulder. "Or we can wait and let him talk us into … what was the plan again – a walking architectural tour of the city's lesser-known buildings? And didn't I hear something about the city's recycling program?"

She almost takes my head off as she springs from the bed. "I'm up!"

Downstairs, we tiptoe through the dark breakfast area and push through the doors into the quiet city morning. We find a sleepy vendor at a lone open kiosk and grab coffee and some pastries that appear to have more chocolate than breakfast food probably should. We practice our *grazie*s and *buona giornata*s, and he mostly indulges us, pointing us in the direction of the Piazzale Michelangelo, where we can watch the sun come up.

A half hour later, we sit on stone steps overlooking the orange-bright city stretched out in front of us. We sip our coffees, devour the pastries, and can't stop saying "Wow," because it's Florence. *Wow* seems the only word that fits this skyline, if only for the way the sunrise deepens the terracotta tiles of the Duomo and the rooftops beyond.

Finally, Riya says, "I'm glad you came."

"Me too." My eyes trace the white ribs of the Duomo. The history geek in me tingles with the thought that I'm sitting where someone like Michelangelo might have sat, staring at something Brunelleschi created when so many people doubted him. So. Cool.

"I wasn't sure if you would," Riya says, fiddling with some loose pebbles on the steps. "Because, well, you didn't respond right away to the package when I sent it."

"I was just surprised, Rye." I clear my throat, my mouth suddenly dry from the pastry. "We said those horrible things and then didn't talk for almost a month."

"I tried to text you! I called. You didn't get back to me." She holds her coffee with both hands, her elbows on her knees, and stares straight ahead.

Defensive knots form in my stomach. "I needed some space. And I couldn't believe it at first when I got your package. I mean, Florence? A multi-city trip? It was a lot to digest. And kind of over the top."

"Well, you know how much I like a grand gesture."

She shrugs, hooking one leg over the other, her foot bobbing.

"I do." Riya's getting mad. Feeling her slow boil simmering, I hurry to insist, "Look, I mostly like your grand gestures. But as you know, I almost always need to process them. I'm not as spontaneous as you are."

She snorts. "No, you're not."

I bite my lip. With Riya, this is a critical moment. She gets mad easily, but she also forgives easily. I've always admired that about her, mostly because I'm terrible at it. "I'm sorry I didn't get back to you sooner after we fought, okay? I was completely overwhelmed."

Riya's dark eyes flick to me. "I know your year—" She takes a deep breath. "Oh, Abby, I don't really know what to say except I'm sorry your year was so awful. I'm sorry about your parents. And that I said those horrible things. But I kept waiting for you to talk to me about it. Not just tell me, actually talk to me. When I asked you, you said you were fine. You seemed like you didn't want to talk about it. I was trying to respect your whole space thing!"

I look at her sharply. "You never asked me what happened."

"Yes, I did!"

I shake my head, my own anger bubbling up. She didn't ask. She told me she was sorry, that I would get over it, that things would get better with time. She sent chocolate. But she did what Riya always does with difficult things. "You went straight to the future," I tell her now. "You told me I'd be okay. That time would make it better. You didn't try to help me live in it. And you never asked what happened."

Her brow furrows. "I meant it the same way."

"But it's not the same." I blink away the tears that threaten behind my lashes and take a deep breath. The air is thick, and I want to believe it's the steadily rising heat, but it's more likely from the memory that suddenly floods me. The day my mom sat us down after New Year's and told us she needed "a change." My parents have never needed changes. We've had the same furniture, the same cars (silver Volvo sedan circa 2007, Datsun pickup circa "older than dirt"), even the same beach towels for as long as I can remember. Things don't change in the Byrd household. My dad shaved his mustache when I was nine, and Kate still tells him to grow it back every time she sees him.

Riya clenches her hands around her coffee, denting the cup. "Abby, you knew I meant it the same way. You should have told me. Don't wait for me to ask. We've been friends too long to worry about stuff like that."

"Maybe I needed you to dig it out of me!"

She sets down her coffee and turns to me. "So tell me now. I'm digging now. What happened?"

Sitting here, all these months later, I can still feel the air leave the room, see the bare trees out the January window, dark and wet with the rain that had soaked them that morning. Still see the look on my dad's face as he leaned his elbows on his knees, staring at the floor, saying nothing. He's barely said anything since. "My mom said she needed a change, that this wasn't working for her anymore, that she needed to move on. And then she left."

Riya curls her hand over mine. "That sounds awful. What did Kate do? Did she start screaming?"

"No one screams in our house, you know that. Everyone was so … polite. It was weird. And then it was silent. We all just sat there in the living room until it started to rain again." I stare out at the city in front of me, at the windows of the far buildings reflecting the morning light. "The weirdest part was, right before Mom left, she asked Kate if she could borrow her rain boots. Blue ones with bright yellow flowers. And Kate said sure, and then Mom left, wearing them. The next day, Kate went back to college early. And Mom wore her boots all winter. That's weird, right?"

"Maybe she felt closer to Kate because of them?"

I blink at more rogue tears. "You know what I didn't tell you? She's *living* with Dr. Restivo now." Dr. Restivo was Riya's dentist, too, before she left. Robert Restivo, DDS. He gives out stickers with smiling molars and lets you pick what color toothbrush you'd like. After a 100 percent checkup when I was a kid, I got a balloon looped around my small wrist, a proud beacon bobbing through the waiting room as I left, smiling my 100 percent smile.

Now my mom lives with him in a condo by the city park.

Riya shakes her head. "Last I heard, you said she was 'taking it slow' with him or whatever. When did that change?"

"A few weeks ago."

She hesitates, then asks, "Do you ever stay with them?"

I swallow over the lump in my throat. "I've had dinner there a few times. It's so bizarre – all small talk and silverware clinking too loudly on plates. But I haven't stayed over. I have to take care of my dad. When she moved in with Dr. Restivo, it sent Dad straight back into his work-sleep-repeat mode. Total zombie. You wouldn't recognize him. I'm worried about being so far away from him now."

"He'll be okay. He wanted you to come on this trip."

"I know. But he doesn't remember to do the most basic things. Like taking out the garbage or emptying the dishwasher. Even walking Henry."

Riya searches my face, and I wonder if now is when we talk about what's happening between us, why we can't seem to keep each other in our close orbits. It's more than just what happened with my parents. She has to know this.

Chewing her lip, she says instead: "Dr. Restivo always spits when he talks. And that's just not what you want from a dentist."

I start to laugh-cry, leaning into her, my hair spilling

onto her shoulder. She puts her arms around me, and I can't seem to tell her how much I miss this, this way she says the just-right thing in certain moments, that I'm still hurt she wasn't there when I needed her to say it most.

Riya

My phone buzzes. Neel again. All caps.

WHERE ARE YOU? I AM QUITE CONCERNED.

Even his texts sound like a strict old professor. I've been ignoring him all morning. I got a text as we wandered along the Arno. Another one as we admired the jewelry as we crossed the Ponte Vecchio, a medieval stone bridge. Finally, I'd turned off my phone, not turning it back on until we found a patch of shade to sit in near the Fountain of Neptune in the Piazza della Signoria.

Abby shifts next to me. "Neel again?"

"The Professor is quite concerned." I hand her my phone so she can read it. "We're officially in trouble. This is the first one in all caps."

"Your screen has a huge crack in it," she tells me.

I glance over her shoulder. "Oh, that's old."

She hands my phone back. "He sent another one."

It reads: Don't think I won't call Aji!!

"Who's Aji?" Abby asks, scanning the square.

"Our grandma. Nani for me since she's my mom's mother. Aji for him since she's his dad's mother."

"Gotcha."

"Let me see the skirt you got at the market." I motion to her backpack. Earlier, browsing the eclectic booths of clothes and bags and jewelry at the Mercato del Porcellino, I'd discovered the skirt alone on a rack of jackets and told Abby it was a sign that she should buy it.

Now Abby hands me the bag with the matching ceramic masks we also bought. "Hold these for a second." She fishes out the short, maroon, leather miniskirt. Inspecting it, she gives me the same doubtful look she gave me back at the booth. "I'm still not sure about this. I'm not really a leather miniskirt kind of girl."

I motion for her to try it on again. "You're in Italy. It doesn't matter if you're a leather miniskirt kind of girl. You're anything you want to be here." Humoring me, she stands and tugs it on under her yellow sundress. "See," I assure her. "It fits perfectly."

She peers down at it. "Maybe you're right. Besides, the pig did say I'm returning to Florence someday, so I can always just wear it here." Before the market, we'd rubbed the snout of the famous pig at the Fontana del Porcellino, putting coins in his mouth. When the water washed our coins into the waiting grate, a woman told us we'd have good luck and return to Florence.

"The pig *has* spoken." I nod. "It's a great skirt." My

phone beeps with what is now Neel's eighth text of the morning. Speaking of luck, I'm going to need it when he catches up with us.

Abby raises her eyebrows. "Why won't you just tell him we're fine and doing our own thing today? So he doesn't think we drowned in the Arno or got kidnapped by art smugglers or something."

"Both of those things are preferable to spending the rest of our trip with him. I'm going to call Nani and talk to her. She promised he wouldn't turn into Neel the Controller."

Abby sighs. "I still don't see why it's such a big deal to text him."

"It's the principle of it." I don't miss Abby's eye roll. I know she thinks I'm being melodramatic about Neel, but we had such a nice morning. For the first time in almost a year, we felt like the friends we used to be and not the ones who had the last ten months wedged in between us. Neel is getting in the way. It's not his job to decide how our day looks just because he thinks he owes it to our "moral and intellectual growth" (text three). What a prig.

"Riya?" Abby has gone still next to me, her sundress still partly tucked into the waistline of the miniskirt.

"Yeah?"

"Do you see that guy over there?" I follow her finger, to where a boy slightly older than us in a black T-shirt and jeans slumps against a far wall of the square, texting on his phone.

"Oh, yeah, cute," I say, perking up.

"No, not cute. I think he's following us."

My body tingles. "What?" I look more closely. He's muscular and, upon closer inspection, gorgeous, with dark, wavy hair. Every minute or so he seems to glance toward us, but when he notices us watching him, he slips suddenly around a corner. "Why do you think that?"

Abby studies the corner where he disappeared. "He was near that pig fountain when we were there, and I saw him earlier at the market."

My heart twitches. "Are you sure?"

We wait to see if he reemerges, but he doesn't. Abby shakes her head. "Maybe I'm just imagining things."

And she thinks *I'm* melodramatic.

But then, there he is again. On a different side of the square, leaning and texting, trying to seem like he's not peering at us. "Um, Riya?"

"I see him." I'm on my feet next to her. "Let's go." In a flash, we're around our own corner and checking to find out if he's noticed.

He's running across the square.

Running.

Toward us.

"Go!" I shout, and we take off, our sandals slapping against the stones.

"I'm definitely not sure about this skirt," she gasps at my heels.

A half hour later, we're sitting at a café table on a quiet side street. Neel stands in front of us, arms crossed over his chest, doing his best Angry Dad expression. He's scarily good at it. Black T-shirt Guy's name turns out to be Damiano, and, yes, he was following us. When Abby heard his name, she nervously announced that Saint Damian is the patron saint of physicians. History tidbit. Of course, this guy seems to be the patron saint of buzz-kills. I don't care how hot he is.

Neel frowns. "I called Aji, and your parents, Riya. Thankfully, Abby's parents don't even know you went missing. We didn't want to alarm them unnecessarily."

"'Went missing' makes it sound like we were kidnapped, or did something wrong," I tell him. "Which we didn't. We're allowed to explore the city on our own terms, Captain Control Freak."

"Actually, Dora the Explorer," Neel says, not to be outdone in the name-calling department, "you aren't just allowed to disappear without so much as a note or a text." He pulls out a chair and joins us at the table. Abby glances at me, her eyes shining with *I told you we should have just texted him back*. I look away. "To not even answer my texts is childish."

I cross my legs and sigh dramatically for his benefit.

"Thanks for the maturity lesson. Tell me again what it's like to be old before your time?" Damiano grins at this, and Neel shoots him a death stare. Maybe Damiano's not so bad after all. His smile gives me confidence. "Speaking of which, where'd you come from anyway?" I ask him. "Italian stalkers for hire?"

Damiano starts to answer, but Neel cuts in. "He's a mate from uni and was born and raised here. He's home for the summer. It wasn't hard for him to spot two clueless American girls wandering around Florence. It's not that big a city. He was going to be our guide today before you two took off."

Maybe I was a little hasty this morning. Damiano might be a buzzkill, but he looks like a god. An Italian one. All the chiseled clichés properly in place. He would obviously make an excellent tour guide.

"Well, it's only one o'clock," Abby reminds us. "Day's not over yet."

I glance hopefully at Damiano. This can't be the guy who was going to show us the recycling program. I'm guessing architecture.

I guess wrong.

We spend the next couple of hours learning about the history of garbage in Florence. Still, with Damiano's dark eyes, an Italian-British lilt to his English, and that easy laugh leading the way, refuse has never been this interesting. This guy just made me care about garbage for two straight hours. He should probably have his own reality television show.

At the end of our tour, Damiano deposits us on some shady steps in the Palazzo Vecchio and disappears to find us gelato. I peer up at Neel. "He's cute. Can we keep him?"

"I think his girlfriend would miss him. She's a model, by the way. And a doctoral candidate in anthropology." He pockets his phone, enjoying my pout. "So stop flirting with him."

I feign surprise. "Was I flirting?" I glance at Abby, who toggles her flat hand back and forth to say *ehh*.

Neel rubs his hands together. "Okay, my turn to teach you something." He leads us to a corner of the Palazzo Vecchio near the Uffizi. A small crowd of people stare at a carving in the bricks that looks like a man's face. "The Palazzo Vecchio is the 'Old Palace' and the town hall of Florence."

"We were actually both at the tour with Matteo yesterday," I remind him. "We know this already."

He narrows his eyes at me. "Can I talk?" When I motion him on, he continues, "Legend has it, this is a carving that Michelangelo made on a dare. The dare: that he couldn't carve the likeness of a man's face behind his back, without looking. So he did. Right into the wall."

I nudge Abby. "Wow, Neel, way to promote vandalism in the name of ego."

His words, though, have the desired effect on Abby. "Can I touch it?"

"Sure." Neel grins smugly at me. You'd think *he* carved the face.

Abby runs her fingers over the grooves worn through time and then motions for me to try it. As I track my hand over the ridges, I try to play it cool so Neel doesn't think he's made some big impression on me, but I shiver despite myself. This is something Michelangelo carved hundreds of years ago, and hundreds of years from now, some futuristic girl might trail her fingers over the fading hollows, wondering why he took the dare. Abby always says that history isn't just Wikipedia entries and documentaries and pages in textbooks – it's something you can touch. She's right. It is.

"Ah, yes, Michelangelo's dare." Damiano comes up behind us carrying four gelatos, already starting to drip in the heat.

I snap my hand back, feeling like I probably shouldn't be touching such a famous landmark. "Neel said I could touch it."

"Yes, yes. Many do." He hands out the *bacio* cones (which taste like Nutella grew up and became the best ice cream ever). "Here, eat these and then we'll go up in the tower. Our reservation is at four. Best views of the city."

I'm pretty sure there aren't any bad views in Florence. There's certainly no bad gelato. "I would make out with this gelato if it wouldn't alarm those small children over there," I announce loudly, mostly to bother Neel, but also because it's sort of true.

"Classy as always, Riya." Neel glances at Damiano apologetically. "But it's good to know you have lines."

I scowl at Abby when she cracks up at this. "What?" She shrugs, chasing a drip on her own cone. "It *is* good to know you have lines." I don't enjoy the knowing look she exchanges with Neel.

The narrow climb up the brick tower stairs leaves my legs burning, even with the short break we take in the prison halfway up. Ten minutes into Damiano's vivid description of the wretched prisoners who spent their last moments in the bleak cell, I feel sick and leave Abby and the boys behind to head up the rest of the steps. Abby finds me a few minutes later. "Too gruesome?"

"I think I ate too much gelato." We stare out at the city, our hands matching curls on the stone edge of the tower wall. It's a wider, more aerial view than the one we thought was unbeatable this morning.

"Wow," Abby breathes. Again, the only fitting word.

"Yeah," I agree. "I love Europe." She shoots me a funny look, so I ask, "What?"

"You sound so wistful."

"I just really like it here." And Berlin. And Paris. And Zurich. And London. All of the places I visited this year just seem to keep making me want more of them.

Abby shrugs. "It's not Yuba Ridge, that's for sure."

"No, it's not."

Frowning, she presses slightly into the wall to let a group pass behind us. "So, what's next for us, then, on this grand tour of yours?"

"Already sick of Florence?"

"Um, that would happen never." Only her face holds a shadow of ache. It's an expression I had a lot my first month in Berlin. Dad called it my *missing* look. Missing the river, missing my bunk bed, missing the light in the sky above the pines. I haven't had that look at all lately, but I recognize it.

"I'm worried you're not having fun. Is it Neel?" I ask her.

She shakes her head, pulling out her phone and scanning it slowly left to right to take a panoramic picture. "Neel's bothering you, not me. I mean, he can be a pain, but he's fine, really. He's kind of funny and sweet when he wants to be."

"Which is never."

"He's not so bad. And he's giving up part of his summer to take us on this trip."

"Yeah, rough life he leads."

Abby sighs as she looks out at Florence. "This might have to be our first wonder, this view."

It's cliché, staring at views, but there is something wonderful about being made to feel small and expansive all at once. "If views could speak, this one would say:

Here you go, ladies – your future awaits!"

"And our future is in..." she prompts hopefully.

"Okay, you win." My stomach flutters with the secret of our next stop. "I was going to wait until dinner, but here goes: Tomorrow we're taking the train to Zurich!"

"We're not staying in Italy?"

"Nope. You are going to love Zurich. I went with my parents a few months ago and you'll see – we're heading for the best hot chocolate you've ever tasted." I frown at her silence. "Wait. You're not excited?"

"It's too much, Riya." Abby returns to the view, the Duomo, the river, the swirl of tiny toy people in the square below. "Too expensive. I feel like I should help pay for some of this."

Oh, Abby. How many times has she tripped on her own practicality our whole lives? "If you keep worrying about the money, it's going to be a long trip."

"Right." She takes a few more pictures, and I can practically see her mind spinning. Finally, she turns to me, her eyes serious. "Earlier you asked if Kate started screaming at my mom when she told us."

I'm caught off guard. "Yeah?"

"You think she should have, right? You think one of us should have yelled at her? Told her she was ruining the family?"

I hurry to say, "Abby, I wasn't there. I don't know what I would have done."

She tugs absently at her low ponytail for a moment. “I’m so mad at her, I feel numb.” Before I can reach out to her, she abruptly heads for the stairs. When she reaches the top stone step, she hesitates and waits for me. When I catch up, she tries to smile. “I won’t mention the money again, okay?”

“Okay.”

the second Wonder

ZURICH, SWITZERLAND

Abby

We take the fast train to Milan, where we switch for our final leg to Zurich. Riya sits across from me, reading a novel, her bare feet kicked onto the seat between Neel and me. Neel reads the *Economist*. Having failed to get Riya to keep her feet on the floor, he uses them to prop up his magazine. I stare out the window, trying to absorb the shifting countryside as we slip from the terracotta palette of Italy to the lush greens of Switzerland.

Out the window, Switzerland looks like a life-size set for model trains, the kind my dad used to take us to at the county fair with the miniature houses and trees, the people the size of a hard candy waiting at a miniature railroad stop or restaurant. Kate would roll her eyes every time we went. "This is so lame," she'd whine. "Can we please go do something less lame?" But I liked the precision of the model train world, the way the engineers considered every diminutive detail. My favorite was the snowcapped mountain in the middle of it, with its dark tunnel, the train's light glowing for a blink before it emerged into the dim glow of the fluorescent-lit room. Switzerland has the Godzilla version of that mountain, and now I'm the one in the tiny train shooting through it.

"What are you reading?" I ask Riya.

She studies me over the pages of her book. "You wouldn't like it. It's not written before the 1950s."

"I like books written after the 1950s." As long as they are historical fiction set before the 1950s.

She knows me too well. "Sorry, it isn't *set* before the 1950s, either."

"I'm out."

Neel laughs but doesn't look up from his article. Riya returns to her book, and I stare out the window at the blur of green. I try to get into the book I brought about ancient Alexandria, but it's pretty dry, even for me, and I can't seem to stay focused. The scenery keeps drawing me back to it. After another hour of passing through storybook villages with patchwork fields and sheets of striking blue lakes, we near the urban center of Zurich. It doesn't look like the cities I'm used to. More like Santa's village. The buildings seem made of gingerbread. Flags, mostly Swiss, flutter along the ordered streets. Leafy trees shade people sitting at outdoor cafés on the wide sidewalks. Pots of geraniums bloom in containers and smartly dressed men and women chat on their phones.

Soon, we're swallowed by the enormous train station

and pull to a stop. As we gather our bags, Neel's cell buzzes. "That's Will. He's picking us up."

We follow the herd into the vaulted space of the station, which is lined at the top with pale orange-slice windows. I attempt to maneuver my bag to my other side so I can give my shoulder a rest. "Who's Will?" I ask Riya, rushing to keep up with her.

She slows, letting me catch up. "A university friend of Neel's. He's from here. We're staying at his parents' while we're in Zurich."

"Neel has stalkers for hire in all cities, huh?"

"Apparently."

Around us, people hurry through the station, which is more like an upscale marketplace than any train station I've been to before. "Wow," I mutter to Riya, "I could live in this train station."

"Just wait until you taste the hot chocolate." She hurries after Neel, who has not stopped once to make sure we're still following him.

I pick up my pace. Hot chocolate has always been a thing for Riya and me, and not in that normal little-kid way. Most kids probably like hot chocolate, but not like *we* do. Over the years, it's evolved into a sort of science for us, actually. A quest for the perfect chocolate, the perfect amount of milk, the perfect temperature. Many a Yuba Ridge Sunday has been devoted to the execution of the perfect cup of hot chocolate.

And I thought we'd agreed on one. "Better than the Brandon Special?" I ask Riya when we step outside into the overcast light of Zurich.

"Just wait."

"Nothing is better than the Brandon Special."

"You'll see."

Neel's friend Will waits for us on a bench outside the train station. He lifts a hand in greeting, moving his lanky body toward us as he adjusts the heavy black-framed glasses that rest against his thick eyebrows.

Riya gapes up at him. "How tall are you?"

He grins as if he's used to the question, and hunches his wide shoulders forward. "Six six – six four from years of practiced bad posture."

Riya lets out a bright burst of laughter that suggests he's just told the most hilarious joke in the history of comedy. Then she tosses her hair and asks him to "tell us about what we're looking at here," and motions to the city around us. Uh-oh. Peal of laughter. Hair flip. And she's doing that glance-up-through-her-lashes thing Riya does when she thinks a guy is ridiculously cute or interesting. Not just her average, recreational flirting. She's bringing her A game. I don't blame her. He's cute, this Will, and as he starts to point out elements of the city, I can practically swim in the easy, rich tenor of his voice. Listening, I fall in step behind them, enjoying the fresh air, the overcast sky. It must be at least ten degrees cooler here than in Florence.

As we cross a bridge over the Limmat River, Will points out the tower of the Fraumünster Church. "Built on the ruins of an abbey from 853 that Louis the German built for his daughter, Hildegard."

"That's so interesting! Abby, it's history tidbit, Zurich edition," Riya calls over her shoulder, her roller bag bobbling over the uneven ground as we reach the other side of the bridge. "I wish my dad would build me a tower."

"You've done okay," I say to her back. "Your dad built you a river cabin." But she doesn't hear me. She's too busy hanging on Will's every last word. I watch him lean toward her to answer a question. He has good hair. The thick, floppy kind that always seems to know right where to fall across his forehead. Gotta give Riya credit. For the most part, she has good taste. On the train, Neel told us Will's studying to be a banker. He seems too tall to be a banker, which I realize is an absurd thought. As if bankers have height restrictions. I take a deep breath of cool air coming off the water, trying not to let Riya's over-bright and sudden interest in history annoy me. She chatters away, finding everything Will says "fascinating!" or "incredible!" and commenting on how gorgeous the landscape is. Right, the *landscape*.

I catch Neel's eye and can tell he's thinking the same thing. He falls into step beside me. "What do you think of Switzerland so far?"

I study the scenery – the gray river, the cloudy sky, the intricate old buildings. "Stunning."

"Right, nothing if not picturesque, Switzerland." He watches Riya and Will chatting up ahead, then nods at the corner of the Alexandria book poking out of my bag. "Been meaning to ask you, why the Seven Ancient Wonders?"

Like Will is used to being asked how tall he is, this is one of the questions I get asked the most. Maybe it's a strange sort of hobby, loving the Seven Wonders of the Ancient World, if you're not a seventy-year-old archaeologist or something. Of course, people always forget that the seventy-year-old archaeologist first fell in love with the ancient world at some point in her life and it was probably as a kid. "It's strange, I know," I say, matching his steady steps along the sidewalk. "But my dad and I saw this show about them on the History Channel when I was seven and they just captured me. I love the imagination it must have taken to create them, the vision, but also there was all this human suffering that went into building them; that contrast has always intrigued me. And I love the myths and legends that blur the historical parts, you know?"

"Quite." He grins sideways at me, his bag rolling along behind him. "It's an absorbing hobby, I'm sure. Probably leads to other intriguing parts of history."

"It does." His acceptance of it sends a shot of warmth

through me. Most people don't get it, are usually quick to tell me why it's not worth my time.

When we reach Will's building, we climb the narrow steps to his parents' third-floor flat. He opens the door, revealing an airy, open room with smooth hardwood floors. Will motions at a futon-style mattress against the far wall spread with a dark maroon duvet. "For you girls." Then he points to a narrow, modern couch and tells Neel, "And for you." Neel will have to fold himself in half to actually sleep on it.

"Are your parents here?" I ask Will.

"They are traveling with my sister in the States. In New York."

"I've never been to New York," I admit.

"You should visit. It's a wonderful city."

"Oh, I *looove* New York," Riya gushes. I know for a fact that Riya has been to New York once, when she was nine.

Neel leans into me, whispering, "He could recommend the fourth circle in Dante's *Inferno* and she'd start Googling available Airbnbs."

A traitorous giggle slips out. When Riya frowns in my direction, I hurry across the room, dumping my bags on the futon.

Riya peers at her phone again. "We should be there. Look for a white awning on the Bahnhofstrasse."

"You just like saying Bahnhofstrasse." I scan the pale

stone buildings that look like all the other pale stone buildings. Switzerland is nothing if not uniform. "Maybe that one?" I point across and down the street to a building with gold-swirl writing on its windows.

"Yes! That's it. Confiserie Sprüngli!" The sweets in the window grow into sharper focus as we near the shop. Giggling, we pull open the door, hit with the sugar-sharp smell of chocolate. Inside, we gawk at the massive rows of elaborately displayed truffles and cakes and pastries. "Oh, wow – chocolate has a heaven."

Riya nods in agreement and tugs my arm. "Let's go upstairs and find a table."

Fifteen minutes later, we're sitting at a round marble table near the tall second-story windows, watching the bustle of the street below. A waiter sets two cups of steaming hot chocolate in front of us, bits of shaved chocolate melting into a swirl of foam. I'm almost giddy at the thought of the first sip.

Riya raises her cup and waits for me to do the same. "One-two-three!" We both sip at the same time, simultaneously uttering our own versions of "Mmm." This is true hot chocolate, not just water mixed with powdered cocoa. We breathe it in before setting our cups down with a clink.

"Verdict?" I ask, studying her reaction.

Riya wipes some foam from her lip, announcing, "Winner! Best one ever. It even tops the Brandon Special."

For me, nothing will ever top the Brandon Special.

After a full day of skiing a few years ago, Riya and I had settled into cozy seats at the Squaw Valley High Camp restaurant. Outside, snow drifted across the wide windows, frosting the landscape. Our muscles aching, we waved down the bartender. "Hot chocolate?" he asked, coming to our table. "It's the best in the world."

"It's not," Riya told him flatly. "We've had it here before." He smiled slyly, assuring us he could make us the best hot chocolate we'd ever tasted. Skeptical, we waited for this miraculous hot chocolate to arrive. When it did, we took our first sips. It was delicious – smooth, rich chocolate with just the right amount of fresh whipped cream and a dusting of cocoa powder. The bartender laughed at our surprised looks. "That's the Brandon Special. Just remember to ask for it." But the next time we went to Squaw, Brandon didn't work there anymore, moving on to snowier pastures, and we never had hot chocolate like it again.

Until (almost) now.

Riya fiddles with one of the small spoons that came with our drinks. "You don't think it's a winner?"

I take another sip. "This is incredible. But it's a definite second place."

We drink in silence, knowing a hot chocolate is always best in the first few minutes.

"I think," Riya says finally, setting down her cup, "that

you have romanticized the Brandon Special and no hot chocolate will ever possibly live up to it."

The air shifts between us. "Are you picking a fight with me?" I try to joke, but there is an edge underneath her statement and my question.

"Maybe."

I set down my cup. "Why?"

She tucks a loose strand of hair behind her ear, her eyes on her half-finished hot chocolate. "Do you realize that since you got to Florence, you haven't once asked me about Berlin?"

I stare out at the Swiss flag, bright red and white, fluttering from a building across the way. Perfect that Riya waited until Switzerland to bring this up. Neutral ground and all that. "You haven't asked about Yuba Ridge." I shrug. "Maybe we're just doing a good job of enjoying the moment."

Riya narrows her eyes. "I'm not sure that's what we're doing."

All year, a dark pool has collected in my belly when I think of her living in Berlin. I've tried to be the better person, to be the good friend, but mostly I get caught in the eddy of that feeling. It's why I haven't asked her about Berlin, about her life there. So I try to sound upbeat. "What's new in Berlin these days?" But it comes out sarcastic.

"Forget it." She doesn't look at me, instead fishes around

inside her bag until she pulls out a silky cobalt-blue scarf and winds it around her neck. Add it to the list of ways Berlin has changed her. A chic new haircut, double espressos, and now she's also the girl who knows to have a glamorous scarf in her bag just in case.

I stop trying for cheery and shoot for honest instead. "You've changed."

"Only for the better." She signals our waiter for the check.

"Maybe. But nothing was wrong with the Yuba Ridge version of Riya."

Her dark eyes settle on me, something serious waiting there. "What is the saying, we have to move forward or we're stuck?"

Her words echo her eyes, so I lean in, try to prepare to hear what's behind them. "Okay, tell me, then. About Berlin."

She eyes me for a moment. "Berlin was a thousand amazing, intense, complicated things. And I feel like you don't know about almost any of them—"

"Well, I don't live in Berlin—"

"I know! Because you never let me forget that part. The part where you're pissed that I moved there. You shut me out because of it. All year."

"I shut you out?" My voice is louder than I mean it to be and two old women at the next table raise their eyebrows. I lower it, leaning in so she can hear me. "I think it was the other way around, Riya. I'm not the one who acts like Yuba Ridge doesn't exist anymore."

Riya inhales sharply and holds her breath in, just for a moment, but I see it, and know it means tears. She blinks quickly, and the whole display would be funny in its familiarity if I didn't feel like crying myself. "I don't act like that."

My heart races. I hate this, hate the out-of-control electric surge in my limbs. "Can we walk or something? Before this becomes the worst cup of hot chocolate we've ever had?"

Riya

We find a path along the river that leads to Lake Zurich, the water growing wide and metallic in front of us. The air turns chilly against my bare arms and clouds flex across the sky, dotting our faces with a sprinkle of rain. I pull my scarf closer, Abby's words thrumming in my ears. Her implied preference for the version of me I left in Yuba Ridge. The one I left there on purpose.

After a minute or two of walking in silence, we duck into a grove of trees near the water. "It's cold." Abby shivers. "Not like Florence. I might need a sweater." It's warmer here under the trees, though, and she doesn't make a move to head back toward Will's flat. She stands staring at the lake, her face blank.

I watch the blue chop of the water. "We can go back," I say. "To Will's." I add this last bit hastily, realizing the first part of that statement said aloud sounds too much like a promise. And not one I'm willing to keep.

She doesn't make a move to leave. I think Abby's love

of history, of all things ancient and past, has built up a barrier between her and whatever is happening right now. No matter how hard something is or how emotional or intense, she has always been able to pull down the blinds on it, retreat into her mind. I've never been able to build that sort of wall against the world. Sometimes, I'm jealous of her for it.

"Actually," she says, turning to me, "tell me about Berlin." No wall. Just her wide river-green eyes.

The leaves rustle above us in the wind coming off the water, and they sound like whispering, like people talking before a play starts. I avoid her gaze. "Okay, big news here." She looks at me expectantly, and I tell her something for the first time out loud that I've imagined saying to her a dozen times in my head. "This year I realized I want to be an actress."

She blinks. "You want to be an actress." It's not a question.

"I do."

"Meaning, you like acting as a hobby or you want to become a professional actress?" This one is a question for sure. Typical Abby, gathering research.

"As a career."

"Hm." She chews her lip, and I can tell she's considering what to say to me, cycling through her options. Finally, she asks, "And you just realized this? How? You're always telling me about looking for signs. Is that what happened? You were walking along the street and a bolt of lightning hit you. Flash: Be an actress! Out of nowhere?"

"No lightning bolt. It didn't just happen. I took some classes."

"Oh, right – classes." She twirls a strand of loose hair around her finger. "And you didn't tell me." Again, not a question. Just a murky underscore of hurt. Even Abby's armor has cracks in it.

"I wanted to tell you in person."

Her eyes drop from mine. "Right." She checks her buzzing phone, then holds it out to me. "Neel."

His text reads: Sorry to bother you, Abby, but my dear cousin isn't checking her phone. Grateful if you'd give her the following message: START WALKING BACK NOW!!!

"How nice that he switches to all caps for his dear cousin."

"I guess we'd better get back." She turns and heads at a fast clip in the direction of the flat, and I hurry to catch her, our unfinished conversation left floating in the cool lake air behind me.

To make matters worse, we get lost trying to find Will's place, and eventually end up back at Confiserie Sprüngli, standing in front of the glossy window of treats.

We pause, the silence between us thickening. Then,

with a shrug, Abby reaches for the door. "I'm thinking this is one of those signs you're so into. Hot chocolate do-over?" She attempts a smile.

My heart lifts. "The universe can be very persuasive." I follow her inside.

We're taking our first sips when Neel texts me: Where are you? Did Abby get my text? We have plans in a half hour.

I pick up my phone. lost in zurich, send helicopter, I text back, showing Abby, who grins and scoots her chair over to see his response. Neel must be writing a novel because it takes him almost a minute to write:

Getting lost in Zurich is like getting lost in Disneyland. There is no excuse for it. It is the easiest city in the world. Read the signs.

I write back: like the sign that says, ausfahrt!

Neel: Grow up.

Me: awww, don't be like that. it's a funny word.

Neel: Where are you? We'll come to you.

Me: sprüngli.

Neel: Of course you are.

Me: ich liebe dich, neel.

Abby's eyes widen. "What did you just call him?"

"Nothing. *Ich liebe dich* means *I love you*. I'm being a dear cousin."

"Sure you are." Abby leans back into her seat, her hands curled around her cup. "Mmmm, okay. I'll give it to you. This is officially the best hot chocolate I've ever had." I glance up from my phone, and she's watching me with apologetic eyes.

Before I can respond, Neel buzzes back, and I burst out laughing at his text. "Now it is." I show Abby.

She gapes at the angry emoji making a vulgar gesture that probably means the same thing in every language. "Wow, that's a side of Neel I haven't seen before."

I flag down the waiter for our check. "Oh, I've seen it."

Will pulls his silver BMW into a parking spot in the lot for a lakeside restaurant. "Hopefully they didn't cancel our reservation," Neel grumbles, closing his door and following Will around the side of the building, where people sit at weathered picnic tables along a wide graveled eating area. The lake stretches out to the hills beyond, which are dotted with houses. I strategically move up alongside Will into the perfect position to sit next to him when we get to our picnic table. "Great place."

He nods down at me. "One of my favorites."

A waitress leads us to our table, chatting with Will in soft Swiss German. I can't follow much of it – it's so different from the German I've been learning – but I think I hear something about rain and something about … a horse? That can't be right. "Water's on the table." She motions to a glass carafe filled with water and cucumber slices.

"Thanks, Alina." Will smiles at her in an affectionate, familiar way, and I try to ignore a childish pang of jealousy by burying my face in the menu. I scan the items, aware I'm already crushing way too hard on this guy. I try to distract myself with food. Okay, much of this I can actually read. Abby fiddles with the silverware wrapped in an orange cloth napkin. I realize she probably can't read the menu at all.

I lean across the table, pointing. "These are mostly small plates that we can share." I pause at an item. "That's fish, so you won't want it."

She glances at Neel and Will. "Oh, I'm good with anything," she says airily. "I like fish."

That's not true. "You've hated fish since you were six and obsessed with *Finding Nemo*."

"My dad and I actually eat a lot of fish now. My mom's the one who hates fish."

At the edge in her voice, Will hurries to ask, "Shall we just order some meat and cheeses and salad?"

I squeeze his arm. "Great idea!" But it comes out like a cheerleader after five energy drinks. Taking it down a notch, I add, "And I'd love to get some of that bread." I point to a basket at another table.

"Yes, of course." Will flags Alina over. She smiles down at him, her hand resting on his shoulder, and I instantly regret the bread decision. It wasn't supposed to come with a pretty waitress attached. They chat back and forth, laughing, and she motions to an empty wooden stage nearby, fiddling with the tie of her apron. Kind of a long conversation to get some bread. I look out at the lake, at the moored sailboats bobbing in the darkening waters, until she leaves.

Neel pours cucumber water into each of our waiting glass tumblers.

"Would you also like wine?" Will asks us.

"Not for these two," Neel tells him.

Will nods. "Ah, yes – sorry. Americans." He says *Americans* with a sort of pitying head tilt, the way someone might say *abandoned puppies*. It helps me like him slightly less. For about five seconds.

Because then he says, "This is a nice scarf," and tugs lightly on one of the silky blue ends. Letting go, he adds, "It's no problem. No wine tonight."

Abby wrinkles her nose. "I think wine tastes like window cleaner."

"You make a habit of drinking window cleaner, do you?" Neel teases her, leaning his elbows on the table.

Abby flashes him a sly sideways look. "Have you tried it? It was all the rage last year in California. We're very cutting-edge."

Wait, what is happening across the table? Is Abby *flirting* with Neel? Gross.

"You'll have to suggest a vintage," he flirts back.

Stop it!

"Are you feeling okay, Riya?" Abby squints at me. "You're making a weird face."

"I'm just hungry."

Neel sips his water. "Yes, well, contrary to popular belief, hot chocolate does not constitute a full meal."

I stare darkly at the table. I'm not sure what is bothering me more: Abby and Neel flirting, or what happened earlier with Abby – the dark edge of her voice when she told me I've changed, her subdued response to my news.

During dinner, I attempt to join in on the pepper of conversation around me, nodding along to the stories, trying to add something here and there, but I feel lost in memory, in the dark, rain-washed streets of Berlin, in the way it grabbed me and shook me. Abby thinks I've changed and she's right. Only she can't seem to see that the changes are for the better.

You haven't asked about Yuba Ridge.

She's right about that, too. I haven't.

I know Abby thinks Berlin changed me, that Berlin forced me to, in her words, forget Yuba Ridge, but what she doesn't understand is that Yuba Ridge began feeling like part of my past long before I moved. Don't get me wrong, I've always felt lucky in my life, and for so many years, I loved my small world by the river. But something started shifting in Yuba Ridge for me years ago. Something that made me *need* to leave it behind if I was ever going to feel hopeful or grateful or that completely overused and simplified word, *happy*.

I think it started in middle school, that growing ache for something else. Something outside of Northern California. Maybe it's because middle school was when being excited or open-minded or grateful started to evaporate for so many of my classmates. It was when we downshifted into a wry lifted eyebrow anytime someone did something goofy or strange. Every year, we seemed to judge one another just a little more harshly, seeking out divisions, separating into groups. People always blamed becoming a teenager. "Oh, middle school," they said knowingly. "Oh, teenagers." It made me sad. Why were we all acting like this? Suddenly, we had to choose a camp, a persona, and slip into the proper uniform for whatever we chose. The sporty kids. The drama geeks. The honor students.

Choosing one never had felt right to me.

It hadn't for Abby, either. Her skepticism of the whole shift had been what rooted her to me. We talked about leaving someday, about college, about beyond. She was always on my side because I knew she felt it, too.

Those were the years Abby saved me over and over, even if she didn't know that's what she was doing.

The night of eighth-grade graduation, I remember sitting on our favorite rock at the river, our dresses tucked up under our knees so our feet could dangle, talking about how weird everyone was acting, how strange it was to have to pretend we didn't like our parents, or certain people who used to be our friends, how it felt like we had to tone down the stuff we liked, make-believe we didn't care anymore about fairies or *Star Wars* or the YouTube star we'd been obsessing about for two years, about *any* of the things we loved as kids.

Abby had listened, nodding, tossing small rocks into the eddy and swirl of the dark water. "I feel like that all the time," she told me.

Now, staring out at the darkening water, I realize it was an incremental ache. First middle school. Then high school: different hallways, same faces. All of us continued to separate into specific blobs of oil in our claustrophobic social pool. Looking back, my biggest fear was knowing that in Yuba Ridge, those groups have a way of fixing themselves in cement, and every part of me pulsed with the knowing that I had to get out of there before they set for good.

Because the only one worth being cemented to was Abby.

If I'm honest, I wasn't fully aware of biding my time. I had fun. I distracted myself. Lots of parties. Hanging out at the river. Boys. Always boys. Some sweet, like Ryan Hoffman, whose heart I might have broken freshman year when I told him I just wanted to be friends. Other boys were pushy and self-centered like Greg Newman, who thought an invitation to homecoming allowed him full groping advantages. When I threatened to call his mother, the mayor, he dropped me off at home and never talked to me again. No loss there.

By that point, though, the ache had found its way into my outer limbs.

Then, one night, my mom sat by my bed and told me, "It would be helpful to your uncle if I could be in Berlin for a year while the company transitions into the new offices there."

I'd jumped at the chance.

"You're quiet." Will trails his fingers across the top of my hand to get my attention, and it jolts me back to the present.

I turn to him. "The water looks so pretty right now."

As I watch the light change the color of the lake from blue to ink, I wonder how I can explain to Abby that because of Berlin, I see light like this differently now.

"We're going to stay for at least the first set." Will's gaze slips to the two musicians who have started tuning their instruments on the stage. The guy wears a suit and tinkers with a violin. The girl wears a vintage shift dress under the thick strap of her guitar. They seem like hipsters, early twenties. Lots of these duos in Berlin.

"Do you play an instrument?" Will asks me.

"I used to play the piano, but I quit before middle school." I study his long fingers. "Do you play? You have the hands for it."

He shakes his head, splaying his hands out on the table. "Just numbers for me. I'm afraid I am terribly tone-deaf."

The duo takes the stage. Soon, their jazzy, indie-folk sound floats across the twilit evening. Neel and Abby turn around to watch them, their backs leaning against the table now. I try to concentrate on the music soaking into the space around us, and scoot a little closer to Will, until his knee grazes mine beneath the table. I try to focus, but I keep noticing the way Neel leans into Abby, pointing out a boat strung with lights gliding slowly across the water or whispering something to her I can't hear over the hum of the song, and that earlier annoyance flickers like the start of a fire.

When the musicians take their break, Will excuses himself and disappears inside the building. A few minutes later, Alina appears with two sticks of pale blue cotton candy, almost glowing in the last of the twilight. "What?" Abby clasps her hands together in front of her heart. "Seriously?! Cotton candy delivered straight to the table? I love Switzerland!" She pulls a delicate thread from her stick and pops it in her mouth. I do the same, and it begins to coax me out of my funk – I mean, it's cotton candy delivered right to our table.

"Did you do this?" Abby grins at Neel.

"It had to be Will." The burnt-crisp taste on my tongue might be sugar, might be my tone.

Neel hears it, gives me a funny glance before answering Abby. "It's all Will, I'm afraid, though I'm happy to take the credit before he comes back."

"Try it." Abby pulls away a wisp and holds it out to him.

He waves her off. "I think not."

Abby laughs at his pained expression. "Don't be such a baby. It's delicious. Especially compared to the cotton candy at our county fair, right, Riya?" Her smile is tinged faintly with blue. "Remember when that guy convinced you to try the banana flavor?"

"Ugh." My stomach curls at the thought. "There is no banana anywhere in the whole world of bananas that tastes like that cotton candy did. They should have called it what it was: armpit flavor."

"Window cleaner and armpit flavor?" Neel shakes his head. "I'm growing increasingly concerned about American dietary habits." It's not all that funny, but Abby and I do that thing we do sometimes where we catch each other's eye and burst into giggles for no reason. The ease of it, its suddenness, loosens the knot in my chest.

Neel looks delighted we find him so funny. "Whatever do they put in that candy floss?" he asks Will, who has just returned to the table.

Will climbs back onto the bench next to me. "Fairy dust. Unicorn laughter. The usual magic." He lets his hand linger for a moment on my back, sending its own magic tingling up and down my spine. "Shall we stay for another set?"

I nod, pulling another strand of candy from the stick, and hope these musicians play for the rest of the night.

Abby

The next morning, I wake as the light creeps under the living room curtains, a breeze from the open window fluttering them and sending sun spangles across the wood floor. Riya snores, shifting as I scoot out from under the covers. I pluck my phone from my bag and log on to the Wi-Fi. Today, Will plans to drive us to Lucerne to see the famous bridge and the Old Town, and I want to do some research before we go so I know what I'm looking at when I get there.

"You're up early." I jump. Will leans against the door frame of the kitchen in dark jeans and a plain black T-shirt. He holds a white ceramic cup with his long fingers. "Coffee?"

"Yes, thanks." I follow him into the narrow kitchen. Will fiddles with the espresso machine, sending it whirling, and turns to set a plate of small croissants (*gipfel*, he tells me) with butter and jam in front of me on the counter. I bite into one. "Mmmm, did you make these?"

"No, no – went to the bakery this morning." He washes out his cup in the sink and sets it in the stainless-steel drying rack. "Good, yes?"

"Delicious." I dab some currant jam on my next bite.

Neel appears in the doorway. "Someone needs to wake Sleeping Beauty in there before she snores a hole in the floor." I laugh. We can even hear her in the kitchen.

Will hands him a coffee. "Let her sleep. No need to rush out of here. Lucerne isn't too long a drive. Especially for a Californian." He winks at me. Riya seems pretty gone over him, and I can't blame her. Neel has cute friends. Actually, Riya would kill me for even thinking it, but Neel's pretty cute himself. Not as obvious as Damiano the Italian Stalker, but there is something about him – his dark eyes, his thick black hair, his lean forearms. Okay, is it weird that I'm noticing his forearms? Who cares about a guy's forearms? I bite into a second *gipfel*, trying not to notice the casual way Neel rests against the counter, holding his coffee as he and Will make plans for the day. He's animated with Will in a way I haven't seen before, telling him a story about a mutual friend they know who started an internship in Norway this summer. He's grown up from the photos of the skinny, fussy cousin Riya had pinned on her wall at home. Relaxing against the counter, the sleeves of his shirt rolled to his elbows, he's practically handsome.

"Abby?"

"What?" *Not looking at your forearms!* I manage not to shout.

Neel sets his cup in the sink. "We'll head out in a half hour or so. Think you can wake the beast in there?"

I slide off the chair. "I'm on it."

"And, Abby?"

"Yeah?"

Neel points the *gipfel* he's about to eat at me. "Wear some decent walking shoes. Not those floppy things you two try to pass off as suitable footwear."

Even good forearms can't save a guy sometimes.

An hour later, I peer through my window in the backseat of the BMW as we move along the highway out of Zurich and into the surrounding area, passing neat towns with their orderly boxes of geraniums, the snowcapped mountains a constant fringe on the horizon. In the seat next to me, Riya wears black-and-white-striped socks pulled to her knees with her running shoes and a belted denim dress. She's listening attentively to the music blaring from Will's car stereo, her head bobbing. "I like this," she tells him. "Is it new?"

"Old." He glances at her in his rearview mirror. "I'll make you a playlist later."

I turn again to the window. Yesterday we had clouds and rain, but today is bright and clear. Will drums his fingers on the steering wheel along to the song's bass-thump and chats with Neel about their classes for next fall. "I can't believe this weather," he keeps saying, scanning the clear skies. "Okay, slight change of plans – I'm taking you to the Rigi first. It's usually clouded over and you can't see anything, but today is incredible."

Riya sits forward, elbows on knees. "What's the Rigi?"

Will changes lanes. "It's a section of the Alps. We'll go to Weggis and take the cable car up. Seriously, on a day like this, it's one of the best views in Switzerland."

Riya grins at Will through the break in the seats. "Sounds amazing."

I check my phone. "Queen of the Mountains."

Will nods. "That's right, good. Have you studied Switzerland much?"

I hold up the evidence. "I'm iPhone smart."

Sitting back, her voice holding a trace of annoyance, Riya mutters, "I hope you have an excellent roaming plan, Queen of the Google."

"I do, thanks." I slip my phone into my backpack. "Nice socks, by the way. Very hiking appropriate. You'll be all the rage in the cable car." She answers by stretching her legs across my lap and waggling her running shoes in my face.

"So about this cable car..." Neel's voice catches. "Like gondola-in-the-sky kind of cable car or a tram?"

"Sky." Will follows signs to Rigi Kaltbad before glancing over at Neel. "Okay?"

Neel doesn't answer him, just looks quietly out the passenger window.

Turns out, Neel has a water-and-oil sort of relationship with heights. A half hour later, ashen-faced, he sits glued to a bench in the cable car, his eyes shut tight, as we soar toward the town of Rigi Kaltbad. "Neel, you're missing it!" Riya exclaims, her face so close to the glass she leaves small patches of fog on it. "You're missing the view of the lake!"

"I've seen a lake," he says, grimacing.

He hasn't seen this lake. And not from this vantage point. As the car lifts us higher, I gawk at the landscape below us – the mountains, the wide blue water, the houses peppered along its edges merging into the green of meadows.

"This is Swiss engineering," Will assures Neel, giving his shoulder an encouraging pat. "You are very safe."

Neel shakes his head. "I will be very safe when I'm standing on the ground."

A few minutes later, he gets his wish as we bump into the Rigi Kaltbad station and walk into the car-free village. I breathe in the mountain air, crisp and green. In the distance, I hear a sporadic, dreamy sort of clanging that I realize must be cowbells. Cowbells! We follow the path through some trees toward a lookout Will wants to show us, the air scented with pine, like home.

The weekend before I left for Florence, Dad took me

hiking on the Pacific Crest Trail in Tahoe. When the four of us were living under the same roof, our family had hiked almost every clear weekend, but I hadn't been on a trail in months. That Saturday, Dad and I set our alarms for seven, grabbed breakfast to go, and drove the hour to the trailhead, listening to the CD I gave him for Christmas, *Mozart for Hikers*. Dad always played classical music on long drives, but I bought that particular CD before Mom had packed the Volvo with hanging clothes and boxes of books and a laundry basket full of her shoes, and then suddenly there it was playing in Dad's car. I had to turn to the window, my eyes stinging.

As we hiked, Dad pointed out types of rocks and various animals: a tree squirrel, a hawk. Finally, as we stood gazing out at Lake Tahoe from the crest of the trail, he turned to me, his Squaw Valley baseball hat shading the green eyes I'd inherited, the eyes that for months had been sad and worried at their edges, and he asked, "You holding up okay, Bee?"

He'd finally given me a chance to tell him that I hadn't been holding up okay all year, that things weren't right with Riya gone or that it was weird without Mom at home. I could have told him how it felt like Kate seemed to be slipping more and more into her college life or even just that junior year had been harder than I'd expected. He finally asked me. But instead of telling him what I truly felt, I pointed out a shadow of another hawk passing over us and told him, "Fine. Really, Dad, I'm fine. I'm your Bee."

Why had I done that?

Riya falls in step beside me. "Okay, serious face – what's up?"

"This is just my face," I try to joke, holding my backpack straps like a parachute. "I'm perfecting the intellectual gleam in my eye – see?" I give her my best smarty-pants stare, adjusting my glasses. We walk in silence for a moment.

She's waiting for me to ask about her announcement yesterday, I can feel it radiating from her. I know I didn't react the way she'd hoped. But Riya has never been a theater kid. We knew theater kids. They passed out flyers for fall shows and spring plays and abridged productions of Shakespeare. Growing up, we watched them at the boxy community theater downtown or outside on the cement stage at the fairgrounds. Each spring, they paraded around the stage dressed as fairy-tale characters or villagers or pirates, while we sat on an old quilt watching them. Later, we went to some of their shows at Yuba Ridge High.

But we never joined them onstage.

"So, an actress, huh?"

Riya's eyes light up. "Okay, I know I told you about Kiara."

About a thousand times. Most of my communication

with Riya since November has had a *Kiara said the funniest thing*, or *Kiara and I went to this amazing club*, or *Kiara and I saw this cool French film*, so, yeah, she's told me about Kiara.

I strangle my backpack straps. "What about her?"

Riya's excitement quickens her pace. "She's part of this theater collective in Berlin. She goes four days a week after school for improv and acting classes and theater-as-social-change workshops."

"Theater as what?"

"As social change. It's a type of theater that acts as a vehicle for social justice. Storytelling to create a better world. I started going with Kiara to these workshops, and, well" – she glances at me nervously – "I fell madly in love."

Riya is always falling madly in love. For about ten minutes. She's like that with everything. Each new find is a fierce burst of love. In high school alone, she's gone through at least a dozen "life-altering" interests. Freshman year, she was certain she wanted to be a vet, so she volunteered at the Yuba Ridge animal shelter. For a month. That's how long it took her to realize she had to clean up after the animals and not just post cute pictures of them on Instagram. She has been *madly in love* with ceramics (a three-month class she didn't finish), swim team (one season), and with bookselling at our local used bookstore (quit after two months). It's a long list.

But that's Riya – she crushes and obsesses and moves on to the next incredible thing.

I've always felt honored she's kept me around all these years.

"So acting's your newest love?"

She shakes her head. "I know what you're thinking, and it's not like that. This time it's for real. I finally realize how you feel about ancient history. I've always been so jealous of you, with how you always knew what you wanted to do with your life."

I slow my pace so the guys move farther ahead of us up the trail. "What do you mean?"

She slips her arm through mine. "You've *always* known your direction. That you want to go to college and study ancient history and work in a museum and then be a college professor, right?"

"We've both always known we want to go to college someday."

Riya's eyes glow. "Yeah, but I've never had anything to love the way you love history, nothing I've ever felt certain about. Until now. I finally understand."

I bite my lip to keep from saying, *we'll see*. Instead, I nod and say, "That's great, Rye. I'm happy for you."

I study our feet as they fall in a natural rhythm along the path, hers in bright green Nikes and mine in worn low hikers, and think about the things she listed for my own life – college, a museum job, maybe a professorship someday. I do want all those things. Eventually. I do plan to study ancient history in college. Only lately, I feel like college can't be too far from home. How can I leave my dad the way everyone else has? I'm just glad we have another year of high school left to figure it out.

"Oh, wow – look!" She points ahead, where the trail opens up to a railed viewing area with benches, a telescope, and a panorama of Lake Lucerne and the surrounding area. Neel hangs back by the bench. Maybe even solid ground isn't enough when we're up this high.

We let the view melt into us, and I realize I'm holding my breath. Letting it out, I say, "Wow, Will. You didn't tell us how ugly it would be up here." Riya and I join the guys at the bench.

"Feel lucky," he says, scrutinizing the snowcapped mountains beyond the spread of blue water. "I'm sure there are Swiss who've never had the chance to see it so clear."

"It looks fake," Riya insists. "Like the whole country is masquerading as a postcard."

Will laughs. "You are not the first to say this."

"Expensive, though." Neel crosses his arms over his chest. "And I'm from London."

Pulling a metal SIGG bottle from his backpack, Will takes a long drink. "There is a joke about this." He motions at the view with the water bottle. "When God was making Switzerland, he asked the people what they wanted from their country, and they said, 'First we would like mountains to surround and protect us from wars and strife.' So God made the Alps to protect the Swiss people. Then he asked, 'What else?' And they said they would like 'crisp blue water in rivers and lakes,' and he made them beautiful lakes and rivers. 'Anything else?' he asked them. And they said, 'Green pastures so our cows can produce sweet milk and we can grow good food,' and God made the pastures the greenest of green. At the end, God was very tired, and he said to a farmer, 'There, I have done everything you asked, may I please have a glass of that milk for my hard work?' And the Swiss farmer said, 'Certainly; that will be five francs.'"

Neel and Will nearly double over laughing.

I glance at Riya, who shrugs. Maybe we don't know enough about Switzerland yet to get why it's so funny.

Neel and Will wander off to read a sign, but I just want to stare at these mountains. I know it makes me a nature dork, but I could sit here for hours, imagining that this view has looked the same for thousands of years. One of my favorite things about history is it doesn't care a hoot about all of us silly humans trying to figure out the right-now. Oh, wow. *Care a hoot*. That's my mom, creeping in. She says things like *I don't care a hoot* and *What the palm tree* instead of their curse counterparts. My stomach knots. I tried calling her last night, but she texted that she was out to dinner "with Rob" and would call me this morning. Instead, though, she sent another text: *Missing you! Hope you're having a great time. Hug Riya for me!* And she tacked on about a thousand kiss-heart emojis. Classic Byrd avoidance strategy. I texted her back a picture of our hot chocolates from yesterday and didn't ask about dinner with Dr. Spits-A-Lot.

"So, what do we do up here?" Riya fidgets next to me on the bench.

I motion at the landscape. "You marinate in the view."

Her marinade lasts approximately five seconds. "Okay, officially bored. Beautiful view. Well done, Switzerland God! Let's go find something fun to do." She pops up and heads back toward the path, and I start to follow her.

But not before I notice Neel rolling his eyes at her exit. "Attention span of a fruit fly, that one."

Even if I sort of agree with him right now, I shoot back, "Well, not all of us can be born fifty years old with a pipe in our mouth, Gramps." I head off after Riya.

"I don't smoke pipes! Smoking kills."

Something in his voice catches me and I pause, turning around. He's teasing me, and his silhouette against the mountains with his hands casually in his pockets sends that same shiver through me I got this morning in the kitchen.

"Abby!" Riya calls from up ahead on the trail. "Let's go!"

I hurry to catch up with her.

For the rest of the day, we walk across the famous geranium-lined wooden bridge in Lucerne, explore the Old Town with its cobbled streets, and spend an hour in the Picasso and Klee museum making grotesque faces at one another until Neel, his Angry Dad expression firmly back on his face, ushers us outside.

"I can't take you anywhere," Will says to Riya as he opens the car door for her, but he's smiling, his hand resting longer on her shoulder than it needs to.

When we get back to Zurich, Will and Neel drop us at the flat and head to dinner with another university friend, so Riya and I have the evening to ourselves. It's the perfect moment to give her the present I've been secreting in my bag during the trip so far. I slip the flat package, wrapped in glossy silver paper, out of my bag, and set it next to her on the futon, where she sprawls on her back, scrolling through her phone.

She sits up. "What's this?" She tears open the paper, her eyes curiously scanning the laminated back of the handmade book in front of her. "Oh, no way, is this—" She flips it over. "It is!" The cover, hand-lettered with colored markers, reads: *The Adventures of Riya the River Fairy and History Girl!* by Ms. Riya Sharma-Collins and Ms. Abby Byrd. Our fourth-grade graphic novel we spent the whole year making, all eighty-seven pages of it.

I sit down next to her on the futon. "I had it bound.

And I made a copy for me, too. Ms. Riya Sharma-Collins and Ms. Abby Byrd. We were such fancy fourth graders." We're both grinning like idiots at the glossy front.

"Where did you find it?" She begins flipping through the pages. "I can't believe this. Oh, do you remember this part? Where we find the Magic Tablet of River Dreams in the Temple of Artemis?"

I nod with fake gravity. "That was a close one. The river almost lost all its dreams."

"Right?! Good job, River Fairy and History Girl!" She closes the book and gives me a teary look, a stripe of afternoon sun through the window lighting her face. "This is the best present of all presents in the entire world of present-giving."

I wave her off, a flush of warmth heating my cheeks. "Good thing Riya the River Fairy hasn't lost her sense of hyperbole." But she's right. It is.

She tucks the gift into her bag and grabs her phone again. "Okay, what to do, what to do. A whole evening without Neel. Let's go celebrate." She scrolls through some options. "We could go to a club, or see a play. Or – hey, this looks fun. And it's so hot today. Want to take a stand-up paddleboard lesson on the lake?"

"I don't really like paddleboarding."

"You've never tried it!"

"It looks kind of silly. I like kayaking."

"Come on. They're open until eight." She shows me a

website advertising rentals and lessons. "And the instructor looks cute."

"What about Will?"

She ducks her head, overly scrutinizing the website. "What about him?"

"You two seem like you're connecting." She's avoiding my eyes, which is strange. Riya usually can't stop talking about a guy when she's crushing.

"I think I might love *this* guy." She holds out the ad again. He's not my type, all glossy muscles and board shorts, but he's clearly gorgeous.

"I think you love that he's not wearing a shirt." I dig through my bag to locate my bathing suit. "But fine. Yes. Let's do it. Only we don't need lessons. It's standing. And paddling. How hard can it be?"

An hour later, I find out.

Every time a big wave comes our direction, I can't stay on the board and go tumbling into the blue water. Over and over. Riya doesn't seem to be having this problem. After my tenth fall of the evening, she paddles up to me. "You're too rigid. You have to roll with the waves."

I cling to the side of my board, water streaming into my eyes, the safety strap digging into my ankle. "I *am* rolling with it. Rolling *off*. Isn't it time to return these things yet?"

"We've barely gone anywhere. Get back on that board!" She bobs on her board, relaxed, holding her paddle in both hands, the lake sparkling with evening sunlight around her. She hasn't fallen in once. When I don't move, she splashes into the water and swims her board over to mine until she's peering at me over it. "The water's so nice."

I rest my chin on my board, letting the waves move past me. "It must be nicer when you don't keep falling into it."

"Do you hate it?" she asks.

I lift my head. "This paddleboard? Pretty much, yeah."

She sets her paddle lengthwise on the board. "You're so grumpy. This is supposed to be fun."

I sigh, following her lead on the paddle. "I'm just tired. I might have exhausted my trying-new-things limit for the day." My teeth chatter; the water's starting to get chilly as the sun slips in the sky. Riya seems like she's about to say something else, but instead she pulls herself onto her board, waits for me to do the same, and we both paddle into the shore on our knees.

We're returning our boards to the guy who rented them to us earlier. *Not* Mr. Muscles. An older guy in a straw hat. Behind us, someone says, "Riya? Abby? Are you kidding me? Is that you?!"

We turn to a boy our age, also returning a board. He wears an NYU sweatshirt and board shorts and grins at us from under a mop of wet brown curls.

Riya recognizes him before I do. "Ian?!" He engulfs her

in a bear hug and the light goes on. Ian Campos. Fifth grade comes spilling back, flashes of our shared table in Mr. Waclawski's room. Ian Campos, the human embodiment of a teddy bear, with a blade-sharp sense of humor and an enormous heart.

"Ian? What on earth—" I start before he silences me with one of his trademark hugs. It's a consuming hug, as he now resembles what happens if a teddy bear hits the gym a few hours a day.

"Wow," he says, releasing me and taking a step back. "What are the odds?"

Today, returning paddleboards at a beach on Lake Zurich, we have officially beaten any and all odds. Ian was only at our school for fifth grade before he moved again with his family to upstate New York, and we didn't stay in touch. But during that fifth-grade year we grew close. It started by bonding over a common enemy: Horrible Noah Stevens.

I will never forget the first day of school, when Mr. Waclawski gave us our seat assignments. Riya and I couldn't believe our luck to find ourselves seated at the same table of four, our names side by side in black ink. Then we frowned at the label across from Riya: Noah Stevens. Our spirits dropped. We scanned the room, seeing Noah over by the water fountain. He hadn't changed much over the summer, still had his trademark blank stare and a low-grade-fever flush to his thin face.

We already had a long list of Things That Make Noah Stevens Horrible dating back to first grade when he joined our school, but he didn't waste time adding to the list as he slid into his seat, giving my brand-new map-of-the-world backpack a swift kick. So much for that peach in my lunch.

"Did you just kick Abby's backpack?" Riya demanded. Shrug from Noah. "Say you're sorry!"

"Don't hold your breath," I muttered, inspecting my peach.

"Yeah, right." This time he gave her seat a kick.

"You're such a Neanderthal!"

"Don't insult Neanderthals," I said, glaring at Noah.

Noah sneered at Riya, and then said to me, "Okay, sorry – wouldn't want your bodyguard to do some sort of tomahawk chop on me." Riya's fists clenched in her lap. For four years, she had endured this brand of boorishness from Noah. Each time, she would remind him that she was Indian – from *India* – but that his comments were insulting to *everyone*. Of course, he ignored her, continuing to make racist jokes that involved whooping and disparaging references to headdresses. Brain-dead jerk.

Then an angel appeared in the form of a new student seated across from me. Ian Campos. He slid in next to Noah. "Hi," he greeted us, his eyes widening at Noah's whooping. "What are you doing?"

I explained our situation.

Noah shrugged. “It’s just a joke.”

Ian stared at Noah, his dark eyes serious. “Not a funny one.” Stricken, Noah shrank in his seat. That year, Ian continued to be popular with the other boys not just because he was twice as big and could throw a football farther than any of them, but because he was simply a good person. To everyone. Even Noah. And, of course, he had the football thing going for him.

Now Riya fills Ian in on her year in Berlin and our grand tour as they exchange Instagram accounts. “What about you?” he asks me.

“Oh, Abby doesn’t do the whole social media thing,” Riya tells him. “She doesn’t approve of this sort of modern technology.”

Ian gives me a look that could be either impressed or weirded out. “Really?” I choose to take it as impressed. “That’s interesting, I guess.” Okay, maybe *impressed* isn’t the right word.

“It’s not that I don’t *approve* of it. It’s just not my thing,” I clarify, wondering why I’m explaining anything to a boy I haven’t seen in six years. “I think it creates a false sense of knowing people, just seeing flashes of their lives but not really being in them for real, you know?”

His gaze flicks to Riya for a moment. To me, he says, “Sure, sure. I just like seeing other people’s pictures. I guess I haven’t thought that much about it.”

My face burns. Noticing, Riya steps in. “I admire her

for it. I mean, mostly I end up getting totally jealous of other people's posts; their lives always seem cooler than anything I'm doing at the moment. I should probably stay off it, but" – she holds up her phone – "screen addict!"

I smile at her gratefully.

He holds up his phone. "Well, now we can stay in touch, which is great. You two should be posting pictures of this trip of yours. Then everyone else can be jealous of *you*." Ian has a smile that occupies every curve of his face. Right now, he can't take his eyes off Riya.

She beams at him. "What are you doing now? Do you want to hang out? Too bad we didn't get to paddleboard together." Her eyes slide over his wide chest. Subtle. Straw Hat Guy hears her and quickly locks his rental shack and wheels a rack of boards toward the parking lot.

Ian looks genuinely disappointed. "Wish I could. But I'm late to meet my mom. It's our last day here, and we're heading to the airport tonight for a red-eye. We just finished a weeklong hut-to-hut hike. The lake felt amazing after all that hiking."

Riya pouts. "Bummer. I would have really liked to catch up."

"I know. Seriously, though," he says, stepping back and taking us in, "I can't believe I ran into you two. Riya and Abby. Nice to know some things never change."

And I accuse social media of not telling the whole truth.

Riya

At dawn the next morning, Abby and I tiptoe quietly out of the flat. We'd planned to join Will and Neel at a club last night, but we both fell asleep on the futon when we got back from paddleboarding, like ninety-year-old grandpas. We woke to Neel jostling me awake at one in the morning. "I texted you six times!"

"Sorry," I mumbled, sitting up, still dazed from our power nap. "I guess we're sort of tired."

Abby punctuated this with one of her epic yawns that sound like a sick ocean bird. But it had its normal comic effect, too. Hearing it, Neel's expression softened. "I thought you'd run off again."

Nothing remotely that interesting.

Now we leave a note on the kitchen counter to avoid a *Neeleurysm* (Abby's word, which she said is a hybrid of *Neel* and *aneurysm*). I include it in the note. *Don't have a Neeleurysm,* I write. *We're out for a walk.*

We slip into the quiet of the Zurich morning, walking

down the street, until we find our way to a park a few blocks from Will's flat. Abby stops so suddenly I walk several more feet before I realize she's not by my side. "I need to tell you something," she blurts, a pale lilac beanie pulled down over her ears against the chilly morning.

I eye her warily. After we saw Ian yesterday, she'd been quiet, distracted. Even more so than her normal Abby self. "Okay."

She steps aside to let a woman with a stroller pass us. "Do you remember our Skype call at Thanksgiving?"

Since they don't celebrate Thanksgiving in Berlin (obviously), we set up a Skype call so I could join her family for a Turkey Day chat. It was almost midnight in Berlin, but before the meal even started, the image just blinked out and they were gone. About a minute later, I got a text from Abby saying that Henry had somehow managed to upend an entire pitcher of gravy onto the laptop, ruining it. I never did get to celebrate with them because no one else had a charged laptop, and Abby said her phone was almost out of power and she couldn't find her charger. Such a Byrd thing to happen since they all basically live like it's 1982.

I nod. "Did you guys ever get that gravy out of your laptop?"

"I lied about the gravy."

I blink at her, confused. "What?"

She studies a man walking his full-size poodle through

an arched entrance of the park. "There was no gravy."

"Why would you lie about gravy?"

Her eyes slide to mine. "I didn't want to have Thanksgiving with you."

Unease ripples through me. "Wait, what?"

"Look, I'm not proud of this. I wasn't even going to tell you about it. But then, I don't know, seeing Ian yesterday, having him say 'some things never change' or whatever, I just felt like—"

"What, Abby?" I push.

"I know I said you changed, but it's not just you."

"Right, your parents—"

"No – not just my parents. Us. You and me. We've changed." She takes a shaky breath. "This year, the *whole* year, completely sucked. I'm not blaming you. I know it wasn't your fault you moved to Berlin. I'm not trying to guilt-trip you. I'm just trying to figure out how to tell you about how I feel without you getting defensive or telling me I should have talked to you about it sooner because I *know* I should have talked to you about it sooner. We both should have done a lot of things differently. Because it kept getting worse. It's like you were on a dock and I was in a boat and you pushed me out onto the water and each time I didn't talk to you or tell you something or call you, I could see you getting smaller and smaller on the dock—"

"Wait," I interrupt. "In this random boat metaphor, I *pushed* you?"

Her gaze cuts over my shoulder. "Maybe it's a bad metaphor, but it's what it felt like."

"Like I *pushed* you? In a boat."

Exasperated, she says, "Don't get hung up on the boat, okay? I'm just trying to explain how I felt last year. How I still feel. I don't really know how else to say it, and maybe I'm saying it wrong. Which is probably why I don't say things in the first place because I say the wrong thing and then you focus on the wrong thing and not what I'm trying to tell you. Forget the boat." Her voice has been rising in pitch, but she quiets it. "What I'm trying to say is, it felt like I spent every day just losing you more and more. And then everything happened with my parents, and I already felt too far from you."

I gape at her. Abby doesn't use this many sentences unless she's discussing something that has an official brass plaque attached to it because it's been buried under a pile of rubble for thousands of years. "You framed your dog."

She stares at her shoes. "I know." She's already putting her Abby Armor back on, I can see it. I need to keep her talking before she seals herself back inside it.

"That's messed up, Abby." I watch a tear trace the curve of her cheek. "Why did you feel like you had to do that? We tell each other everything."

But even as I say it, I know it's not true. Not anymore. The realization settles over me like fog. I pull her to a stone fountain ringed with a cement bench, and we sit, the water splashing softly behind us. "Tell me what happened with Thanksgiving. Please. And be honest."

She pulls her knees to her chest. "Remember when I went to Fall Formal?"

She'd sent me a picture. In it, she wore a hunter-green dress, almost Roman style. Super cute. "I loved your dress. You went with Amanda and Sydney, right?"

She nods. "Yeah. I even wore makeup." I exaggerate a gasp at this information, and she smiles through her tears. "I know, right? Me and eye shadow." She fakes a shudder. "I even used a curling iron."

"Well, that's where you went wrong. Curling irons are for your hair."

"That hairstyle was cute, right? There were bobby pins in play."

"You looked amazing."

She swallows. "But I didn't tell you what happened at the dance."

When I'd texted to ask her how it went, she'd replied: typical school dance, blah, blah, blah.

typical abby, I'd written back. She'd never been big on school spirit. "What happened at the dance?"

A faint stain of red colors her cheeks. "Okay, so I was at the dance and it was all the usual suspects, acting all the expected ways—"

"Of course."

"And I started dancing."

"In public?! Abby Byrd! I'm totally taking you to a club in Berlin."

She grimaces. "Careful, you haven't heard the rest of the story yet. So, we're dancing and I go to get some punch and, well, end up standing next to Derek Ayala by the snack table."

I widen my eyes at her. Abby has been crushing on Derek Ayala since sixth grade, even if she never admits it to anyone but me. "Um, is this about to be a love-over-the-cookie-platter story?"

"You forget this story is about me and not about you." Her face definitely doesn't have a ride-off-into-the-sunset hue to it. More of an I-might-puke-thinking-about-it shade. I motion for her to keep going. "So, Derek and I start talking," she says. "Turns out, we both love history movies. For him, he mostly loves spies and war, but he's a total sucker for ancient Rome and hidden treasure and secret societies."

"Just like you!" I can't help but still be hopeful, even knowing this doesn't have a happy ending.

"He's a total closet history geek! His favorite author is Steve Berry."

"You *love* Steve Berry."

"I do." She nods sadly, staring at the tops of her knees. "We ended up sitting at one of those round plastic tables in the outdoor cafeteria until the dance was over. At one point, it got really cold, and he gave me his suit jacket."

"And?" My voice squeaks.

She drops her face into her hands. "It was horrible," she mumbles through her fingers. "I kissed him."

"The kiss was horrible?"

She peers at me through her fingers. "At first it was fine. Even sort of great, but then he got really weird and stood up and told me he was planning on going out with Tori Hollister. Not that he was going out with her. He was *planning* on going out with her. And then he asked for his jacket back and left. Seriously, he set some sort of track record getting out of there, and I just sat there, in that empty outdoor cafeteria, with water dripping somewhere, echoing like I was the next victim in a horror movie. So I texted Sydney and Amanda and told them I was coming down with the flu and going home and couldn't sleep over at Sydney's house. Then my dad picked me up by the football field parking lot."

"Oh, Abby." She's been into Derek as long as I can remember. In the whole time we've been friends, she's kissed three other boys. Sixth grade she kissed Mike LaFont at a birthday party as part of a dare and said it was gross. Eighth grade she kissed Joe Colley after the graduation dance because they'd been flirty all year and she thought *why the heck not, it's graduation* and Joe Colley is the sweetest boy on earth. And sophomore year she kissed her chemistry lab partner, Kevin Bryant, on and off for about three months, but it had seemed more scientific than romantic, so when he started dating Becka Mackley, Abby had seemed mostly relieved.

Derek Ayala was another thing entirely.

And she hadn't told me.

"And this has what to do with gravy?" My skin feels cold in the early light of the park.

Abby sighs, straightening her legs out in front of her. "I didn't realize it at the time, but that's when I began to not tell you things. That's what I meant about the boat. That push away from you. I went home that night and crawled under the covers and stayed there until two the next day. When I got up, all I could think about was how that kiss was the most embarrassing and disappointing thing that had ever happened to me and *Riya isn't here*. And then the next week, I went to school and there were Derek and Tori making out by her locker, and all I could think was, *Riya isn't here*. I couldn't nudge you and say, *Ugh, get a reality TV show*, but you would know it felt like someone had just kicked me. You would have known my brave face was a fake face. You would have made me my favorite red mango curry and bought Americone Dream ice cream and watched *National Treasure* and we would have rolled our eyes about stupid Derek and Tori. But we didn't because you weren't there." Her voice crumbles.

"That's not fair. You didn't even let me try. You went silent. You made up fake gravy. You pushed the boat, Abby. Not me."

She starts to cry again, tears spilling down her cheeks. I know I should do something, say something, maybe put my arm around her, but I can't. So I sit, staring out at the park, listening to the fountain splashing behind us, until her tears stop coming. "We should probably head back to Will's," I say, standing.

As we walk silently back toward Will's flat, my head spins with conflicting thoughts. In some ways, she's right; I wasn't there. It wasn't my fault, but I wasn't there. Still, she didn't even let me try to help her. And she wasn't there for me, either. For the last few months, she completely shut me out. I keep taking deep breaths, attempting to soothe the competing feelings of anger and guilt fizzing inside me in the cool air of Switzerland. Finally, pausing before the closed door of Will's flat, I blurt out, "I didn't push the boat."

Her shoulders slump. "Just stop with the boat, okay?"

Will sees Abby's face when we walk into the kitchen, where he and Neel are leaning against the counter drinking coffee. "Oh – what?" But I just shake my head at him and he does what the Swiss do so well – strategize solutions – and thirty minutes later we find ourselves in Bärenland, a gummy candy store in Old Town Zurich. Around us, we find cakes made entirely of gummies, a whole shelf of gummy pizzas, platters of shrink-wrapped gummies, gummy frog princes and unicorns and trolley cars and hearts and roses. We fill our bags, and Neel buys one of the gleaming platters to send home with Abby. I try to ignore my sour gut at the smile she gives him, try to blame it on too many gummies on an empty stomach.

Outside, we walk the cobbled streets. There is something delightfully disturbing about biting the tiny heads off gummy creatures, and I see it begin to work its magic on Abby, her face softening into a laugh at something Neel's saying to her about the Grossmünster Church we're strolling past, but I'm not listening to Neel. My brain's still sifting through the shredded pieces of our fight, and I can't seem to shake her stupid boat metaphor.

Maybe because I know she has a point.

How did I miss the push?

Abby has always been comfortable with being alone. More often than not, on Friday or Saturday nights, Abby would bow out of a party to watch a documentary on the History Channel or take extra shifts at the Blue Market, encouraging me to go without her. "Go on, butterfly," she'd tease. "Get your social on." Sometimes, I even skipped out early from those nights and went to her house, crawled onto her bed, and listened to music with her, telling her about all the people acting like idiots that night. She'd have a foot on her desk, painting her toenails, always listening, nodding, and smiling knowingly at the antics of our Yuba Ridge classmates. One of the best things about Abby was that she never felt even remotely guilty about not having to be a part of all that. She never apologized or doubted herself.

At least that's what I've always thought.

the third Wonder

BERLIN, GERMANY

Riya

Will hands me my suitcase as I prepare to board the night train for Berlin. Neel and Abby have said their good-byes and already disappeared inside the train, but I take a last look up at Will. He smiles at me, hands in the pockets of his jeans, slouching in a way that makes him just the tiniest bit shorter. Before I can chicken out, I stand on my tiptoes, pull him close by the back of his neck, and kiss him, not too quickly but not too long, on the mouth.

"Oh!" His eyes go wide with shock behind his lenses.

Still close to his face, every nerve alive with the kiss, I whisper, "Now I can tell my friends I kissed the cutest boy in Switzerland. Not many girls can say that."

"Happy to help." Grinning, he attempts to smooth his tousled hair. As I step into the doorway of the train, he calls to me, "Maybe I'll see you when you visit Neel at uni?"

I wave through the glass of the train window, watching

with a familiar pang as his long body turns and moves away through the swarm of people in the Zurich station. I know some people think this side of me is one of my more shallow parts. I've had people say things like, "Don't be one of those boy-crazy girls." But they're wrong. It's not shallow. I know that now.

In one of my favorite acting classes last spring, my teacher, an old British man named Niles, with holes worn in his jeans from actual use and not for fashion, told us that actors must absorb both the best and worst of people around us. As students of human behavior, we must try to see everyone for their flaws and unique talents and quirks. It is in this exploration that we can discover the source of each of our characters. Sitting there in the front-row chairs of the darkened black box theater, his words sent a warm rush of recognition through me. I've always done this, studied people this way. Even more, I often fall for people, instantly, for all the small ways they are strange or beautiful or interesting. Not just boys, but all sorts of people. I fall for someone's gait or the way they wash a dish or the edges of their smile. With Will, it's the way his gaze seems like he is automatically on the side of whoever needs him most. Of course, this instant crushing (romantic or otherwise) has gotten me in trouble before. Especially with boys. It can get mistaken for something else: interest or obsession or love. But I was never able to explain it until Niles said those words.

Up until then, I'd just let people call me boy-crazy or flighty or melodramatic. It's been easier than trying to defend it, because, ironically, maybe they are too shallow to understand that if it isn't love, it's a version of it.

I find Abby waiting in our narrow train cabin. She motions to the bunk beds. "So, we fall asleep here and wake up in Berlin? I love this idea." She smiles at me, and it feels like a genuine Abby smile, free of ghosts, and I think maybe this trip is helping her. This is the smile of our childhood nights spent curled together in bunk beds in California or huddled together in sleeping bags on the floor of the family room, letting the flickering light of the TV lull us to sleep.

This is the smile I've been missing.

She peers at me with amused eyes. "I take it you had a good send-off with Will?"

"Does it show?" I shoot her a mischievous look.

"You're glowing."

"I kissed him."

"Of course you did. Top five?"

"The very top."

But she must see something genuine in my glow, because she adds sincerely, "He's great, Rye."

It's one of the reasons we're friends. Abby crushes on history and ideas and experiences the way I do on people. She gets it. But she also gets when something is special. Excitement for the night ahead floods me. We won't sleep.

We'll stay up talking all night, filling in the rest of the cracks from the year behind us until it's smooth so we can tuck it away behind us.

Neel brushes by me in the doorway. "I'll take this one." He tosses his suitcase on the bottom bunk. Shrugging, he adds, "Heights."

It's only now I notice there are *three* bunks stacked on top of each other. Wait. Neel is *not* sleeping in here with us. "Why don't you have your own room?"

He unzips his bag and starts rooting around for something. "And pay for a whole other cabin when we're just going to be sleeping for one night?" He reads the disappointment on my face. "Ah, come on. It'll be brilliant." He holds up a trashy gossip magazine someone must have left on the train. "I can tell you about whatever celebrity is currently in rehab while you dish about boys and paint each other's nails."

"Wow, sexist and condescending in one obnoxious package."

He feigns innocence, his gaze slipping from me to Abby. "No takers?"

"Wouldn't have pegged you for a celebrity gossip sort of guy." Abby sets her bag on the second bunk, her smile turning coy. "You could also start by telling us about British microeconomic theory, and we'll be out like a light in no time." She snaps her fingers. "Instant sleeping pill."

"You put on a good cover, Ms. Byrd." Neel rolls up the

magazine and points it at her. "But you know you find me irresistibly fascinating. I can see it in your enamored expression."

"That's indigestion," she tosses back. "Does anyone have a Pepcid or something?"

I narrow my eyes at the way he looks at her, at the slight tilt of his head, the smile at the corners of his mouth, his enjoyment of this verbal sparring game of theirs. He's an idiot if he thinks I can't see it. "Weren't you supposed to call Moira an hour ago?"

His face morphs to panic. "Oh, right – bloody forgot." He darts from the room.

Abby turns around, her hands across her stomach. "Seriously, Tums, anything?" She crawls up the ladder and onto her bunk. "Can you die from gummy overdose?" She curls into a ball. "I'm so glad you made me leave Dan's Reese's Peanut Butter Cups in Zurich. I never want to see sugar again."

That night, Abby and Neel fall asleep to the shifting and sway of the train. Their breathing, steady and deep beneath me, rumbles through the cabin like a couple of Darth Vader impersonators. Even with the erratic sleep we got the night before, I lie awake in the narrow top bunk, hyperaware of the night sounds of the train. I realize I forgot to brush my teeth. Gross. But I don't want to climb down, dig through my bag, and turn on the light in the wedge of bathroom. I'll just brush them twice in the morning.

An hour slips by with no hint of sleep, the kiss with Will playing over and over in my mind. I'll never get to sleep if I keep this up. Trying to clear my head, I think about arriving in Berlin tomorrow morning. My parents will pick us up at the Hauptbahnhof, and I'll finally be able to show Berlin to Abby. I've rewritten our itinerary about a thousand times in my head, adding and crossing off dozens of possibilities. We only have three days, but I know she'll have her mind blown by Berlin's intense and massive history. She'll geek out in the way only a history nut can. But I want to leave enough time for her to meet the friends who helped Berlin grab me by the shoulders and shake me.

In three days. Even if we don't sleep, it's a tall order. I squeeze my eyes shut. Go to sleep. Go to sleep. No deal. Neel and Abby have officially entered into a dreamland snoring contest. *It's a tie,* I want to shout. *You both win, now shut up so I can sleep!*

My phone glows with a text. I pull the duvet over my head to mute the light.

Kiara: home yet? abby with you? did you tell her about the show?

I text: no, yes, and no.

Kiara: !!!!!?

Me: night train, berlin tomorrow.

Kiara: did you tell her about london?

Me: NO!! i've got a plan.

Kiara: okay.

Kiara: IMHO you should tell her.

Me: didn't we have this discussion already?

Kiara: okay, she's your friend.

Me: trying to sleep. tschüss!

Kiara: tschüss!

I turn off my phone, my stomach blooming with nerves. Tomorrow morning, my two worlds will officially collide. Old and new. No better city than Berlin for that, but my stomach churns. As the train rocks us ahead, I start to doubt some of my plans, especially after everything Abby told me in Switzerland. As I squint into the dark, I consider calling Nani, canceling the rest of the trip, and sending Abby back to Northern California.

Because that would be easier.

Maybe even better?

Frustrated, I sigh loudly in the hope that it wakes the Snore Factory down below. It doesn't work. I chew my lip. Sometimes, I miss how simple it was to spend our summers by the constant swirl of the river, lounging like lizards on the warm granite. Simple and sweet.

Before the world grew huge and began to swallow us whole.

But like this train, I can't turn around now. I just hope Kiara and Abby are a good mix. What is it about the dark that grows a worry into a shadowy, evil shape even when there is probably nothing to worry about? I've rarely seen Abby be possessive. If anything, she will be distant when she doesn't like someone. And she's never needed us to like the same people. But that's just it. I want her to like Kiara. I almost need her to. Because what would I have done this year without Kiara? Berlin bodychecked me on arrival, but Kiara threw a much-needed blanket around me. She filed the edges off an autumn tipping dangerously into disappointment (despair, even, when I let myself get melodramatic about it).

The first two months at my new school, I cried almost every night. No one knows this. Not Abby. Not my parents, though they suspected. At the breakfast table many mornings, her espresso cup halfway to her lips, Mom's eyes would track my face for signs of distress. I would smile brightly and chatter on about a new gallery Dad had shown me or a film I'd seen recently. I hadn't wanted them to know I wasn't handling things, that the city seemed huge and cement-blocked, the language sharp and stabbing at me on the underground or at the grocery store. I couldn't admit I was struggling. Not to them. Dad was busy with a show at a gallery. Mom was busy wearing suits and taking meetings. Her brother, Neel's dad, had carried the family business on his shoulders for years so his younger sister could live by a river in Northern California with her artist husband and small child. It was Mom's turn to pick up some of the slack.

And it was just for a year.

Only sometimes a year can feel like a lifetime.

Then one rainy Thursday afternoon in November, I was packing my books into a maroon leather satchel I'd found with Mom in a vintage shop on Oranienstraße, when a girl in my social anthropology class stopped by my table. "Hey." She had multicolored streaks in her chopped blonde hair. "You're Riya?"

I nodded. "Yes, Riya. I'm sorry, I don't know your name."

She put her hand flat against her chest. "Kiara." She wore jean shorts over ripped purple tights and vintage Doc Martens and a tight leather jacket buttoned to her throat. "I really liked what you said today about globalization, how we're becoming blind to cultural specifics. Very cool." She grinned wide white teeth at me. Like a spotlight.

"Oh." Caught off guard, my cheeks heated. "Thanks."

"I'm going to a forum now." She paused, adjusting her own black shoulder bag, studded with safety pins. "At the Collective. It's a talk about social theater. Want to come? It'll be in English."

The heat from my cheeks had receded, draining into my limbs. "I would love that." Since that afternoon, I've spent three to four days a week at the Collective, studying the role of social theater, taking improv and technique classes, reading and studying plays, and steadily letting a path I'd never known existed light up the world in front of me.

Now I shift in the train bunk, thinking about what Abby said in Zurich. About the boat. Maybe that rainy afternoon in Berlin was the moment where Abby and my life in Northern California began to slip through my fingers, spooling away on the dark water of my past, instead of staying a fixed part of my life. Even if I didn't realize it at the time, maybe that was the moment I pushed the boat.

My parents are easy to spot in the crowded train station, espccially with Dad holding up a huge sign with his cartoon drawing of two traveling girls and the word *Wilkommen!* in bright orange letters. I warm at the sight of him. Not just the sign but his paint-spattered jeans and T-shirt. Dad uniform. Mom, looking glamorous in jeans, a bright geometrically patterned top, and wedge sandals, waves enthusiastically when she sees us. As we get closer, Abby drops her bag and runs to hug them both at the same time, crushing Dad's sign between them. She steps back. "Oh – sorry about the sign."

He folds it in half, waving away her apology. "It's done its job. How's the grand tour?"

Abby beams at the sight of my parents, her words spilling out. "This trip is incredible! I can't believe it.

We had the best hot chocolate in Zurich, and we saw the most beautiful art in Florence, and I bought a leather miniskirt – a *leather* miniskirt, me! And we took a gondola up a mountain in Switzerland—" She stops to catch her breath. Abby has always adored my parents, and it hasn't changed. "Just, well, wow."

Grinning, Mom picks up Abby's bag. "Wonderful, girls." She leans in to kiss my cheek. "Hi, sweetie." Up close, I see the dark patches under her eyes. She told me work had been busy when I talked with her yesterday. And they have both started packing to go back to California in August, so she's probably exhausted. Her eyes slip to my outfit. "Cute dress."

"Thanks." I look down at the cerise-pink maxi dress I slipped on this morning, wrinkled from its time wadded in my suitcase. It was cool on the train, but Berlin will be hot by midmorning.

Dad leans in to give Neel one of those awkward side-body hugs guys are always giving each other. "Good to see you, Neel. Have these girls been behaving themselves?"

Neel makes a snorting sound. "Troublemakers, both of them."

Dad laughs. "Right, I'm sure. Let's go. We brought the car." We follow him through the massive, glass-ceilinged train station, Abby's eyes popping at the multi-levels and shops. "We can stop for breakfast if you guys are hungry?"

The train-weary three of us unanimously agree.

Forty-five minutes later, we sit at an outdoor café half-way through breakfast, staring out at the Spree River. A boat packed with tourists moves lazily past us in the blue water before disappearing under an arch in the nearby bridge. Neel's phone buzzes on the table, and he snatches it up, eyeing it warily. Grimacing, he excuses himself and moves away down toward the water.

Abby takes another bite of her eggs Benedict and glances at my plate. "Aren't you hungry?"

I realize I've been picking at my scrambled eggs in an absentminded way that leaves them looking like accident victims. I shovel a forkful into my mouth. "Sorry, just thinking about our day."

Mom hands me an envelope. "Here's tickets and such. I know you're anxious to get sightseeing, so Dad and I thought you could head out from here and we'd take your luggage back to the apartment."

Before I can reply, Dad's phone rings. Checking it, he says, "It's the gallery, excuse me," and leaves the table.

Mom raises her eyebrows. "We're losing the men!" She studies Neel pacing near the river's edge, gesticulating widely. "That doesn't look pleasant."

"Moira," I mumble through my eggs, no other explanation necessary.

"Right." Mom's gaze slips back to me. "She's here, you know."

I set down my fork. "What?"

"In Berlin. She's here to see Neel while you two explore the city."

I push away my plate. "Well, that's just great."

Abby looks interested. "I want to meet her."

"No, you don't."

"You're in luck." Mom finishes the last of her espresso, clearly enjoying my reaction. "We're all having dinner tonight. After you go to Museum Island."

I drop my forehead to the table.

Bemused, Abby notes, "Museum Island sounds promising," then adds, "You have scrambled eggs in your hair."

Abby

I like cities in theory. A city seems cool, a constant invite to stay up all night on a rooftop, soak in the theater, try new cafés, all the while moving through a constant throng of busy, vibrant people. I love visiting cities, but I've always wondered if I'd actually enjoy living in one. Maybe it's the press of so many people. Or the grime. Or the noise. Or the underlying smell of urine. But, for me, city life seems like living perpetually at the end of an overcrowded day at Disneyland. I adore Disneyland, but I wouldn't want to live there. Still, I could see myself in a city for a while. Because cities have museums. And museums have all the things I love.

Speaking of love, after breakfast, Riya takes me to Berlin's Museum Island.

Museum Island.

Apparently, Berlin sent out a Bat-Signal for museum geeks, a flash against the sky to say, *There's an island just for you.*

Riya claps her hands in front of my gaping face. "See! Look at you. I knew it! I knew you would love it. The first time I came here I thought, it's like Abby's mother ship."

"If friendship had a museum, it would be the Riya Sharma-Collins Museum."

She hugs me. "This is true. Okay." She waves the envelope her mom gave her at me. "Tickets, tours, maps, recommended lunch spot. Mom organized the whole thing. We have until dinner at eight with Moira the Monster. What do you want to see first?"

I shake my head at her exaggeration. "Moira the Monster. She can't possibly be that bad."

Riya blinks at me. "Right, optimism. Okay. Let's go enjoy that for a while."

A few hours later, I stand transfixed in front of a gold coin in a glass case in the Bode Museum. One of the Seven Wonders of the Ancient World is the sculptor Phidias's seated statue of Zeus at Olympus. It's not my favorite of the wonders. I've always thought while reading the myths that Zeus acted like a sexist, overtired toddler who needed anger management classes, so I never really focused much on him. But Phidias's statue was a wonder, the biggest statue of ivory built over wood at its time. The coin I'm gaping at now features Phidias's Zeus, holding a tiny figure of Nike in his gold hand.

Riya squints at it. "Who was Nike again?"

"Goddess of victory."

"Oh, that makes sense. I guess they wouldn't name a shoe after the goddess of sleeping late." She inspects her own Nikes. "Do you think she cares that she's now the goddess of sweaty feet?"

I shrug, the coin holding me in a history trance. Like all the Seven Wonders except the Great Pyramid of Giza, the statue of Zeus doesn't exist anymore. As with many theories in history, people disagree: Some say it was destroyed in a fire, some argue it was lost when Constantine the Great ordered it dismantled and a collector had it moved to Constantinople. How someone loses a forty-three-foot statue is beyond me, but who knows, maybe FedEx runs into this sort of problem all the time. Yet somehow, this tiny coin survived and made it all the way to right now, right here, in front of my face. It might be the coolest thing I've ever seen. Like standing in front of the lost wonder itself.

Riya yawns, inspecting her cuticles. I can't blame her. She doesn't have museum stamina in the same way I don't have loud-music-and-too-many-people-at-a-party stamina. Today, I've already dragged her through rooms of Byzantine art and spent the last hour poring over about four thousand coins in the Bode collection. I peel my eyes away from this beautiful coin. "Want to move on?"

She brightens. "Are you sure? I'm sorry – I didn't sleep so great last night on the train. And that currywurst from lunch isn't sitting so well." She clasps a hand over her belly. "But I want to make sure you see everything you want to see. And I know this Zeus thing is a big deal."

"How many coins can we look at before our eyes start crossing?" *All of them,* I don't add. *I want to see every single one.* "Let's hit the next museum."

Riya looks relieved. "Great. I'm ready to go, too."

I don't mention I could spend the next month basically living here.

We wander through the Pergamon Museum for the rest of the afternoon, our eyes bugging at the sheer scale of the artifacts. Standing in the Aleppo Room, we pause to take in the intricate panels, the paintings containing the oldest Syrian home collection from the Ottoman period. "I don't really know much about the Ottomans," Riya admits, turning a slow circle to soak in the detailed scenes that merge Islamic and Christian stories in bold red, black, and mustard yellow.

"They basically ended the Byzantine Empire," I tell her, leaning in to examine a panel detailing the story of Saint George.

"Well, that's super helpful, thanks." She follows my gaze. "Is this a story I should know?" She points to Saint George and his dragon.

"Saint George? It's damsel in distress and imperialism all rolled into one!"

"Charming." She doesn't try to hide the sarcasm. Right

now, Riya's clearly having her own paddleboard moment. Time to bring the boards to shore.

"Oh!" She grins, glancing at a new text on her phone. "Will says hi."

"Hi back."

His message puts the first genuine smile I've seen on her face all afternoon. It's nearing five, and she's obviously had enough museum air for one day. We head for the exit. Outside, we walk into the hot light. Riya slips on her aviator glasses. "This whole area was bombed in World War II. Seventy percent of it was ruined or something like that. We came here with my school. It's been a huge restoration project."

I tuck the slim book I just bought on the Pergamon's Islamic art collection into my backpack. "I've been reading a lot about Berlin this year. Interesting city; such a sad history. It's crazy to think about how much of it was bombed and divided. But it seems like Berliners aren't afraid of their past. Like it just makes them more determined." As I prattle on, Riya withdraws into her phone, grinning at an exchange she's having with Will. I bite my lip, knowing I need to shut up and let her show me the city she's been living in for a year without all my research babble clouding the air around us, but I wish she'd put the phone away. I study our sandaled feet as we continue along the cobbled paths of Museum Island. "Everything good with Will?"

She looks up. "What? Oh, sorry. Actually, it's not Will. It's Kiara." She slips her phone into her bag.

I try not to let a spark of annoyance creep into my voice. "Should we go back to your apartment? I can't wait to see it."

"Great idea. We can walk along the Spree to Hackesche Höfe, do a little shopping on our way. Then we can walk from there to Alex. Or we could rent bikes? Do you want to rent a bike?"

"I think walk. Who's Alex?"

She shakes her head. "Alexanderplatz. It's the square near our apartment named for the Russian czar's trip to Berlin in 1805. Ha! History tidbit for you. See, I can be a wealth of historical knowledge, too." She motions at the Neues and Altes Museums as we pass them and then the blue-domed Berlin Cathedral with its wide green lawn. "Museum, museum. Church!"

I shake my head, but can't help but smile. "You're a detailed and thorough tour guide."

I peer through the dim lighting of the restaurant, my mouth watering at the savory scent in the air, and sip sparkling water, my eyes on the door. Despite Riya's warnings (or maybe because of them), I'm looking forward to meeting Moira. If Riya's to be believed, I should be looking for a harpy with fangs. As I wait, I scan the menu again. My parents are not adventurous eaters. Going out to dinner usually means pizza or Mexican. This past year, I've missed going out with Riya's parents, who always seem to try something new. Tonight, Anju and Dean bring us to a Turkish restaurant in the northeastern corner of the Tiergarten, Berlin's central park. On our way here, they pointed out the famous Brandenburg Gate, and I noticed Nike again, that busy goddess of victory, atop Berlin's famous monument. But I couldn't seem to focus on those massive passageways Hitler famously marched his troops through when he became chancellor, the sound of goose-stepping like thunder. My rumbling stomach distracted me. And the promised Moira sighting. The suspense is killing me.

"Maybe he can't find the restaurant," Dean muses, checking the time on his phone. "Neel's not usually late."

"Moira likes to make an entrance," Riya mumbles into her water.

"Maybe she's grown up a little since the last time we saw her." Anju adjusts the napkin in her lap, the light of a low-hanging chandelier flashing on the necklace of green glass beads she wears, sending pale spangles of light across the table. "Maybe we all have."

Riya sets down her water. "She was nineteen the last time we saw her. Do people grow up from nineteen, or do they just fine-tune their annoying habits?"

"I guess we'll soon find out," Anju says brightly, leveling her gaze at Riya in that way she has that says, *You're answering your own question right now, my darling*. I've been the recipient of that look before. It's gentle, but effective. Then she's rising a bit out of her chair, waggling her fingers at the couple coming through the door. "Hello, Neel! Moira!"

Moira is no gnarled, green-skinned harpy. This creature floats through the restaurant, short and narrow-faced, wearing a simple pearl-pink sheath dress, her white-blonde hair slicked into a low knot at the nape of her slender neck. She's beautiful, like a blade, thin and sharp. The table stands to greet her and Neel, air kisses filling the space around their cheeks, a European habit that makes me feel like I missed a necessary choreography lesson that would allow me to execute this custom with any style or grace. I stay seated and avoid the *kiss, kiss*. Moira slips into the seat to the right of me. She has deeply sunken eyes the color of pool water, and translucent skin. She must burn easily, and for some reason realizing this makes me feel marginally better about her perfect skin. I'm not proud of this flash of meanness, but it flared unexpectedly.

Moira plucks her napkin between two French-manicured fingertips and deposits it in her lap. "So," she says more to me than Riya. "Aren't you two cute with your grand tour? Neel's been telling me all about it, haven't you, darling?" She beams at Neel, who is already buried in his menu.

Riya rolls her eyes in a way we grew out of in late middle school. "Well, so long as it's cute, my mission's accomplished. One must be cute at all costs – ow!" The table is not so big it doesn't keep Neel from kicking her under it. Riya narrows her eyes at the back of his menu.

Moira arches an eyebrow at their exchange, but then turns her attention to Riya's parents. "How are you, Anju? Dean? Enjoying Berlin?"

Anju leans in. "It's been a lovely year."

Moira picks up her menu. "Well, better you than me. It's such a gloomy city. I'm sure you're looking forward to your exit. All the *graffiti*. I know it's supposed to be artistic and evolving, but—" She runs her pool-water eyes across the restaurant's offerings, her tongue tsking. "Ugh, Turkish food. So much of it tastes alike." I exchange a look with Riya, and her look back says, *I warned you*. A waitress comes to our table and Riya and I order some dumplings to share and a pide, which is a type of Turkish pizza.

Moira doesn't look at the waitress when she asks, "What can I order that isn't choked with spice?"

"She has a sensitive palate," Neel adds, his eyes flicking to me and then back to the waitress.

The waitress starts to point out a few options with the tip of her pen, but Moira waves her off. "I'll just have the çoban salatasi salad. And a glass of white wine." She snaps her menu shut like a gunshot. Dean hurries to order his meal, ramping up the charm, even winking at the waitress as he hands her the menu. Dean is not a winker. There are beads of sweat at his temple.

Moira eyes him across the table. "Neel took me to see your show today, Dean. It reminded me of one we saw last year at the Whitechapel Gallery." She slips a hand onto Neel's forearm. "Who was that artist?"

Neel searches for a name. "I can't quite remember—"

"Of course you remember. You *loved* the show." He shakes his head apologetically, and she sighs. "No matter. It reminded me of that. Really vibrant, Dean."

"Well, thank you."

"Do you get inspiration from other artists?" she asks.

Dean shifts uncomfortably in his chair. "I try to keep the work original rather than derivative, but of course I have sources of inspiration."

She nods coolly but doesn't ask anything else. Riya has gone silent, staring at her lap. Moira and Neel sip their wine. The evening might have teetered into an inescapable crevasse of awkward silence except that Anju, in her graceful way, steps in. "I heard it was raining in London when you left. Must be nice to see some sun." Anju continues to carry us through the rest of the meal, asking Moira about her chemistry studies at university, her family, and finally about her internship this summer at a pharmaceutical lab. "Neel told us the lab is quite prestigious."

Moira casts him a haughty look, like a lioness staring

affectionately at a fallen gazelle. "Oh, how sweet of him to say that." She picks over the cucumbers and tomatoes dressed in lemon juice and olive oil on her plate. "It's quite dreadful, really. I'll be thrilled when the summer's up."

Neel hurries to say, "Impressive, though. To be selected."

She allows him a thin-lipped smile. "I suppose." She proceeds to describe her work as if she's been toiling away in a war-torn country full of hostile revolutionaries instead of working in a sterile lab outside of London. Everyone at Grimes Pharmaceuticals, it seems, has a personality flaw Moira finds "distressing" or "abysmal," or they are simply "imbeciles."

"There's a reason you call it the Grime Farm, right, love?" Neel chimes in, smiling at her over the last of his kofta.

She squeezes his arm. "Quite right!"

"Why do you continue with it?" Dean asks. "If it's so terrible."

She looks confused. "It's a wonderful opportunity. Even if the director is a lazy cow."

Dean almost chokes on his wine. "What?"

Moira sighs. "She's always rushing off on the dot of six, even in the middle of a meeting."

"I think she has young children to fetch—" Neel tries, but she interrupts him.

"She should have thought of that before accepting the

director of analytical chemistry position, for which she is grossly underqualified." She takes quick sips of her wine, two pink spots appearing on her pale cheeks.

Neel puts a hand over hers. "Quite."

Riya widens her eyes at me over her glass of sparkling water as Anju flags down our waitress and orders coffee and dessert. The waitress clears our plates. When she's done, Anju folds her hands under her chin, her face thoughtful. "I think finding balance in family and work is a challenge. It changes priorities."

"And there's a double standard," Dean adds. "If a man left work to get his children, we'd commend him for being a good father, but we don't always do that with women. And he'd never be criticized for *not* leaving, that's for sure."

Moira groans. "Oh, feminism. How Californian of you to mention it."

I can't help it. I start giggling.

Neel frowns. "Abby?"

Oh no. This happens sometimes when I've grown too uncomfortable in a situation, inappropriate giggles start slipping out and I can't control them. Sometimes, I can pass them off as hiccups. The look on Neel's face assures me this is not one of those times. "Sorry! Just thinking about, um, something we saw earlier at the museum." I shoot Riya a desperate look. *Help!*

Dean clears his throat. "Oh, well, I hadn't realized

Museum Island had started including humorous exhibits, but good to hear they're branching out."

Riya snaps out of the social coma she's been in the entire meal. "Oh, it was this weird man we saw on our way out of the Pergamon. You're thinking about that guy, right? In the toga?"

I follow her lead, nodding. "Right! The guy. In the neon-yellow toga. And clogs! I mean, clogs and a neon toga?! Togas are just naturally hilarious."

"Yes, I'm sure the Romans wore them for their comedic value," Moira remarks, arching an eyebrow at Neel. At the sight of that eyebrow, I take Riya down with me and we both succumb to giggles. Under Anju's hot gaze, we excuse ourselves to pull it together in the restroom. Once there, we lock eyes in the bathroom mirror and completely dissolve.

Riya wipes a tear from her eye. "Was I right or was I right?"

"She's the worst."

"The currywurst!" Riya chokes out, sliding down the bathroom's tiled wall, hysterical, because now we're in that place where anything is funny. Including terrible currywurst puns.

I wave my hand, adopting a fake British accent. "Order anything – it all tastes the same. They're all imbeciles anyway."

Riya's still curled against the wall. "Yes, funny how

people around her all just happen to be idiots. So convenient!"

"Quite!" But I freeze when I see Moira standing in the bathroom doorway, watching us.

Even as she tries to keep her composure, I'm sure I spot a gloss of tears in her pale eyes. "Dessert's arrived." She lets the bathroom door fall shut behind her.

Our laughter dies in our throats.

We slink back to the table.

Riya

"She had it coming," I mumble from the backseat of the silver Mercedes my parents leased for our year in Berlin.

"The goal, I think," Mom says as she turns onto a darkening main street leading away from the Tiergarten, "is not to stoop to her level."

"I'm a teenager; I'm still learning these things."

"That old excuse," Mom replies dryly, but I see the smile at the corner of her mouth.

"Use it if you got it." Outside, the lights of Berlin blink on around us. It's my favorite time of day in the city; everything starts glowing, and it blurs some of the city's harsh edges. Abby reaches across the seat and sets her hand on top of mine. Her squeeze means *thanks for saving me back there*, even if we both screwed it up in the bathroom.

"Moira doesn't make it easy." Dad leans his arm on the edge of the open window, the night air coming through, still warm. "It's like she gets more annoyed with humanity each time we see her, like the world is a constant affront to her existence."

I reach forward and slap his shoulder gratefully. "Well said, Daddy-o!"

"Where is this place?" Mom slows, turning onto a side street shadowed by tall cement apartment buildings. "Is it someone's apartment?"

"Where are we going?" Abby sits up, trying to hide a yawn.

"I have a surprise for you." I motion to Mom. "Over there, by that green awning." She pulls the Mercedes into a parking spot across the street.

She turns to look at me over her shoulder. "You sure you don't want us to come see it?"

I shake my head. "It's pretty much the same workshop you guys saw last month. Another theater group is letting us borrow their space for the night."

We wave as the car pulls away. I tug Abby through an entryway into a musty lobby and past the door for an elevator. We take a sharp right down some stairs. "What exactly are we doing?" Abby follows me down the tight staircase, our way vaguely lit with a wall sconce that looks like something from a medieval torture chamber.

"I'm in a show tonight."

"A show?"

"It's called *Gerechtigkeit*."

"Which means what?"

"A good translation is equality. Or maybe justice?" The staircase opens into a basement room where six rows of battered folding chairs face a single black curtain and an open area that serves as our stage. I love this room.

"So, not sure this counts as a history tidbit, more history rumor, but supposedly in World War II, American and British spies held secret meetings here basically right under Hilter's nose."

Her eyes gleam as she scans the room. "No way; how cool." I can practically see her imagining the years falling away, the room suddenly quiet with spies sitting at tables, their shoulders hunched over maps or secret documents, murmuring, strategizing.

I wave to a small knot of actors standing near the stage. "There's Kiara and Jonas. Come on, I'll introduce you."

But Kiara beats me to it. She hurries over. "Rye!" She embraces me, kissing both cheeks. "You made it!" She turns to Abby. "I'm Kiara."

"Hi." Abby nods, her voice guarded, and she scans Kiara top to bottom: the scuffed Doc Martens, the red velvet short-overalls over the black bra. "Nice to meet you," she manages a beat or two late.

Kiara doesn't seem to notice. She's beaming at Jonas across the room. "We're so glad you're here. This show will be wild! As Riya knows, Jonas is a visionary."

Okay, visionary might be a tad much, but I'm not surprised. Kiara thinks Jonas invented the sun. Don't get me wrong, he's talented, but he kind of knows it and that gets annoying. The majority of the girls and half the boys in the Collective are in love with him, but I'm not big on the beard. Or the narcissism. The first time he told me he was a sociology student at Humboldt, he caught me off guard since we have a Humboldt State back in Northern California. His Humboldt, though, is the oldest university in Berlin, where people like Albert Einstein and Karl Marx once walked the halls. Jonas often reminds us that when he's there, he can actually *feel* their ghosts prodding him along in his studies. When Jonas talks, many of his words come with audible italicization. He *feels* us watching him now and gives us a crisp wave. As usual, he's dressed in tight black clothing and pushes obsessively at the heavy lime-green frames that keep slipping down his nose. I'm pretty sure he doesn't need glasses. Just wears them because, well, sociologist playwrights wear heavy-framed glasses in ironic colors, right?

People start wandering in, filling up the twenty or so seats. Tavin, one of my favorite friends from school this year, emerges from the stairs and lumbers over, his line-backer build disguising his sweet nature. "Hi, hi!" He throws an arm around me. "Shouldn't you be dressed in black clothing and waving a puppet around?"

"Um, spoiler alert!" I hug him, breathing in his familiar rain-and-spice smell. "This is my friend Abby. From California."

"Hello, Abby from California."

Tavin has the kind of smile that often gets reflected back at him, and Abby's reaction is no exception. "Hi."

I *knew* Abby would like him. "Tavin helps run our student government," I hurry to tell her. "He's an expat. His parents are both from the States, but now they live here. How cool is that?"

"Cool," she echoes unconvincingly, and I want to shake her. Tavin is cute and totally Abby's type. History geek. Funny. She needs to try harder. I'm hoping the look I'm shooting her right now drills some of this telepathically into her brain before he gets bored and leaves.

But Tavin just grins and replies, "I'm not sure how cool it is. It's just geography."

"Tavin was the first person to show me Museum Island," I tell her pointedly. "He *loves* museums. He's planning to study history in college."

Abby brightens. "Me too."

"Let's find some seats and talk about old stuff." He grabs her hand and leads her toward the rows of chairs. That was almost too easy.

Smiling, I slip behind the curtain.

After a whirlwind show (yes, both black costumes and puppets made an appearance), I meet Tavin and Abby where they wait for me in the audience. Abby's face is hard to read, but she smiles when she sees me. "Not sure I got most of that, but it had some serious energy."

"Thank you!" I'm still pulsing with adrenaline from the show, from the feel of throwing myself into someone else's world for seventy charged minutes. And it was especially challenging for me because it was in German. "What'd you think, Tav?"

He nods his shaggy head. "Weird, but I liked it. I've always felt the themes of aggression and poverty find their true connection through puppets made out of milk cartons." I punch his arm in mock protest. "It's true," he insists. "And it added a much needed environmental angle."

Kiara bounces up to us, still flushed from the performance. "We're heading over to Jonas's flat – hi, Tavin! – want to join?"

Tavin checks his phone. "I'm in."

Abby yawns down at the program in her hand, each one created on a piece of paper that had already been used for something else – a pharmacy receipt, a napkin, the tagboard backing of a checkbook. Abby holds what looks like an old flyer from a furniture store sale.

Leaning into her, I whisper, "Are you too exhausted? We don't have to go."

"Oh, I'm fine," she assures me, sneaking a look at Tavin. "It'll be fun." Her phone rings. "Sorry – it's my mom." She picks up with a "Hey, Mom" and wanders over to a corner of the room. "No, I can hear you—"

When she's out of earshot, I grab Tavin by his arm. "She

doesn't know about London yet, so don't say anything."

"Wow, vise grip." He looks down at his arm, frowning, and when I ease off the pressure, he asks, "She doesn't know?"

"No, so don't tell her."

He holds up his hands in defense. "What's the problem? It's good news, right?" He follows my gaze, to where Abby listens to something her mom says over the phone, her brow furrowed, her free hand over her ear to block out the buzzing postshow audience.

I shake my head. "Just don't mention it."

"No problem."

Jonas lives with three other guys in a tiny flat near the university. It looks like many flats I've hung out in over the last year: mattresses on the floor, stacks of books, student art on the walls, folding chairs around a card table, empty bottles posing as paperweights for various scripts. Only one of Jonas's roommates, Arik, is home when we come spilling in. Arik reads mostly thick, dark Russian novels and rarely feels the need to talk. He makes a mean pot of coffee on the single-burner stove and sneers if you add milk. He nods a vague hello to us and disappears into the room he shares with Oskar, who I've never met, closing the door behind him.

Kiara, Abby, and I settle onto a mattress, our backs against a wall, while Tavin studies the various stacks of books. In the tiny kitchen, Jonas makes herbal tea in a clear glass kettle. Jonas is one of the only guys I've met in Berlin who doesn't drink. And unlike Arik, who seems to live on nothing else but his thick coffee, Jonas is caffeine free. He's also vegan, which isn't always easy in a city that seems to subsist on beer and meat.

Kicking his shoes off into a corner, he brings out a tray with ceramic cups, the steaming kettle, and a bowl of raw cashews. Setting the tray on the floor, he fills five cups with tea. As I take one, I hide a smile. Jonas doesn't have an actual couch, but he has a serving tray for tea. Which seems about right. He settles, cross-legged, on the hardwood floor in front of us, his eyes expectant. "So? What did you think of the show?" he asks Abby as Tavin continues to examine the book selection behind him.

Abby stares into the still surface of her cinnamon-hued tea. "Really interesting."

Jonas nods for her to go on. "Which part caught you?"

Abby's gaze flicks to me. "Um, the red half masks?"

Oh, great. Jonas and his red masks. "Yes!" He looks at me triumphantly. "See how powerful they are?" To Abby, he adds, "They represent muzzles."

I try not to roll my eyes. "I didn't have a problem with the symbolism, Jonas. They're just really hard to speak through and you kept getting mad that you couldn't hear me." I sip my scalding tea.

"Not mad," he stresses. "Notes. Directors give notes. And I couldn't hear you."

"Because I was wearing a muzzle."

Kiara takes a handful of cashews. "I think that's part of the power of that scene. That you can't really make out what we're saying when we wear them. It adds confusion."

Tavin leans down to take a cup of tea. "Is confusion what you were going for?" he asks Jonas, and I can't tell if he's being sarcastic. After the last performance he saw with the milk cartons, Tavin expressed that perhaps Jonas's work was the other stuff that comes out of cows.

Jonas nods earnestly. "Yes and no. Theater should be about creating thought, which then creates change. When we perform, we add to a greater conversation, a greater social discussion. If it's confusing, that's okay. That's still inspiring a kind of mental challenge, a thoughtfulness." As Jonas explains this, I narrow my eyes at Tavin. I don't always love Jonas's pretentiousness, but he cares deeply about theater as social change. He's the real deal.

Tavin takes my hint. Sort of. "Well then, I think you have a winner." He holds up his cup. *"Prost."*

Jonas holds up his cup in answer. *"Prost!"*

The door bangs open and Jonas's third roommate, Leo, stomps in with two girls in tow. Leo is in many ways Jonas's opposite, a beefy, tattooed, found-objects artist who always seems to have two or three girls in his orbit. Which is not the problem. The problem is that the second girl who stumbles in behind him is Tavin's ex-girlfriend, Rilla.

"Okay." Tavin plops his teacup on the tray, his eyes slipping to me. "I'm going to take off. Thanks for the tea, man." He blasts out the door. Abby and I hurry to follow him. But when we get to the street below, he's gone.

Abby stares at me with wide eyes. "What was that about?"

I scan the streets for signs of Tavin's big frame. "That girl in the red top is Rilla. Or as I like to call her, Wreck-It Rilla. She trashed his heart about two months ago."

Abby looks worriedly up and down the street again. "Poor Tavin."

I sigh, more annoyed at Tavin's disappearing act than worried. He's ruining things with Abby before they can start. "Yeah, but he really needs to get over it."

I get a text from Kiara: ???

I text back: gone.

Kiara: come back up.

Abby is yawning again but trying to hide it. I text back: i think we'll call it a night.

Kiara: :)

Me: dream sweet!

Kiara: tschüss.

Later in my room, after we've both taken showers, Abby and I sit facing each other on my single bed. I'm painting my toenails on a towel and Abby texts with her dad, wet hair combed back away from her face. Finally, she tosses her phone on the bed. "Dad says hi." She's wearing a pair of my emerald silk pajamas that look pretty with her eyes.

"You should wear that color every day," I tell her, capping the nail polish and blowing on my toes as best I can.

"Thanks." She pulls out the glossy book she bought in the Pergamon gift shop but doesn't open it. I grab a hairbrush, flip my head forward, and give my hair three quick strokes from underneath. When I come back up, Abby's watching me. "You know I've probably seen you brush your hair like that a thousand times on your bed back home, but never in Berlin."

I lower the brush. "Wow, nostalgic much?"

She sets the book aside and stretches her legs out in front of her. "Isn't that the point of this trip – the grand nostalgia tour?"

Her tone sounds sharper than it should. "You okay? Did your dad say something?"

A dark expression clouds her face. "Ugh, I don't want to talk about it right now. Too tired." She climbs off the bed and starts digging through her bag on the floor. "I have travel fatigue or something."

I hesitate. "You sure you don't want to talk about it?"

She shakes her head. "Let's talk tomorrow. Speaking of which, what's next? Are we staying in Berlin for a while or off to somewhere else?" But she immediately holds up her hand. "Wait – don't tell me. That's the point, right? That I don't know what the next day holds for us?"

I nod, and she tries to smile, but that watercolor wash of sadness is back behind it. "I could tell you the whole plan. I just thought it'd be more spontaneous this way, more fun."

"It *is* fun."

Before we can say anything else, we hear the front door open, then close quietly. I scurry off the bed, and Abby joins me at the doorway, both of us hanging back in case it's a crazed murderer with an ax or something. But it's Neel. He tiptoes his way through the shadowed living room, holding his shoes.

"We thought you were a lunatic with an ax!"

He jumps at my voice. "Geesh, Riya, you almost gave me heart failure!"

"Course we'd have preferred the ax murderer." Crossing my arms, I lean into the doorjamb. I get a closer look when he falls into the square of light spilling from my room, at his rumpled clothes and exhausted expression. Abby and I exchange a guilty look. "You look awful," I say to Neel. "Trouble in paradise?"

"You should know since you started it," he snaps. His black hair stands on end, as if he's been running his hands through it for the past few hours.

"We're sorry about that, Neel. We—"

I cut Abby off. "Oh, please. Moira started it years ago." At the sight of his pained face, I swallow the rest of my remarks and take a tentative step into the living room. We were horrible to Moira, laughing at her in the bathroom, which was bad enough even if she hadn't caught us. But she had. Which makes it mostly our fault if she's now chucked him out of their hotel room. "Look, I'm sorry about Moira, too. But she's such a pill, Neel. And by the looks of those phone calls you've been on the last week, we didn't actually start it. Threw gas on the fire is more like it. I honestly don't know what you see in her. What can possibly be in it for you?"

He flops onto the couch, pulling the sapphire chenille blanket Mom keeps there over him. "Go to bed, children. I'm tired." He throws an arm over his eyes.

"Ugh, maybe you're a perfect match after all."

"Are you still talking?" he mumbles from where he has his head turned into the couch cushions.

"Idiot." I shut my door, careful not to slam it. I wouldn't want to give him the satisfaction.

The next morning, we almost sleep through my alarm but force ourselves to get going before the day gets too hot to enjoy it. I leave Mom and Dad a note on the coffee table next to a snoring Neel, and we head out. I plan to fill our morning with some of the usual tourist spots, even consulting Lonely Planet to make sure I'm not missing anything. We start again at the Brandenburg Gate so we can follow the former course of the Berlin Wall south on Ebertstraße, growing quiet as we arrive at the Holocaust monument, the Memorial to the Murdered Jews of Europe.

It's this sort of frankness that initially caught me off guard when I came to Berlin, but I've come to admire it; it's a long cry from the California tendency to euphemize, well, almost everything. Berlin, as a city, has a tendency to hold your face up close to the glass of the past. In my time here, Berlin has never stopped reminding me that humans do horrible things and that it's our job to put something worthwhile into the future to combat them.

Abby and I agree to take different paths through the disorienting headstone-like blocks and undulating ground of the memorial. Within moments, I find myself alone in its isolating and towering maze. As I wander through it, I think about how Dad told me the last time we came here that the memorial has its critics; some argue it's not specific enough, or it's too metaphorical, or that children aren't properly somber, playing hide-and-seek through its two thousand blocks of gray stone (which isn't the memorial's fault). One of my teachers at school told us she feels like it takes emphasis away from the Nazis with its passive title. I brought this up with Dad while we walked through it, and he told me that this sort of discussion is one of the important things about art: No matter what, it should inspire debate and ideas.

As I wander out of the labyrinth, I find Abby sitting on a low gray slab, something broken etched on her face. I settle next to her. "You okay?"

She takes a ragged breath. "Not really. This is … intense, what it represents. I wasn't prepared for this." She swallows, folding and unfolding her hands in her lap.

"You can't prepare for it." I put my hand on her arm, already warm in the late-morning heat. "It crushes me each time I see it or walk by it." I follow her gaze as she watches a couple pass us, quietly whispering, their cheeks slick with tears. My stomach clenches. "It's supposed to have that effect."

She folds her arms across her stomach. "I know people think I'm a big dork for loving it the way I do, but this is why history is so important to me. Sometimes, though, I get too comfortable in the distance of it. I mean, yeah, I read about things, but they are stats and facts, removed – it's the past. This kind of place reminds me that history is happening around us all the time. Somewhere in the world right now, this kind of evil is still happening. It's completely overwhelming when you let yourself think about it."

"I know." I close my hand over hers and gaze at the western edge of the Tiergarten, at the neat green trees. It's difficult to think that a city this beautiful holds such terrible ghosts. I squeeze her hand. "We studied this one-act play a few months ago at the Collective. It was set in a Japanese internment camp in Oregon during the war. In it, the father of the family made flowers out of scraps of paper for his son and daughter, because, he told them, they needed to know they could always find the beautiful parts of the world no matter what. It was such a sad, hopeful play. That part really stuck with me. That choice. To put any sort of beauty in the world is an active, maybe even aggressively subversive act, I think, even if it's just for one other person to see. It's one of the things I fell in love with most about theater."

Abby drops her head onto my shoulder, her hair tickling my chin. "I think you've always been that person, Rye. I mean, I'm glad you found this whole acting thing, but you've always been that person to me. When the world throws a Crap Party, you show up with awesome decorations and snacks. It's just who you are."

"Thanks." Her compliment warms me, but I can't help but think that when she had the biggest surprise Crap Party of her life thrown at her, I sent chocolates and RSVP'd no.

She clears her throat. "It's hard, though."

"What is?"

"To keep trying to put the good stuff out there. I mean, we can say over and over *be positive* or *look on the bright side*, but it's tricky work to actually do it. I didn't realize until this year how hard it is. Because the world keeps throwing stuff at you. Not just the big world stuff – but the smaller, individual stuff, too. My parents split up this year, and I joined the ranks of kids with divorced parents. I know it's nothing special or new—"

"Abby, when I said that I didn't—"

"No, it *is* ordinary. I know that. But it *feels* brand-new to me in this terribly extraordinary way. It's hard to explain. One minute, we're a family, and the next minute…" Abby makes an exploding sound and her hands become a puppet bomb. "People keep telling me things will be okay, that it will all work out in the big picture, but I can't seem to figure out how to get out of the small picture." She waves at the slabs in front of us. "Which is annoying, because it's not like we were ripped apart by a fascist government or something. We did our own ripping." She frowns at this. "I guess I still don't even totally understand what happened to us."

"Maybe there isn't a rational reason. People grow apart."

"Right. Kate says that, too. I mean, I know that intellectually, but I didn't truly believe love could just do that. You think it's something that sticks, but you'd be wrong."

I take her hand. "Sometimes, it sticks."

"But does it even matter? When we're ultimately just a stat on some record book somewhere?" She swallows hard, and I can tell she's a little embarrassed about her ramblings. "Ugh, listen to me."

I assure her she's in the right city for this kind of existential reflection. "It matters. My acting teacher Niles says that in theater we tell both small and big stories, and that it often takes the small stories to understand the big ones. Yours is one of those small, important stories. This" – I motion out to Berlin – "is a big story, but there were millions of small ones inside it. It's one of the reasons I want to be an actor, to tell those stories." She nods but doesn't say anything. We sit in the hot quiet of the sun for a moment. "Abby?"

"Yeah?"

"Did you really like the show last night?"

She widens her eyes. "Of course I did!"

"It's just, when Jonas asked you, I wasn't sure if you really thought so or if you were just being nice." I hate how insecure my voice sounds, but I need to know she understood it, that she sees how important this is to me, that it's not just a whim.

She gives me a funny look. "Well, I might have missed some of it because it was in *German*. I didn't even realize those puppets were made out of milk cartons until Tavin said something. They were just boxes with cows on them. I thought maybe the play had something to do with cows."

"It was about oppression and poverty!"

"*Bovine* oppression and poverty?" She leans into me in that way that tells me she's opened her heart too wide and needs to dilute the moment with humor.

I decide to let her, decide to help her lighten the mood. "You shouldn't joke about it, you know? There are plenty of oppressed cows in the world." I pull her to standing, and we start walking toward Ebertstraße. We can grab lunch in Potsdamer Platz before heading to Checkpoint Charlie.

She links arms with me. "Well, I will be the first to buy a ticket to your Power to the Cow play."

"That's actually a pretty good title."

Abby

After lunch, we walk to Checkpoint Charlie, which during the Cold War was the Allied name for the best-known crossing point between divided Berlin. In the sixties, a human activist established this controversial museum near the famous guard station. In it, I read the terrifying account of how the Wall went up in 1961, basically overnight, with soldiers unspooling rolls of barbed wire, and it remained for almost three decades until it finally came crashing down. I wander around the hot space of the museum. There are dozens of stories written in small, dense print, of families being trapped on opposite sides of the Wall, trying to reunite, of people disappearing, of fear and pain. As I read them, goose bumps crawl over my skin even though the museum is oppressively hot. The weight of it all threatens to overwhelm me, and my stomach churns and knots, beads of sweat breaking out across my face and the back of my neck.

Riya notices. "You look kind of green. Hope you didn't

get a bad kebab at lunch." When I can't even laugh at her joke, her face shifts to genuine concern. "Seriously, you don't look so good. Are you going to barf?" Her eyes dart nervously around at the other tourists. "Please don't."

"I won't," I hurry to promise, and her face relaxes. We both know Riya's fear of puking is a borderline phobia. She will do anything to avoid it or any proximity to it. I take a few deep breaths, the stories from the museum racing through my brain. I try to close my eyes against them, try not to think about how it feels like our own sort of wall went up between us this year, about how we're still pulling it apart. The metaphor's so obvious I'd be embarrassed to mention it to Riya. "It's probably just a bad cramp," I lie. "Like those stabbing ones I used to get when we ran twenty wind sprints in Ms. McGrath's gym class, who never believed me, by the way, when I got them."

Riya puts an arm around my shoulders and leads me away to some shade cast by a nearby building. "I'm pretty sure she only had us run about ten of those, but glad to see you're not hanging on to it." She peers closely at my sweaty face. "You're probably too hot. It's ridiculously humid today. We should go somewhere cooler." She perks up. "I know! We can go to Galeries Lafayette."

Riya's answer to everything. Shopping. "I don't know—"

"It will be nice inside. It's like a ten-minute walk, but we could hop in a taxi."

"I'm okay to walk as long as it's slowly."

As we move sluggishly up Friedrichstraße, Riya fills me in on some of the history of the Galeries Lafayette, an enormous French department store with a famous central glass-and-steel funnel designed by the French architect Jean Nouvel. I nod along, mostly concentrating on taking one step at a time, the cramp shifting like a knife between my ribs. Maybe it was just the kebab, and not that horrible wall. Either one of them.

"You're probably dehydrated." Riya eyes me, keeping her pace slow. "Really weird stuff can happen when you get dehydrated. Have you had enough water?" I shake my head, wincing as I trudge alongside her. "See! Dehydration." Without stopping our pace, she roots around in her bag, extracts an aluminum water bottle, and hands it to me. "Sorry, it's kind of warm." I drink it anyway, little sips, and it does help. "Yes? Is that better?"

I hand it back to her. "Do they have air-conditioning in this city?"

Somehow, I make it inside the Galeries Lafayette and downstairs to the upscale food court, the air a welcome change – not arctic in the way of many American malls, but much cooler than the humid heat outside. Riya deposits me at a blond wood table and disappears, leaving me to admire the French pastries in the glass dessert cases, and I start to feel better just sitting here amid the subterranean sweets.

Riya returns with a glass of what looks like ginger ale

and a plate with two butter cookies. "Drink this." She plunks the glass down in front of me, and I take a sip. It's delicious, with hints of lemon and ginger, but not too sweet.

My stomach starts to unwind. "Thanks, Rye. I think I was too hot. Or maybe I'm just worn out. Too many intense things back-to-back. I'm such a bumpkin."

Riya runs her fingers through her dark hair, which has grown curly in the humidity. "Did I plan too much? I wanted to make sure we got all the history stuff in that you'd like. No offense, but I don't need to see any of it again. I'd rather take you shopping."

I watch shoppers mill around us or sit at nearby tables, enormous bags resting at their feet as they murmur to one another across their own tabletops. "Sometimes, I get depressed thinking about all the amazing historical things in the world and how I probably won't get to see even the tiniest fraction of them. Even if I Google all the checklists of what I should see."

Riya grins. "I Googled Ten Best Things to See for each of our cities. Even though I've been to most of them. But you can't possibly see everything anyway."

I sigh. "Maybe I just feel guilty. I know I should want to see as much historical stuff as I can, but it starts bumming me out after a while."

"Don't feel guilty! We're allowed to have fun. We don't have to be so productive all the time. We're not Neel."

I reach for a cookie. "Maybe this cookie represents the best part of Berlin for me." I take a bite. "Yep, this is my wonder of Berlin."

Riya shakes her head. "Well, that would make me the world's lousiest tour guide." I throw the cookie at her. "Hey, you're wasting our wonder of the world!"

Tears threaten to surface. Clearly, I'm having some sort of emotional heatstroke today. "Forget it." I should tell her that it feels like it's been a long time since anyone has taken care of me the way she has on this trip, has stopped whatever they were doing to make sure I had water or a cool department store to sit down in, but I don't tell her, and the moment passes as she points out a cute handbag hanging from the shoulder of a woman walking by us. I grab the other cookie on the plate. "Don't underestimate how good these cookies are." The sad truth is that more often than not, I don't say the things I should in any given moment.

But I'm lucky. Because I have Riya, who can mostly read the thoughts shooting through my messed-up head even if I don't say them aloud. She motions to the crumbs on the plate. "Thanks for saving me one, by the way."

Later, Riya stands next to me by a rack of clothes and studies my find. "You should definitely get it."

I drop the slippery fabric of the top, letting it fall like water back onto its hanger. "Right, because I'm going to spend" – I pause, checking the price tag and running the math in my head – "eighty-eight dollars on a tank top."

Riya pulls it from the hanger. "It's beautiful. And it's on sale. Try it on."

In the dressing room, the mirror confirms my fear: I love it. I turn in circles, admiring the way the silvery fabric spills around me. Riya peers over the edge of the door. "Let me see – oooooh, yes. It will look gorgeous with the miniskirt from Florence. My treat."

"You are not buying me an eighty-eight-dollar tank top. I don't care how much on sale it is." I pull it off over my head and put it back on the hanger.

Riya yanks open the door and snatches it. "Okay, then my nani is buying it."

Before I can grab it back, my phone rings. A FaceTime from Kate. "Hi," I say to my sister, her big eyes blinking at me through the screen. "Whoa, up close and personal."

"Guten Tag!" she shouts into the phone. Older sisters are supposed to be cool and teach you about cool things, but that does not include technology for my sister. She's more of a Luddite than I am.

"Why are you shouting?"

She pulls back slightly from the screen. "Where are you?"

"In a dressing room. In Berlin – hold on." I set the phone down on the ground and quickly slip back into my shirt.

"Nice bra!"

I grab the phone. "What's up?"

"Just checking in on you before I go for my run."

It's almost three in Berlin, which makes it nearly six in the morning in Portland, Oregon. Kate runs five mornings a week at 6:15. She's very committed to it. She got 99 percent of the athletic genes in the family. I can do basic hiking, but nothing that takes actual skill or endurance or a prop of any kind. Or getting up at six in the morning.

I start to tell her, "We saw Checkpoint Charlie today, the most well-known crossing spot for the Allies in the Cold War," but her phone goes suddenly between her chin and her shoulder. She's tying her shoes. "Hello, this is a video call," I remind her.

Her face reappears. "Oh, right. So you met someone named Charlie." My sister got zero percent of the interest-in-history genes.

"Yes, he was dressed in lederhosen and wielding a beer stein the size of a small car. I might move in with him here in Germany and learn to herd goats. Could you tell Mom and Dad for me?"

She rolls her eyes. "Sorry – I had to tie my shoes. How's Riya? Did you see Dean and Anju?"

"They're great. Dean's taking us to see his work at a gallery here tomorrow."

"They're too cool to be parents." I hear her filling up a water bottle.

Someone knocks on the dressing room door. "Okay in

there?" the matronly saleswoman asks me when I crack open the door, her hair in a perfect gray bun. I show her my phone, and she smiles understandingly, moving off down the row of dressing rooms.

"And the cousin," Kate continues, "how's that going?" To my horror, heat rushes to my cheeks, visible even to distracted Kate in Portland. She perks up. "Oh, well, what do we have here? International romance?"

"Eww, no. He's *almost* twenty years old."

"I'm twenty-two. Am I *eww*?" She mimics my face.

"Yes."

She grins. "He sounds intriguing. An older, British chaperone?"

"He and Riya are always at each other's throats. Cousin baggage because he's so bossy and condescending. Besides, he has a horrible girlfriend."

This kills her smile. "Off-limits, then."

"Yes, I know." Kate has always been clear on this subject. Which makes her unrelenting support of Mom's choice even more annoying. I know Mom claims she and Dr. Restivo didn't start dating until after she and Dad decided to split, but it seems like a technicality.

"You should call Mom." Another of Kate's annoying habits: reading my mind.

I exit the dressing room. "I talked to her last night."

She tries a different angle. "She said you still won't talk to Robert?"

"I don't currently have any pressing dental needs." I see Riya across the store, finishing up at a cash register. She holds up a white, red-handled bag and gives me a thumbs-up.

"You're being a baby about this, you know?"

"Says the girl who conveniently lives in Portland."

"Abby—"

"Look, you haven't had to deal with the fallout, okay? You don't know what it's like."

"So you've said."

"I have to go," I tell her. "Riya's waiting for me."

"Abby!" Her expression is as worried as her voice, and it keeps me from ending the call even if I don't respond. She really doesn't get it. Kate got to grow up with her childhood intact, move away, and is now off living her own life, our parents existing in the backdrop for holidays and long weekends. She hasn't had to survive in the same house with Dad for the last five months, see his face each day as he wanders like a zombie through the rooms. She hasn't had to make sure he eats right or puts the garbage out. She has the luxury of neutrality because she doesn't get dropped off each week for Sunday dinner with Mom and Dr. Spits-A-Lot.

"Don't worry about it, okay?" I tell her. "Have a good run."

That night, I feel sort of awkward standing in front of Nachtlicht on a busy Berlin street wearing the beautiful silvery tank top, my leather miniskirt, and a pair of borrowed heeled sandals that include an elaborate zigzag of unnecessary straps that Riya had to help me fasten.

It also feels exhilarating.

"You look incredible," Riya keeps telling me, squeezing my arm. She tugs on one of the curls she somehow managed to pile on top of my head in a way that didn't make me look like a deranged sprinkler.

Giddy, I wonder if the makeup she applied still looks as good as it did in the mirror back at her apartment. I hope I'm not sweating it off. "Thanks. *You* look fantastic." She does. Black platform combat boots, lemon-yellow satin shorts, and a tight, subtly glittered black T-shirt.

"You look like a tarty bee," Neel declared as we left earlier.

"Buzzzzzzz," Riya tossed out as she shut the front door on his response.

"There they are!" Riya releases my arm, waving wildly at Tavin, Kiara, and Jonas as they cross the street toward us.

"What is he wearing?" I gape at Jonas, dressed in a suit that looks entirely made out of pockets. Suit pockets. Dress-shirt pockets. Denim back pockets and the inside white material of front pockets. Big pockets from handbags stitched together with smaller pockets from coin purses – every kind of pocket – to form a full suit. Even his tie is made from tiny pockets.

"Wow," Riya says when they join us. "Mr. Pockets."

He hands us each a slip of white paper and a pen. "Tell me a secret."

Kiara giggles. "You write it down and put it in one of his pockets!"

"I'm a piece of interactive performance art," he tells us proudly, his lime-green glasses slipping down his nose. "Cool, right?" Riya scribbles something down and tucks it into a denim pocket on his right sleeve. Tavin does the same. I can't really think of much, so I write *I wonder what my dog's doing right now* and tuck it away in his chest pocket.

Tavin leans into me, whispering, "I wrote down that he seems to need a lot of attention."

Tingling at the feel of his breath on my neck, I whisper back, "Not sure that's such a big secret."

Tavin flashes his trademark smile at me. "Perhaps I should resubmit?"

"Maybe."

"Nice tank, by the way." He takes the hem of my top and rubs it between his fingers. I follow him into the club, fluttery in the wake of his compliment.

Inside, it's a mix of shadow and spots of neon lights from a hidden source. On the angular corner stage, a three-person band pounds out a driving beat. They seem to be wearing a full outfit between them: the singer in a crop top and high-waisted marching band shorts, the drummer in a suit jacket without a shirt, and the base guitarist sporting a dress shirt that hangs to his knees, no pants, just combat boots and a top hat. He looks a little like a punk version of John from Disney's *Peter Pan*.

Tavin notices, too. "Maybe they don't have enough money to each buy all the clothes," he says dryly. "So they share."

"Music is a tough life." I nod in fake solemnity.

He squeezes my arm. "Riya knew you and I would get along."

My heart picks up a beat. "Are we getting along?"

He leans into me, his lips grazing my ear. "I'm going to get us something to drink." He disappears into the throng, giving me a minute to catch my breath.

Riya, Kiara, and Jonas dance at the edge of the thick pack of dancers. I survey the rest of the room. Some people hang out in clumps by the wall or sit at low tables with drinks, leaning in, heads almost touching to hear each other. I have never been in a club before, and even if this is a special club for sixteen and over and not a "real" club (as Neel informed us earlier) it feels real to me. Of course, I also have absolutely no idea what to do in a real (or fake) club, so I just stand here lamely, searching for Tavin's familiar worn jeans and maroon T-shirt to reappear in the blur.

Suddenly, he's next to me with a pair of Cokes, and I can smell the sweet syrup of the soda. I take a grateful sip, my head more carbonated than my drink. "I'm not much of a dancer," he confides, dipping close to my ear again.

"Me either," I shout into the side of him, his shaggy hair tickling my nose. Maybe this is one benefit of a club: It forces you to get close to someone just to hear them.

"Fancy meeting you here!" A voice bellows on the other side of me. Neel stands there, eyes wide in mock surprise, his hands in the pockets of a pair of skinny black jeans. "Thought I'd join you since Moira's ditched me and gone back to London."

"What? Oh, um—" I can't believe he's here, after the whole fake club comment. He blinks at me and then makes a slight nod in Tavin's direction. "Oh, right, this is a friend of Riya's – Tavin."

"Gaven, how'd you and Riya know each other?"

"What?" Tavin can't make out Neel's words.

"It's Tavin!" I try again, shouting into Neel's ear. "They went to school together last year."

"Ah, brilliant." He moves his head to the music.

Something has shifted. Tavin looks annoyed, sips at his Coke, his eyes scrutinizing the dancers. Neel rocks back and forth on his feet, heel to toe, heel to toe, trying to look interested, but beneath it, he's hurt. He's being casual about Moira, but something happened.

I scoot closer so he can hear me. "What happened with Moira?" He makes a sour face. "Do you want to talk about it?" As I say it, I realize I want him to want to talk about it with me. Somewhere quiet. That can't be good. "Or not – whatever."

He shakes his head. "Too loud!" He motions around us.

I take a long swallow of my drink, choking on the carbonation. Both boys slap me on the back in unison. Smooth. "I'm fine," I sputter. One of my curls comes loose and bobs like a bungee jumper in front of my eyes.

Tavin tugs again at the flutter of my tank top hem. "You want to dance?"

Feeling Neel's eyes on me, I give Tavin a playful nudge. "I thought we agreed we weren't dancers."

"Let's fake it." He pulls me toward the dance floor, and I cast apologetic glances back at Neel, who smiles stiffly, still rocking, heel to toe, heel to toe, like a bored teacher at a dance he wasn't supposed to have to chaperone.

We find Riya with Kiara and Jonas near the stage. Tavin and I attempt some dance-related moves for a few minutes and our joint awkwardness cracks us up. He really goes for it, kicking his legs and arms in random directions, and doing little shimmies that aren't even close to being rhythmically on beat for the music that's pounding the air around us. He's adorable, and the way he keeps looking at me kicks up that fizz in my belly again. Riya dances over to us, giving me a sly smile. She motions at Tavin. "Having fun?" I nod, and after a few twirls, she shouts, "Is that Neel I saw moping over there?" I nod again, and she takes my hands, pulling me into her until our faces almost touch. "What in the name of ancient history is he doing here?"

The band takes a sudden break. Riya lets go of me, and we each take an automatic step back now that we can actually hear each other. She repeats her question.

"Moira went back to London."

Riya shoots a concerned look at her cousin. "So, we actually scared her off? And it didn't even take a spike or a silver bullet. Miraculous."

I glance at where he stands, his face long. "He seems pretty sad about it."

"This is what they do." She fans herself as she heads to the bar.

I follow her. "What do you mean?"

"She throws a fit, breaks up with him, and he coaxes her back. It's a repetitive, boring little game of Duck, Duck, Neel." Riya scans the bar. "Whew, hot. I need water."

Kiara dances up to us, even if the music has stopped momentarily. "Get me one," she tells Riya, and collapses on a barstool. "I love dancing."

I'm distracted, trying to catch Neel's eye, but I nod and say, "Yeah. It's great."

Kiara kicks off a heel and starts massaging her foot.

"You must be thrilled to see Riya. She tells me you two are tight."

My gaze snaps back. "Yeah, super tight. Since pre-school."

She switches feet. "That's cool. I've been dying to meet the famous Abby!"

"Great to finally meet you, too." She's being nice, but the air feels weird between us, and it takes me a minute to recognize the thin tendrils winding their way through my gut as jealousy. I try to give Kiara a bright smile. Back home, Riya has tons of friends and often hangs out with them without me. I've always preferred it this way because I know when she's done with parties and boy-friends and just wants to be herself, she comes to me.

Why should Kiara feel different from all those other friends?

She just does.

Riya returns, balancing three glasses of sparkling water, and hands one to Kiara and one to me. To Kiara, she says, "Apparently, you know the bartender? Sebastian."

Kiara runs the name around her head, trying to place him, until Riya points him out at the other end of the bar. "Ah, yes. He's friends with Ren."

At my confused look, Riya says, "Her brother. One of her *three* older brothers. The middle, right?"

Kiara nods into her water. "Renald. The one who gives my dad all the gray hair. He got a tattoo on his face last week." She shakes her head affectionately.

Riya laughs. "Another one?"

Kiara launches into a story that involves her brother, a German flight attendant, and the Swedish authorities. She has Riya doubled over in giggles by the end of it. "And that's when he said to them, 'Does this mean I don't get my massage?' "

I try to laugh even if it has the feel of a recycled story, one she's told for this very moment, this lead-in to the theatrical punch line. Kiara drains the last of her water. "It reminds me of what happened with Gus at school – remember that?"

Riya has to set her drink down she's laughing so hard. "With the hamburger! That was hilarious."

I don't know Gus or what happened with the hamburger. I try to follow the back and forth of conversation (something about a librarian and a smuggled hamburger?) but they've lost me. I know it's not on purpose – they've disappeared down the rabbit hole of a shared school environment that can't help but leave me out of the mix, but it's never easy to be on the outside of an inside joke.

Kiara finally composes herself, looping a long, bare arm around Riya's shoulders. "What am I going to do when this girl leaves?"

She doesn't really direct the question at me. It's a throwaway question, barely rhetorical, but before I can stop it, something dark sprouts, curling up from those vines in my belly, and her words water it. What will *she* do without Riya? Seriously? She's known her for five minutes. "Do you know where the bathroom is?"

Giving me a funny look, Kiara points at the far wall. "There."

I deposit my glass on the bar and hurry off.

A few minutes later, Riya appears behind me in the cracked bathroom-sink mirror while I wash my hands. Her face seems faintly green in the dim lighting. "You okay?"

"Sure, why wouldn't I be?"

"I thought maybe you got stuck in here?" she tries to joke.

I'm not in the mood. "Nope." I shake off excess water and try to locate paper towels. Do they not have paper towels in Germany?

Riya points at the hand dryer she's partly leaning against. Her tone shifting to annoyance, she asks, "Want to talk about why you fled the scene back there?"

"I didn't *flee* the scene." Maybe being in theater makes people more dramatic than they already are? "I had to pee." I start the hand dryer, and its hum drowns out Riya's response. "What?" I ask when it stops.

"Kiara thinks you don't like her."

"I don't *know* her. How could I not like her?"

"Are you trying to like her?"

Two girls with matching magenta hair burst in through

the bathroom door. Riya follows me out of the bathroom, and I ask her over my shoulder, "What does that even mean?" We wriggle behind a cluster of girls crowding around a mirror hanging in the narrow hallway, holding their mascara wands and lipsticks like unsheathed swords.

"It means you could make more of an effort. She is."

The end of her sentence feels laced with a dare. "Sorry. I left my friendship bracelet kit back home."

"Abby!" She grabs for my arm, but I'm one step ahead of her.

This is one of the times where Riya is trying too hard. She's forcing the whole thing with Kiara and it's irritating. We weave our way through the dancers back toward the bar. A new band has taken the stage, all guys with ink-black hair outfitted in mesh tank tops and bright pink tutus. I see Jonas wandering the crowd with his pen and paper. Kiara lounges on her stool, chatting with the bartender I assume is Sebastian. I don't see Tavin or Neel anywhere.

I'm hit with a wave of weariness. It's loud, I'm hot, and now this whole thing with Kiara is messy. It's too much. "Is there somewhere I can grab some air?"

Riya's face sags. She knows me well enough to know Kiara and I will not be doing a get-to-know-each-other dance with the tutu band this evening. She motions toward the back of the club. "There's a courtyard through that door, but it usually smells like garbage. And smoke."

"I'll just be a few minutes."

She shrugs, already turning away.

Outside, the evening is still warm but feels cool after the muggy heat of the club. The courtyard is more like an alley, smaller than even the stage inside, and a sour-milk smell hangs in the air. It's dark, and water drips from an unseen place against the cobblestones. This is not a place to hang out, which explains why only two people are out here. One guy, dressed in what looks like a blue auto mechanic's jumpsuit, smokes against the shared brick wall of the next building and checks his phone.

The other is Neel, who tucks his own phone quickly into his pocket when he sees me. "Oh, hey – everything all right?"

"Just getting some air. Was that Moira?" I cross to him.

He shakes his head. "I tried to ring her, but she's not answering. She might already be in the air." His eyes look especially liquid in the dark.

I remember Riya's question to him last night. "I know you and Riya don't always agree on things" – he snorts, his eyes widening at the understatement – "but she's not wrong. You don't seem very happy with her."

He slips his hands into his back pockets. "Moira is many things: complicated, fit, opinionated—"

"Critical, self-absorbed," I offer.

He narrows his eyes. "She's brilliant, really. She puts

on a bit of a tough face, but she's smart and interesting and complicated."

I fold my arms across my chest. "You mentioned that one already."

"Did I?" His face cracks into a smile, a concession. "Okay, she can be a real pisser, I know."

"I've met more compassionate wolverines."

He arches an eyebrow. "Have you?"

"No."

This makes him laugh, and I find myself falling into the sound of it. He runs a hand through his hair. "It doesn't matter anyway. She's dumped me. Perhaps I can add failed wolverine tamer to my CV."

"Not sure you want to advertise that one." I think about Riya's earlier mention of Duck, Duck, Neel. "But she's done this before, right? And it hasn't been over."

He gives a rueful shrug. "Riya's told you, has she?" My face flames, and he nods at the admission in it. "I know this isn't the first time she's fallen out with me. I'm sure she thinks I'll go running after her. But not this time. Something about this time." He holds my gaze. "This time is the end."

It dawns on me that while he's been talking, I've been watching his mouth, imagining what it might feel like to kiss him. Heat returns to my cheeks and I clear my throat, trying to sound genuine when I say, "I'm sorry, Neel," even if I don't feel sorry, but then find myself blurting, "She's an idiot, though. She won't do better than you."

He gives me a grateful smile. "Thank you."

"Just don't do anything drastic. When Dido, the queen of Carthage, found out that Aeneas was leaving her, she threw herself on his sword in the middle of a burning pyre." The words tumble out before I can stop them, and he looks startled with this sudden introduction of classical antiquity into the mix. I drop my eyes, mortified. I do this when I'm nervous: spew random history tidbits that are barely related to the conversation because I don't know what else to say.

Still, his surprise seems to melt into something else, his face growing – what is that expression? It could masquerade as affection even if he doesn't mean it to. But I think he might because he steps closer, until our toes are almost touching. "I promise – no swords, no burning pyres."

I force myself to look at him. "Right. That would be hasty."

"You know something? In all of Riya's endless chatter about you, I never expected, well – *you*."

This last word, his velvet delivery of it, sends a delicious current through me, and even though I'm flirting-impaired, I go for it anyway. "Am I complicated and interesting?"

His eyes grow serious. "Yes, actually."

I suck in my breath. The guy smoking against the wall chuckles softly and stubs out his cigarette on his shoe.

He gives us an amused nod as he heads back inside.

I'd forgotten we had an audience and hurry to say, "But I am sorry Moira broke up with you."

He lowers his voice. "Are you?" I shake my head, and another curl comes bobbing down. He tucks it behind my ear. Am I imagining that his face keeps getting just a bit closer to mine?

Riya comes banging out of the door. "Oh, Abby, there you are. I thought you'd been murdered." Neel and I leap apart, and Riya freezes, her eyes narrowing. "I'm not interrupting something, am I?"

"No!" Neel clears his throat. "Right, then – ready to head home?" He disappears past Riya through the doorway. Behind me, the *drip-drip-drip* of the water grows louder.

Riya clamps her hands on her hips. "What was that all about?"

"Nothing." I avoid her eyes, pulling out my phone and checking the time. Only I can't really get the buttons to work properly with my shaking hands. I pretend anyway. "Wow, it's late."

Riya pauses, waiting for me to explain, then gives up when she sees I'm not offering more information. "I'm ready to go. Kiara and Jonas got into a fight because Jonas thought she was all over that bartender."

"Wait. Are they together?" I ask, still trying to recover from whatever just happened with Neel.

She rolls her eyes. "Jonas wishes they were. But he blew it because now she's pissed at him. So Tavin's taking her home. Poor Jonas, he's just sitting in there, crying into his tea."

"He is?"

Riya laughs. "Not really. But he's out of paper, someone stole all his pens, and he's alone at the bar in his pocket suit. I could write *Stop depressing people!* on a napkin, but, you know, the whole pen-theft thing." She pauses again, narrowing her eyes. "You sure I wasn't interrupting something?"

I wave her off, pushing her back inside the club.

"Can we go?" Riya asks the next morning. "Seriously, you don't have to do this. Dad doesn't care."

I shake my head, peering at Dean's painting. Riya had other plans for our morning, but when her dad mentioned the gallery, I'd jumped at the chance to see his new work. Now Riya keeps flashing me skeptical looks each time I beg to stay "just a little longer."

"What are we doing here?" she whispers again, scanning the gallery tucked into a narrow industrial space that seems made entirely of glass and white-painted wood.

"Enjoying amazing art."

Her dad paints large, bright canvases that have always, for some reason, reminded me of the circus. They are never about the circus or feature anything relating to the circus; in fact, Dean and Anju have always been vocal about their loathing of the circus on the grounds of animal rights. And maybe also clowns. No matter, his paintings scream *circus* to me. I just make sure not to mention this.

"You hate art galleries," she reminds me, checking her phone for the tenth time in ten minutes.

"I don't hate art galleries," I insist, even if I sort of do. I love museums, so it seems reasonable that I would also love art galleries. They are essentially the same beast. People wander around staring at beautiful and interesting things, titling their heads, peering in or stepping back, depending on the piece. They both have helpers milling around should people become confused about what it is they are observing or where they should be heading next.

Only art galleries make me feel the opposite of museums.

Instead of relaxed, at home, engaged, I'm tense, dry-mouthed, planning my escape. So Riya has an excellent point. Why am I here?

Because here I don't have to talk about Kiara or Tavin or how I almost kissed Neel last night in a dingy alley.

"I like art galleries."

"Do not."

Maybe because at a museum I can sink into the history and the information, casually buying a postcard or a ten-dollar book upon exiting instead of feeling like I should be considering one of the five-hundred-dollar smaller pieces or I'm wasting everyone's time. Dean has tried to tell me over the years that I should never feel pressure to buy. The artist wants his or her work *seen*. Being here supports the creative world. But I always feel like a woman with a severe chignon and dagger heels expects me to either buy something or get out.

I feel like that now, for example.

Lovisa, with her lavender-dyed pixie cut, four-inch heels, and dress that seems like its own art installation (medium: indigo cling film?) hovers nearby, eyeing Riya and me as if we might suddenly set the place on fire. Or wet our pants. Probably the latter, since she clearly thinks we're still in diapers. When Dean introduced us, she spoke to us in the kind of high, sing-songy voice reserved for babies and small dogs who wear fashion sweaters, then asked us if we wanted some "pressed juice" or "nibbles." I'm not one to turn down snacks of any kind, so now I move around the gallery as quietly as I can with my tiny red metal plate of white cheese cubes and green grapes and try not to say something about circuses to Dean. Or chew too loudly. I'm pretty sure Lovisa can hear me chewing.

Dean steps up beside me. "What does it make you think about?"

Not circuses! "This one's my favorite," I tell him, motioning to a tall swirl of reds, greens, and blues that all seem to move outward from one another with streaks of light. "It's like a firework. But sad."

He seems thrilled with this response. "Yes! It's called *Capitalism Takes a Holiday*."

"Perfect." I nod, not really knowing why it might be perfect. Seems to me it could be named a lot of things. "I like how all the colors are racing one another."

"That's what gives it energy." Lovisa startles me. I hadn't heard her drift over to us, would have thought cling film might make a bit more noise. "This movement here." She motions at a sweep of red. "And here." She indicates a streak of silvery gold.

"What's the red dot?" I motion to a tiny sticker next to the title.

Lovisa smiles proudly. "We sold it the first night we opened the show."

No price tags. I guess if you have to ask, you can't afford it. "That's wonderful, Dean!" I lean to hug him, forgetting my plate, and my three remaining green grapes go rolling across the floor. Lovisa click-clacks after them, bending like a great blue heron to fetch them.

Riya wanders over. "Can we go eat? I'm starving."

I turn to Dean. "Want to join us for lunch?"

As she walks past me, Riya mutters, "I'm onto you, Abby Byrd."

After lunch, Dean walks us past the Gedächtniskirche, the Kaiser Wilhelm Memorial Church. The church was bombed in 1943, but instead of rebuilding it or tearing it down, Berliners did a mix of both. They left it partly destroyed as a reminder of the war, but also built a modern section, rising out of the ruins as a testament to our human ability to move forward, onward, upward.

I've seen a lot of churches. This one, though, feels different. I stare at the chunks of stone missing from its body, a shudder moving through me. I can't imagine living somewhere with a constant threat of bombing, with death falling from the sky at any moment. I know people live like that now, all over the world, but seeing it here in front of me makes it vividly real, which I guess is the point.

"Were any of the ancient wonders a church?" Dean asks me, his head craned up, his hands in the pockets of his paint-speckled jeans.

"Sort of," I answer, studying the modern belfry, rising like a jagged green iceberg out of the church's top. "The Temple of Artemis at Ephesus was like a church, only they called it a temple."

"Same diff," Riya says, scanning her phone again.

I watch people hurry along the Kurfürstendamm, tourists standing out from the locals with their cameras and iPads and wrinkle-resistant travel wear. A girl a bit younger than me sits on the ground nearby with her phone, trying to get a shot of the belfry against the bright blue sky. I take a deep breath, the air already hot and thick. "I love Artemis. Goddess of the hunt. So fierce. She was Apollo's twin sister. When she was born a moment ahead of him, she turned around and helped deliver him."

Riya's eyebrows shoot up. "What the— That's insane. And gross."

"Welcome to Greek mythology. Some pretty disturbing stuff."

Dean smiles at Riya's sour face. She slips her phone back into the enormous red bag she's been carrying around all day. "Can we go swimming now? It's like the surface of the sun out here. Dad, don't you have work to do?"

Her meaning is not lost on him. "This is where I leave you, ladies. I should get back to the gallery." He gives us a wave and then disappears into the mass of people.

Riya locates the bus we need, but even sitting in a seat, the bus rumbling away from the Kurfürstendamm, I can picture the bombed-out places of the church in my mind, like the glimmering imprints behind your eyelids when you've closed them after staring too long into the sun.

Riya

To escape the mounting heat, I take Abby to the Badeschiff, a swimming pool and hangout spot on the Spree. The pool is not in the actual river; it's built directly on top of the river, with its own sand beach and a twisting dock leading to the pool. It takes us about forty minutes to get inside; we change quickly into our swimsuits, and then head out to the pool, winding our way out onto the dock and dropping our towels in heaps. We climb down the ladder into the cool blue water, the shock of it biting at first and then blissful.

"Ahhhhh." I glide into the water. "Perfection."

Abby sinks in beside me. "Exactly what we needed. I like hot weather but not like this."

I swim along the side until I reach the empty corner of the pool, stopping to take in the view of the East Harbor, the old buildings against the blue sky spotted with white clouds. Hard to believe I'll soon be leaving this skyline behind. What a year. A few feet away, Abby leans her back against the pool edge, her arms splayed out like a cross to hold herself up. She kicks her legs out in front of her, then lets them drift slowly back under her. We spend a few minutes in silence, the water hypnotizing us. Finally, I break the spell. "I got a text from Kiara earlier. Tavin is pouting."

"What – why?"

"Because you ditched him last night. To go hang out with *Neel*."

Abby shakes her head. "I didn't *ditch* him." She dunks under the water because she thinks it will hide her blush, but I see it. When Abby blushes, it's a neon sign.

I wait for her to surface. "What were you and Neel talking about?"

She wipes water from her eyes and avoids mine. "Moira. They're over."

"I don't buy it. Moira breaks up with Neel the way most people cancel a dinner reservation. She knows she can always get a table tomorrow. It's what she does."

Abby swirls the surface of the water with the palm of her hand. "He said this time it's the end."

"Why would he say that to you?" I wait to see if she offers what I'm obviously most interested in, but she doesn't, so I say, "From where I was standing, it looked like he was about to kiss you."

"What?! No – that's – just, no." She pushes off from the poolside, diving deep into the blue of the pool.

Oh, wow. He *was* about to kiss her. Why else would she be acting like this? That's just what I need complicating this trip. My stupid cousin kissing Abby. I should have tossed him in the Arno when I had the chance. While Abby's still underwater, I see Kiara and Tavin heading down the dock toward the ladder and wave to them. Just as Abby surfaces, Tavin scales the narrow poolside and jumps in next to her, sending a surge of water into her face.

At her sputtering, he gasps, "Oh, hey – sorry about that."

Abby wipes water from her eyes, but she's grinning a wet face at Tavin and splashing him back. I study them. Maybe she's not lying about Neel? Maybe it's nothing. Abby squeals as Tavin picks her up and tosses her a foot in the opposite direction. Okay, she seems happy to see Tavin. I'm clearly imagining the thing with Neel.

Kiara swims up to me, turning to watch them. "Well, they're disgustingly cute."

"I knew they'd get each other."

"Did you tell her about London yet?"

I glance sharply at her, my face reflected in her mirrored sunglasses. "You're really not giving up on that one, are you?"

She shrugs, kicking her legs rhythmically in the water in front of her, her slick purple toenails standing out against the blue of the pool. "If it were me, I'd want to know that my friend, who is supposed to be moving home with me at the end of this trip, is actually moving to London instead."

"Shhhh!" I check to see if Tavin and Abby heard anything, but they are chatting animatedly on the far side of the pool. I lower my voice even if they're out of earshot.

"I *am* going home with her at the end of this trip."

She gives me a withering look. "And then moving to London at the end of August. Same thing."

"It would totally wreck the trip for her, okay? And I have this whole scavenger hunt planned out to tell her about it, which she'll love."

Kiara shakes her head, her eyes on the East Harbor skyline. "I don't know, Riya. From what you've told me, she's had a pretty tough year—"

"I know what's best for my friend."

Kiara tilts her sunglasses in my direction. "For your friend, or best for you?"

Anger simmers through me. Kiara's like a pit bull sometimes: Once her jaws close over an idea, it's misery to pry them open. "They're coming over here. Just drop it. Be on my side."

"I am."

I know she is. The problem is, I'm afraid she might be right.

When Abby and Tavin swim up to us, Tavin pulls

himself out to sit on the side of the pool. "Let's get something to drink and find some deck chairs," he suggests, the water streaming off his large frame. Ten minutes later we're tilting our faces to the sun, sipping the fizzy, fruity drinks Kiara bought as we melt quietly into the warmth of the day.

Abby's phone rings.

She squints at it. "It's my dad. That's weird. It's so early in California." She answers, and her face shifts from relaxed to worried. "What – when?" She shoots scared eyes at me. Tavin and Kiara sit up, waiting. She listens a few moments more, then whispers, "Henry got hit by a car!"

"Who's Henry?" Kiara asks, her brow creasing.

"Abby's dog." We wait as she nods and pauses, saying things like "yeah" and "okay," and then finally, "call me back." She sets her phone down on the white canvas of the deck chair, her face like chalk. "Dad's in Loomis with him. At animal emergency." Her eyes shimmer with tears. "He might die."

I scoot onto her chair and put my arms around her as Tavin and Kiara sit helplessly by in their chairs. "He'll be okay," I say over and over, because this is what to say even when it's most likely not true.

An hour later at the apartment, Abby sits on my bed, still in her damp swimsuit and a Hogwarts T-shirt, checking updates about Henry.

He's in critical condition.

He's in surgery.

Silence.

We stream a romantic comedy on my iPad that might be funny if either of us could actually pay attention to it. I try to concentrate on the current scene. A man and a woman argue in a restaurant in New York. For some reason, the man isn't wearing a shirt, and the other people in the restaurant keep looking at him. There is a misunderstanding. It might have something to do with the no-shirt thing. As long as it doesn't involve a dog, we should be okay. I glance at Abby, who isn't watching it anyway, only staring at the blank screen of her phone.

We left Tavin and Kiara behind at the Badeschiff, promising to meet up with them later when we knew more information. Her jaw clenched, Abby stared out the bus window as we threaded the streets back to the apartment, and she hasn't moved much since.

Halfway through the movie, Dad comes in with a tray of his famous molasses cookies, still warm from the oven. He sets them down, the room filling with the smell of cloves, cinnamon, and nutmeg. "Any word?" I shake my head. I offer the plate to Abby, but she just stares at a stripe of late-afternoon sunlight falling across my duvet.

Her phone buzzes again, and she quickly puts it on speaker. "Dad?" Her fear is fully present in that one syllable.

"He's going to make it." Geoff's warm voice sounds tired. Abby lets out a whooshing sigh of relief. He continues, "The vet says it's lucky I found him when I did. I need to fix the latch on that stupid gate," he adds guiltily.

"I'm just glad you found him." Geoff had been up early to take out the garbage can he'd forgotten to put out the night before, had found Henry in a heap in the street at the end of their driveway. Whoever hit him was long gone. "Are you still in Loomis?"

"Yeah. Mom's here, too." I notice Abby stiffen at the mention of her, but her dad can't see. "She was great, talking to everyone, getting everything worked out. She's with the surgeon right now. I'm outside." I imagine Geoff standing in the heat of a California July, far from us, but still right here in the room.

Abby peers at her phone. "I'm so glad he's okay. Are you sure you don't need me to come home?"

I bristle at this, grateful when Geoff says, "Don't be silly. Enjoy your trip. He's going to be fine. Might have a limp, but that will make him seem tough," he jokes.

"You'd tell me, though, right? If you needed me there, I can be there."

Why would she go home? Henry's fine. Geoff assures her she doesn't need to come home. "Do you want to talk to your mom?"

"You should get back," Abby says quickly, and angles her back away from me on the bed. She switches the phone off speaker, but not before I hear him say, "Abby, could you just talk to her?"

"I should go. We're meeting some of Riya's friends. Love you!" She ends the call and turns to me. "Don't look at me like that."

I pretend I wasn't. "Like what?"

"I don't feel like talking to her right now."

"I'm not looking at you like anything." I take a cookie and push the plate toward her so she can reach one. "It seems like they're getting along better if they're talking now. That's good news."

She shrugs. "I should have been there. This wouldn't have happened if I'd been there. I would have fixed the gate."

I bite my lip. Henry might have been hit anyway, he was always finding new ways to escape, but she's not in a place to hear that right now.

Later, after we finally abandon the movie, Neel pokes his head into my room. "You two want to go on a covert mission with me?"

"Just because you're British doesn't make you James Bond." I fluff one of the many pillows on my bed, settling back against the pile, and show him the book I'm reading. "We're busy."

Neel glances at where Abby sits on the floor against my bed, flipping through an old *National Geographic* of my dad's. "Yeah, you seem busy. You're not seriously going to spend your last day in Berlin shut up in here?"

Abby looks up from a glossy page. "It's our last day here?" Neel pretends he doesn't notice the knife eyes I shoot at him. He did that on purpose. To get me back for the whole Moira thing.

Abby looks eager. "Where're we going?"

I shake my head at Neel, but not vigorously enough to stop him from saying, "Next stop – Edinburgh, Scotland!"

Abby's eyes practically light up in the shape of old castles. "Seriously?"

"Surprise." I glare at Neel.

"Riya and I used to be quite the Harry Potter nerds."

"Right." I motion at her shirt. "*Used* to be."

"Brilliant." Neel rubs his hands together. "So, since it's your last day, what are you doing sitting around here?"

"Abby's dog almost died today."

Concerned, he steps into the room. "I didn't realize. Is he okay?"

Abby blinks up at him. "He'll be fine. He's out of surgery now." She closes the magazine on her hand to hold her place. "What sort of mission did you have in mind?"

I interrupt her. "Doesn't matter. We have plans. With Kiara and Tavin."

Neel ignores me, directing his answer to Abby. "A collector friend of mine told me there's a shop here in Berlin that might have a vinyl I'm looking for." He peers at his phone. "On Oranienstraße."

I perk up. "There's a cute vintage shop on that street." Checking my phone, I let Abby know we have time.

Abby tosses the magazine aside. "Covert missions are my favorite kind."

She doesn't know how much I hope those words prove true for us, too.

Outside the record store on Oranienstraße, the sky shifts toward evening as cars glide up and down the busy street. Inside, it's hot and stuffy in the crowded space of the shop. Posters of punk and metal bands paper the walls, along with bright graffiti art. Neel seems out of place here. I would have pegged him for Bach or Wagner or maybe even Sinatra. Not bands with names like Danzig or Heavens to Betsy. As we flip through dusty album covers, I ask him, "So it's really over with the Monster?"

He pulls out an album, inspecting the back of it. "Listen." He dials and holds out his phone to me. *You've reached Moira. Leave a message, unless you're Neel. In that case you can piss off.* She then suggests a number of creative places he could put his mobile.

"Wow, those are some specific suggestions."

"Yes, they are." He slips his phone into his back pocket. "After all, she's a technical sort of girl." He clears his throat, his gaze drifting across the store, to where Abby flips through a bin of old cover art. "Sorry I let it slip that it was your last day."

"No, you're not."

He laughs. "You're right, I'm not. Serves you right. What you did to Moira."

"So you ruined the surprise for Abby to punish me. How nice of you."

He frowns, studying Abby across the store. "I didn't see it that way."

I flip through more albums. "Did you know her parents split up in January?" He shakes his head. "This trip is supposed to be relaxing, without a bunch of added drama." I wait, hoping my implication sinks in. *Please,* I want to add, *don't kiss my friend. Don't complicate things.* But I can't seem to find the courage to be direct, so I aim for the outer rings of my target and hope he has the shred of intuitiveness to figure it out. "We're meeting Kiara and Tavin later. Abby and Tavin seem to be *really* hitting it off," I say pointedly.

His gaze slips to me, and he holds it a moment before letting it drop to the albums in front of us. I can't read his face. "Was the split unexpected? Abby's parents?"

He moves down the row with me trailing him. "Out of the blue. At least for her. For me too. I mean, her parents don't seem the splitting type. And now her mom's with this other guy, our dentist actually. She moved in with him."

"That's bloody awful." He motions for me to move my hand from where I have it resting on the anarcho-punk section. They don't have the album he hoped for, but he wants to dig through their collection and see what else he can find. "Oh, I've been looking for this one." He pulls out a dark maroon album. The Barbarellas. "So, she" – he taps the girl screaming into a mike on the cover – "is the daughter of Bart Krow, the lead singer of Her Majesty's Pleasure." He laughs at my confused face. "They were huge in Britain in the eighties."

"If you say so." I study my cousin. It's funny how you can grow up with someone as a family member and only have a vague notion of him as a whole person. I have spent a handful of days with him over the years – at weddings, at holidays, on a trip to India I barely remember because I was six – but I've only ever seen him as this older, bossy, hyperacademic boy evolving through a series of holiday cards and emails his mother sent my parents over the years. His older sister, Darshana, is even more of a phantom to me. Now twenty-seven, she was often away at boarding school and then law school and now lives in Manchester with her husband (also a lawyer) and has a baby on the way. I peer at the cover of the next album Neel pulls out. "I wouldn't have picked you as a punk fan." I follow him to the counter so he can pay the intricately pierced, waif-thin girl behind the counter. She snaps her gum, nodding with approval at his selection.

He tucks the album under his arm. "I'm full of surprises."

To his credit, Neel takes a hint and leaves Abby and me alone to meet my friends for our last night in Berlin. First, though, she and I eat dinner at an outdoor café on the boulevard Unter den Linden, enjoying the ease that happens as the sun goes down and everything blurs in the rose-tinted light, the heat lifting from under the weight of the sun. After dinner, we stroll to the Bebelplatz. I've saved one of my favorite tourist places in Berlin for tonight because I want it to be mostly dark when we see it; it's more beautiful and chilling lit up. Ahead of us, I see people standing around, staring down into a pale light.

"What are they looking at?" Abby slows, her history geek antennae on full alert.

"It's called *Library*," I tell her, pulling her toward the crowd of people. "It's an installation by the Israeli artist Micha Ullman. On this spot in 1933, the Nazis burned over twenty thousand books from the Humboldt University library because they went against their political values." Abby tucks her arm through mine, and edging closer, we find a space to peer down into the glass window set into the cobblestones.

The room below is full of empty bookshelves.

"Enough to hold all those burned books," I whisper.

"They burned books in the Library of Alexandria, too, destroyed it," she tells me as we move aside to allow other people to see the memorial. "It was the ancient world's single greatest source of information, no back-ups. Just gone."

More lights blink on around the Bebelplatz. We wander over to the brass plaques that go along with the memorial. I point out the quote from Heinrich Heine written more than a hundred years before the Nazis burned the books and translate it for her as best as I can remember: "It says, *That was but a prelude; where they burn books, they will in the end burn people.*"

Abby shivers next to me. "Whoa." She has the same reaction as I did the first time Kiara translated it for me.

"I know." I shake my head, feeling the wash of sadness I've grown used to while living in Berlin, the one always lingering at the edges of my vision. I've even grown to savor it because of the way it reminds me to stay aware of the world. "What I don't get is that you would think a government would want its citizens to be educated and well-read."

"Oh, they do." Abby slips her hands into the pockets of her shorts, her eyes sliding back to the window in the ground. Her expression grows thoughtful; it's the one she gets when her mind is whirling a thousand miles an hour back through history. "They just want to control the narrative." Love for Abby floods me, drowning any sadness. Love for my smart and contemplative friend.

We stroll through the busy Berlin night. People ride bikes, hurry past us on the street, sit in outdoor cafés drinking and eating with friends. I soak up the energy of it, feel it run the length of my limbs. The city at night is electricity for the senses; I just want to plug myself in and recharge.

My phone buzzes, and I start to tell Abby, "Kiara found this club—"

But she doesn't hear me. "Oh, the river!" She points out the dark Spree glimmering with the lights of Berlin. We stop on a bridge to watch the reflections.

Abby's glasses reflect the lights, too. "Remember when you got your glasses for the first time? How old were we?" I ask.

"Eleven."

"We spent that whole weekend taking pictures of them. We named that album 'Things That Reflect in Abby's Glasses.'"

"Oh, yeah!" She remembers. "What made you think of that?"

"The river, just now."

"Henry's face was one." Her own face falls. "I feel terrible I wasn't there when he got hurt."

"Oh, Abby, it's not your fault he got hit by a car. And he's fine now." When her brow creases even more, I sigh. "Text your dad to check on him. You'll feel better."

She leans into the bridge railing and says what she's writing aloud: "I'm standing on a bridge on the Spree wondering about Henry."

A minute later, Geoff texts back a photo and caption. It's Henry on their worn brown couch, his leg in a cast, one of those plastic sad-dog collars around his neck. I'm doing fine, Abby! I miss you!

kiss him for me! she texts, and sends her dad a picture of the two of us against the darkening river, the spray of Berlin lights behind us.

Beautiful, he writes. And the river's nice, too.

Suddenly, I'm viscerally angry with Abby's mom in a way I've never been before. Not even the time when we were twelve and she canceled our two-night sleepover because she was mad that Abby hadn't cleaned her room like she'd asked. That time, I even made a rock doll of Stephanie Byrd and kicked it into the river. In this moment, I'm even angrier than when I made rock voodoo. How could she do what she did to Abby's dad? He might be dorky and quiet and care about things like hiking trails and going to boring city meetings to get better streetlamps installed on their street, but he's the world's nicest guy! Watching Abby as she texts her dad, it suddenly dawns on me that she has been taking care of the world's nicest guy for months now.

"You've been doing a lot for your dad since she left, haven't you?"

A slight breeze ruffles the hair around Abby's face as she watches a couple stroll by us holding hands. "He doesn't have anyone else."

"What about Kate?" Abby's big sister can be a pain sometimes, but she's not a terrible person.

"Oh, Kate." She shrugs. "Kate's a million miles from us. She has her own life." She studies the river, a million miles away herself. "Riya?"

"Yeah?"

"I don't really feel like going out tonight with Kiara and Tavin."

My stomach sinks. "Abby, don't let what happened to Henry ruin our last night in Berlin. Kiara found a cool club for us to hang out in."

"It's not that – I'm tired. I'm not up for a club tonight."

"But what about Tavin? You two were having so much fun." A whine creeps into my voice. I want to go to the club, but I don't want to just leave Abby alone with my parents.

She tries to reassure me with a smile that sags at its edges. "Tavin is great, Rye. But we're leaving tomorrow. I don't have any grand notions about Tavin."

"Why do there have to be any notions at all?" I ask, trying to keep the frustration out of my voice. "Can't you just hang out with him tonight and see what happens? I think he really likes you."

She turns to watch the lights wriggle across the water. "I like him, too. He's great. But I just want to put on my PJs and crash out early. Maybe watch a movie or something."

"But I told him you'd be there!"

When she looks at me, the flash in her eyes isn't from the river lights. "Why are you pushing this? What does it matter? You can go if you—"

"I'm not pushing it!" My voice rises. "I'm trying to save you from being your normal self, from being so—" I bite my lip, dropping my volume. "Nothing."

She crosses her arms across her chest, her expression growing stony. "No, say it. You were going to say boring. You think I'm boring."

I throw up my hands. "Maybe a little! I mean, it's your last night in an amazing city and you're going to go get in your PJs and maybe watch a movie? It's like the definition of boring!"

Tears spring to her eyes, and they send a lightning shot of guilt through me. I start to apologize, but she cuts me off. "You know what, Riya? Maybe I don't think your city is as amazing as you do. Maybe I think hanging around in a stupid club with kids I barely know is boring. Maybe I don't need to be a huge drama queen to have fun."

My throat goes dry. "What?"

"Nothing." She eyes a group of American tourists hurrying by us who are actively trying not to notice our fight. "Forget it."

"You think I'm a drama queen?"

"Well, not all of us can be foot models," she tries to joke, but her voice shakes.

And I'm not laughing. "You know what, Abby? It's fine. You do whatever you need to do. Go sit in the apartment or whatever. Do a crossword puzzle. Buy a cardigan. I'm going to go out and have fun with my friends."

Her lip quivers. "Fine."

"Fine." We stare at each other, both of us refusing to back down. Finally, I ask, "Do you need me to take you home?"

She narrows her eyes. "I'm a big girl. And don't worry – I'm sure I'll make it back, even with my elderly lung capacity." Then she turns and heads back in the direction of the apartment, leaving me standing alone on the bridge.

Abby

I knock on the door, but there's no answer. My heart races, even after the long trudge back from the bridge. Maybe partly because of it. But I know it's mostly the fight. I wish I could rewind the clock and take back the terrible things I said, wish Riya could take back hers. Why do Riya and I seem to need so many do-overs this year? I knock again. Still no answer. Maybe her parents are watching a movie and can't hear the door? I try a more banging-on-it approach, but when the door opens, it's Neel, wearing a red soccer jersey and a pair of shorts, his feet bare.

"Abby?" He lets me in. "What are you doing here?" I move past him through the foyer and into the living room. "You okay? Where's Riya?" I sink onto the couch. He's watching a James Bond movie in the dim light of the room, several white take-out containers and a few pairs of chopsticks spread out on the coffee table in front of him.

"We got in a fight. She's with friends at a club."

"She left you?"

"I'm not a puppy. I got back fine."

He motions to the food. "I have plenty. Help yourself."

"We ate, thanks." Most of the apartment is dark, just a single lamp and the blue glow of the TV lighting the room. "Where are Dean and Anju?"

He settles back onto the couch. "They went out with some friends to hear music."

I pull one of the fuzzy couch pillows onto my lap. "See, even Riya's parents are more interesting that I am." Neel eyes me but doesn't say anything. He picks up a white take-out container and plucks out a dumpling. We watch the movie for a few minutes. Someone jumps from a train. Guns are fired. I bet no one calls James Bond boring.

"Thing is" – I motion at the TV – "he lives this extraordinary, crazy life. But he never seems very happy. Why so glum, Mr. Bond?"

Neel mutes the movie. "You want to talk about it?"

I shove the pillow aside, trying to get comfortable on my corner of the couch. "What I want to do is put on my PJs and sleep for nine hours, but apparently, I'm not ninety-seven years old, so that sort of behavior is frowned on in certain social circles."

He hides a grin and kicks his feet onto the coffee table,

fishing another dumpling from the box. "I'm not sure going to clubs makes someone more interesting."

"Tell that to Riya."

"*I'm* not out right now."

I reach for the box he's holding. "That's actually helping her case."

He hands me the box and a fresh pair of chopsticks. "I like the way I am." He grabs a box full of thick, saucy noodles.

I watch him lean forward, careful not to drip any sauce on the couch. Dipping my head, I dig into the box of dumplings with the pair of chopsticks. "I like the way you are, too."

He hesitates in the wake of my words, twirls a noodle slowly around his chopstick. "Sorry to hear about your parents," he says finally. At my surprised look, he adds, "Riya mentioned it. She's worried about you."

I switch out the dumpling box for one with mixed veggies. "Yeah." I spear a piece of broccoli. "Real worried." We watch the muted action of the movie for a moment. "Okay, I know she's worried. I mean, she planned this trip for us. But she just wants me to be normal right now, and I don't feel normal."

"Have you told her that?"

"I think so. She says to give it time; things will get better. But they're not getting better."

"Right, because you're still dealing with the pain of it.

As you should be. Don't let people try to wrap it in a rosy future before you're done grieving it."

My body warms at his insight and I smile gratefully at him. "Maybe it's because my dad hasn't been the same since my mom left. It's like he just flickers in and out, half alive. He's not getting better. And I can't be mad at him for it, right? I mean, she ruined his life."

Neel considers this. "Parents are rubbish sometimes. It's not right when you have to fill in for them."

I pause, a baby corn halfway to my mouth. "What do you mean?"

"Sounds like you're the only one looking out for anyone besides yourself."

Tears prick my eyelids. "That's how it feels. All the time."

"That's exhausting." He grabs the remote. "So, right now it's not going to get solved. But you can just kick back and watch James Bond get chased by thugs." He unmutes the movie.

I catch his gaze, and he smiles in a warm and sad sort of way that feels like he understands, like he might need to just watch James Bond get chased by thugs, too. "Thanks," I tell him.

"My pleasure."

the fourth Wonder

EDINBURGH, SCOTLAND

Abby

Neel refuses to go up the Scott Monument. I don't blame him. It's dicey the higher we climb, but it's the largest monument in the world dedicated to a writer, Sir Walter Scott, which is a great history tidbit, so up, up, up Riya and I go, scaling the narrow, twisting staircase. We still haven't talked about our fight last night. She came creeping into our room around two, and I pretended to be asleep. This morning, we kept busy packing and getting to the airport for our flight to Scotland. Now we pause to take in the view – the fat green treetops, the busy Princes Street Gardens, the dramatic profile of Edinburgh Castle nestled regally on the skyline.

Riya points to where Neel sits on a wooden bench far below us. We can feel his frown all the way up here. "Is he having a staring contest with his phone?"

I hold tight to the black iron grate that should ostensibly keep me from plummeting to my death, though I'm not completely convinced. "He is actively not replying to Moira's text."

"She texted him?"

"Last night. She wants to 'talk' about things." We were almost done with the movie when she texted: Let's talk, okay? Even though he told me he wasn't going to text her back, I'd begged off as tired and gone to bed, not having the energy to wait and see if his willpower would hold up.

Riya lets out an exaggerated groan. "And the cycle begins again. The predictable cycle."

We squeeze together to let a woman pass us. "He said there is no way they are getting back together." I try to say it casually, but even I can hear the catch in my voice. She narrows her eyes, and I hurry to add, "He hasn't responded to her text. Hence, the staring contest."

Riya looks impressed. "Well, okay, then. Good for Neel. Stay strong, cousin!" she shouts down at him, but he doesn't hear her. To me, she asks, her voice thick with implication, "Maybe something happened last night to encourage his sudden determination?"

I shrug, avoiding her eyes, and press my hand flat against the stone wall to steady myself. I turn and start climbing the stairs. "Let's keep going up, okay? I want to text my dad some pictures of this view."

"Abby?" She slips a hand around my wrist, stopping me.

"Yeah?"

"Tavin and Kiara wanted me to say it was nice meeting you."

"Thanks, same."

"They really missed you last night."

Without answering, I continue up the steps, feeling her gaze hot on my back.

After we manage our way down the stairs, feeling just as wobbly as when we went up them, we walk the ten minutes from the Scott Monument across Waverley Bridge and into the Old Town to the Elephant House. The silence between Riya and me has its own crackle. Neel tries to fill the space with random observations about the various sites we see along the way, but we're not listening to any of it; we're too busy avoiding each other's eyes.

"The Elephant House," he announces when we arrive. "J.K. Rowling penned part of the first Harry Potter novel here." He points out the yellow writing on the front window of the famous coffee shop: *Birthplace of Harry Potter.* Tourists crowd the window, taking pictures of its red front with the burnt-gold-lettered name. I grow still at the thought of one writer in Scotland creating a story now known around the world. The power of a single act. Next to me, I can sense Riya having the same thought.

Neel pushes us through the crowd. Inside, it's cozy and warm, with wood paneling, potted plants, and colorful walls. Everywhere, elephants – ceramic, wooden, in paintings – cover most of the available surfaces. People sit at wood tables, clacking away on laptops, reading, or chatting quietly over sandwiches and soup. Neel orders us coffees and motions for us to grab a couch against the far wall that two women are just vacating. They look like local university students, their book bags crammed. The taller one tucks a copy of a James Joyce novel beneath her arm and smiles at us hovering nearby. "All yours." Her accent is American.

Riya settles on the couch, her eyes glowing as she takes in the views of Edinburgh Castle visible through the window. "Can you believe she sat here with just an idea, and then it turned into Harry Potter?!" She scrutinizes the room. "One woman's idea. Incredible." I can tell she's trying to repair some of the damage from last night, have been feeling it in her hawk-like gaze all day.

"Incredible," I echo, trying as best as I can to keep snarky comments like *yep, she wasn't boring* to myself, even as they buzz at the edge of everything I end up saying.

Neel brings us our coffees. He hasn't even lifted the espresso cup to his lips when his phone rings. Seeing his face fall at the caller ID, Riya snatches it. When he protests, she holds up a hand to silence him. "That's at least six calls today! She's relentless. I've got this – we have a family name to think of." She answers mid-ring. "Hello, Moira? Nope, this is Riya. Stop calling, okay? Stop texting. Just stop. No means no." She hangs up, handing the phone back to an astonished Neel.

"No means no?" I can't help but grin into my latte.

"What?" She shrugs. "Solid message there."

Neel drinks his espresso in silence.

After the Elephant House, Neel skips dinner to head back to his room at our hotel, swearing to both of us that he will not contact Moira. After a quick dinner, we leave the Old Town and stroll the streets through the Georgian section of Edinburgh. The sun sets late in Scotland, and the sky grows heavy with pink and orange clouds, the air carrying the smell of rain.

"Do you think he'll call her?" I study the raindrops dotting the sidewalk in front of us.

"Nope."

"You sound pretty sure."

"I took his phone." She pats her bag, pulling her jacket closer against the chill in the air.

I gape at her. "You stole his phone?"

"Had to be done."

I shake my head in disbelief, but I'm mostly impressed. "Still, there are landlines. Our hotel has a computer room. If he wants to contact her, he will." I wander into a shop selling Scottish souvenirs – brightly colored sweatshirts adorned with *Edinburgh* in block letters, tins of shortbread, stuffed Loch Ness monsters, paper models of the castle, ceramic bells boasting the Scottish flag. I head to the counter with a blue sweatshirt. "Have you considered that maybe he loves her?" I ask Riya as the woman runs my credit card. I've thought of it, and I'm trotting it out here mostly to see if Riya thinks it's a possibility.

"Definitely not." Riya fiddles with a rack of key chains. "Their whole on-again, off-again self-sabotaging thing – that's not love. That's something else."

She has no idea how much her words buoy me, but I argue anyway. "Maybe he thinks it is."

She snort-laughs as we step back out onto the rain-spotted street. "I'm sure he does, otherwise he wouldn't have put up with their terrible pattern for the past two years. But I still get to judge him for it." She smiles wryly at me. "Who thought Neel's relationship drama would be his most annoying trait on this trip?" She pauses in front of a store that seems to only sell sweaters and tiny felt versions of sheep before we continue down the street. "Maybe drama queens run in the family," she adds quietly, a peace offering, gauging my reaction out of the corner of her eye.

I step closer to her. "Riya, I shouldn't have said that. I'm sorry."

She hugs me quickly and fiercely. "Thank you. I'm sorry, too. You're not boring. I was just frustrated. Let's not spend the rest of this trip fighting. I want us to have fun."

I untangle from our hug. "Me too. I just think sometimes we have different ideas about what that is. But we've always been okay with that, right?"

"Yes." She tucks her arm through mine and we keep walking. As we peer into shops, I think about Neel and Moira. Whatever messy feelings he's stirring up in me, his situation isn't easy. Even if they are terrible together, he seems to care about Moira. He's tired, true. Fed up, yes. But he cares. And even though he ended it for good, there is always cleanup to be done. "Maybe they will try to stay friends?" I wonder aloud, and when Riya frowns at me, I add, "Neel and Moira."

"Ugh, let's not talk about them anymore. She's such a wretch."

"Maybe she has a nice side that only comes out at special times of the year?"

"Like once a month at three a.m. she does something kind for a sick child?" Riya laughs. "Doubt it." She shoots me an odd look. "Are you looking for reasons he should stay with her?"

"Of course not! They're an awful couple."

She pulls me to a stop in front of another shop window, this one with dresses and shoes. "Because it's hard enough to be a single person. Can you imagine being one half of a miserable couple?"

I try not to think that this might be how my mom felt about my dad.

We grow tired of window-shopping, ending up back near the Scott Monument. We stop to watch a small, roped-off amusement park area with four or five different inflatable attractions: two different-size bouncy castles; a ladder that people try to climb that seems to keep flipping them onto an oversize inflatable yellow pillow; and, at what appears to be the largest attraction, kids racing around like hamsters inside clear plastic balls on top of a raised swimming pool. We can hear their muffled laughter and screams as they slip and fall and scramble to right themselves again.

Riya points it out. "Let's do that."

I hesitate. We're in Scotland, home of castles and feuding clans and monster legends and lochs, not to mention at least a dozen museums. And Riya wants to drop ten bucks to be a water hamster?

Then I think about last night. Why is my first instinct always no? Does that make me boring? "Okay – let's do it." We hurry toward the entrance.

It's not my first hamster ball. I did this once before at our county fair. Riya and I must have been six or seven, and we begged our moms to let us climb into these inflatable transparent balls and fumble across a shallow pool. I remember feeling dizzy with joy and maybe a little bit seasick, but wishing it would never end.

Now it's just the seasick part.

In the translucent ball next to mine, Riya giggles and squeals each time she falls down. I see her in flashes, her fluttering jacket and jeans, her arms flailing, her inky curls bouncing. She bumps her ball into mine, and I scuttle to stay upright, but fail. The whole world turns upside down. Oof. I lie on my back, bobbing, the lights of Edinburgh muted through the plastic bubble, sweating a little in my jeans. Riya spins her ball off in another direction.

Why does this whole contraption feel like one spinning metaphor for my life?

The clouds have blown out the next morning, leaving a blue sky over Edinburgh. I have to shake Riya to wake her. We stayed out until after two last night, cajoling Neel to join us at a sixteen-and-over club with a steady stream of both techno music and a chilled drink that tasted like liquid butterscotch. Riya and I spent last night dancing with our cups aloft, pretending we'd stumbled into a wizarding portal complete with butterbeer. At one point, two Scottish rugby players from a nearby school joined us on the dance floor, both ruddy-faced and proud Harry Potter fans. "Team Hufflepuff!" we shouted at Neel as we danced by the chair where he sat sulking in the corner, and then, "Team Ravenclaw!" on the next time around.

"Can I have my phone?"

"Not until you dance with us," Riya called back.

He scowled into his barely touched cup of tea. Who orders a cup of tea at a club?!

Eventually, Riya grabbed both of his hands and tried coaxing him out onto the dance floor, but he wouldn't budge. "Your sad beverage is having a better time than you are."

His eyes slid to his cup. "It's time to go. Say good-bye to your Quidditch fan club."

Now we find him sitting in the morning light, sipping coffee in the breakfast room, showered but still sour. "Well, good morning to Hermione and her house-elf," he grumbles, making a show of shuffling his newspaper as he directs the latter name at Riya.

Unperturbed, she says sweetly, "Dobby is a free elf, sir," and helps herself to some rolls and a tiny pot of raspberry jam.

"Can Dobby give me my phone back?"

Riya tosses him his phone, and he hurries to check it. "Don't call her."

"I'm not."

"Liar."

He catches my eye. "I'm not," he says again, almost fierce.

"Okay." I smile sympathetically at him. "I'm just excited to see Edinburgh Castle today. And not just because it was part of the inspiration for Hogwarts."

"Abby loves castles," Riya tells Neel.

I do love them. Castles are their own brand of museum. Oftentimes, if you go back far enough, they also come with myths and legends, and some of my favorite periods in history are when historical facts blur with myth. Edinburgh Castle is no exception. Some historians say it was built on the ruins of a shrine, the Castle of the Nine Maidens. One of the maidens was Morgan le Fay, King Arthur's half sister and a magical shape-shifter. I relay all of this to my tablemates. Riya brightens. She's always had a soft spot for Arthurian legend, and Morgan in particular.

"She was a sorceress." Riya picks up her espresso. "Hardcore."

Neel folds his paper into a neat square. "If I remember correctly, didn't she spend most of her time trying to kill Arthur?"

Riya groans. "Oh, right – a powerful woman gets cast as the witch trying to hurt the poor patriarchal king. Figures." She raises her eyebrows at me. "That's history for you."

"Some of it." I collect our plates to deposit on the busing tray near the buffet. "But she did try to kill him."

Riya adds her cup to my stack. "He probably deserved it."

A half hour later, we pass through the Portcullis Gate of Edinburgh Castle, Neel no longer speaking to either of us. This is mostly our fault. On the way over, Riya and I felt the need to yell "Pipers!" every time we saw bagpipers on the walk to the castle. "Could you two just stop?!" he growled as we walked up the steep hill to the castle. "We're late."

Outside the castle walls, Riya nudges me again, stage-whispering "Pipers" at the six men playing in red-and-black kilts. Neel storms off ahead to secure our tickets. Ten minutes later, our guide, a redheaded University of Edinburgh student named Ryan Ramsey, leads us to the Argyle Battery, and we stare out at the city toward Fife, the day hazy but still blue, even as a few clouds begin to form. Ryan explains more about the castle, and about the battery, which was built in the 1730s. When he asks if we have questions, Riya wants to know if they only hire redheads for the tours and if his name is really Ryan Ramsey because it sounds made up.

"No and yes," he answers, his blue eyes flashing a sort of twinkle that would seem CGI'd if he wasn't standing right in front of me. Maybe he's a leprechaun. No, wait, that might just be Irish.

"Do the Scots have leprechauns?" I ask.

"We have brownies," Ryan answers, glancing at Neel, who shrugs apologetically at our silliness.

"Double fudge brownies?"

"Brownies are like leprechauns," Neel snaps at Riya. "Do you have any real questions, or can the man do his job?"

We've pushed Neel too far. I try to catch his eye, but he's ignoring both of us, walking with Ryan up the Lang

Stairs to the summit of Castle Rock. We follow them as they chat, their hands clasped in identical knots behind their backs, as if all boys in UK universities are taught to ascend castles in this fashion.

Giggling behind her hand, Riya whispers, "Castle walk formation, gents!" I nod along, but Neel's annoyance dulls the moment.

We spend the rest of the morning wandering the castle, learning about grisly Scottish historical prison practices and famous battles. We finally pause to gasp at the stunning views of Edinburgh from the Western Battlements. Even Ryan remarks on the clear day, surprised at a rare sighting of the peaks of the distant Highlands. The day has grown warm, so Riya ties her sweater around her waist. "Views have been kind of our thing this trip," she tells Ryan, and describes the one from the Rigi bench in Switzerland. As I listen to her description, it feels like something that happened months ago and not just last week. Staring out at Scotland (*Scotland!*), I realize this whole trip has elongated time for me.

Ryan gives us a moment more to enjoy the view and then motions for us to continue along so we don't miss the One O'clock Gun. We follow him down the steps and across the courtyard. As we walk, he explains that "the gun's been fired every day except Sundays and Good Friday and Christmas since 1861, originally so the ships in the Firth of Forth could set their maritime clocks by it." He finds us a space in the crowd that has gathered near the low black gate that blocks the gun from the tourists. "We are a historically frugal people," he tells us. "So some say this is why the gun gets fired at one o'clock every day instead of at noon. To save ammunition."

Neel looks impressed. "Quite a lot saved since 1861."

Ryan nods, noting the appearance of a guard with a black hat and a red stripe down the pants of his uniform who has just emerged and is now marching to the side of the gun, which actually looks more like a cannon. The crowd quiets. The guard goes through some motions, a half minute passes, and then – BANG! Riya lets out a yelp next to me as I feel the shake of the blast briefly in my knees.

As the rest of the crowd drifts away, Ryan smiles at us, rubbing his hands together in a we're-wrapping-things-up way. "Well, that's it for us, then. You have a one-fifteen reservation for high tea in the Queen Anne."

"We do?" Riya frowns at Neel, but he doesn't see it as he scrolls through something on his phone.

Ryan checks his notes. "Yes, one fifteen for tea. Come along." Riya shrugs at me; this is clearly news to her. We follow Ryan to Crown Square, and he points out the door to the tearoom. "Okay, here you are. End of the line for me. I've had, as I believe you Americans say, a blast." He grins, and we humor his lame joke about the One O'clock Gun because he's sweet and, well, those blue eye sparkles of his make him easy to forgive.

A hostess leads us into a narrow, stone-walled courtyard set with wooden tables. "Neel, did you book this?" Riya begins, but then stops abruptly, her eyes wide moons. "Wait, what? Nani?!" The woman sitting at a round corner table stands to greet us. "What are you doing here?" Their grandma is dressed smartly in a canary-yellow dress with a floral scarf knotted at her neck, her long silver hair pinned in an elegant updo. She pulls a surprised Riya into a hug.

"Hello, Aji." Neel leans in to kiss her cheek.

She releases Riya and turns to me. "Abby," she says warmly, pulling me into a rose-scented hug. "Lovely to see you."

"Thank you!" I slide into the velvet chair she motions for me to sit in, silently cursing my long-sleeved T-shirt, Tevas, and cargo shorts. At least Riya is wearing a sundress and pretty leather sandals. They should seat me at a table that says, *Underdressed Americans Only, Please*. (And it would say please because everyone in Scotland is so nice.) "Riya didn't tell me we were meeting you here."

"I didn't know." Riya glances nervously at Neel. To her grandma, she says, "I mean, I knew you were in Scotland, but I thought you were in Skye?"

"I was."

It might be the flat light, but Riya looks almost chalky. "Neel didn't tell me."

"You had my phone." He shrugs, perusing the high tea menu.

Nani swats affectionately at Neel with her napkin as she unfolds it. "I got into Edinburgh last night. To surprise you. Neel didn't know until this morning." She places her napkin in her lap and blinks expectantly at us, her face perfectly made up. "Well, don't just sit there gaping at me like koi, tell me about your adventures!"

As the waitress brings our three-tiered trays of finger sandwiches, pastries, and pots of tea, we describe our trip so far, often interrupting each other to add to the story. Even Neel seems to come out of his funk, enjoying recounting in dramatic detail our going AWOL in Florence, although we add in our own defense, of course. Finally, a waitress clears the remains of our meal: tiny sandwich crusts, half-finished bowls of jam and clotted cream, scone crumbs. I sip at the dregs of the fruity tea in my china cup, watching the diners around me admire the stone walls, the still-blue Scottish sky.

I'm in a groggy post-tea coma, so I almost miss Nani's comment when Riya thanks her again for our trip. "Well, of course, dear – my youngest granddaughter has graduated high school and is moving into this next exciting bit of her life. It is my absolute pleasure to send you on this trip."

"For my birthday!" Riya hiccups, her eyes cutting to me. "This trip is for my birthday!"

I snap to attention. "Wait." I falter, my mouth suddenly dry. "What did you just say?" I stare at Riya. "You *graduated* high school?"

Nani's palm moves to her chest. "Have I said something shocking? All three of you have seen a ghost."

Riya licks her lips, her words taking on an almost tinny echo in my ears. "Actually, I haven't shared my news with Abby yet. About this fall." She avoids my eyes, folding and unfolding her napkin on the table in front of her.

"What news?" When she doesn't look up from her napkin, I repeat, "What news, Riya?" Neel watches us both carefully, his hand wrapped tightly around his water glass.

Riya takes a visible breath of air and her eyes don't quite meet mine. "I graduated early." She pauses. I wait. There is more. There is clearly more. She swallows. "And I auditioned for a theater academy in London. I'll be moving there at the end of August." Her words sound different from the ones she spilled across the river last year, but they are in essence the same.

How can this be happening again?

Worry creases Nani's forehead. "Oh, girls. I apologize. I thought that you—"

But I can't hear anything else. Stunned, barely aware of standing, I scrape my chair back against the stone floor, my napkin fluttering to the ground, murmuring, "I'm so sorry, please, excuse me, I just have to, I just have to—"

and then, the world blurry and tilting, I hurry from the room into the hot light of the Edinburgh Castle courtyard.

And then I run, my feet slapping against the stones.

Riya

We can't find Abby. I text her. Nothing. I call her. No response. Nani goes back to our hotel to wait in case Abby goes there. Neel and I walk up and down the Royal Mile, checking busy pubs and shops and museums. We try the Elephant House again. No sign of her. Then we walk it all again, my feet aching in my sandals on the cobbled streets as we dodge tourists and school groups. At one point, I step out of the flow of people into the sanctuary of a closed bar's empty doorway to try Abby's phone. Again, no response. I check in with Nani, but she tells me Abby hasn't returned to collect the key for our room. Next to me, Neel tries her phone, too, then texts her. Nothing.

She has disappeared into Edinburgh's Old Town.

Nani felt terrible, but it wasn't her fault. She didn't know I hadn't told Abby, had been waiting until I could give her the news in the way I envisioned at the end of our trip. I thought it would be best: let us enjoy our time together, maybe heal somewhat from last year, regrow a friendship that felt slippery and fragile these last few months. Then, once we arrived in London, our final stop, we'd do the scavenger hunt I created where we'd end up in front of the white-and-black building where I auditioned and I'd say, "Okay, funny story—"

Only it wouldn't have been a funny story. I realize that now. Kiara was right. It was a terrible idea. She would have looked at me, her eyes filling with understanding, and it would be last summer all over again. Have I changed so much this year that I didn't even consider what it would do to her, what this revelation would feel like to her? In my head, I wrote a happy ending that would soften the blow in the rosy glow of London when what Abby deserved was the no-filter wash of the truth. Do other people do that? Withhold or reshape a story, rationalizing that it is best for the person we're not telling, when really, even subconsciously, we just don't want to see their eyes darken when we lay out the truth?

We spend another hour walking the Royal Mile. Still no sign of Abby. Neel's phone buzzes. He hurries to check it. "Aji says she's not back yet." He stuffs the phone into his pocket. "This is useless. If she doesn't want us to find her, we won't." He sighs, his eyes darting around the street, as if Abby might appear from behind one of the glass doors of the shops.

I'm starting to panic, a jittery whirl that bubbles in my

gut and spreads out like a stain. "Don't you have any spies in Edinburgh? You have them everywhere else."

"And they would do what precisely? I'm not in Her Majesty's Secret Service. There are no hidden cameras." He scans the crowds of people.

"Maybe you are and you just can't tell me." I jostle him a bit too hard with my elbow. "*Wink wink*, right? You could make a call?" My voice creeps toward shrill.

"You are mental."

I chew at the side of my nail, my anxiety growing like a sunburn. I have to find her. I can't keep letting her run away. "We need to check every museum. Abby would go to a museum. That's what we should be doing." I pull out my phone to Google "Ten Best Museums in Edinburgh."

"Oi, you lost?"

I peek over my phone into the cobalt eyes of Ryan Ramsey. A girl a bit younger than me with tangled, flame-colored curls and knee-high flowered boots stands next to him. She and Ryan have matching eyes and the same easy smile. "Not exactly," I tell him.

"We can't find our friend," Neel tries to explain. "Abby. She, um, left."

Ryan frowns. "Does she have a mobile?"

"She's not answering." I study the research results on my phone. "She doesn't really want to talk to us right now, but we're trying to figure out where she might have gone. She's a big history nut, so we figured maybe a museum?"

Ryan runs through most of the options we've already tried before offering, "I'm off for the day. We could help you. This is my sister, Wyn."

I slip my phone into my bag; it's getting me nowhere. "That is so nice, but I'm sure you have better things to be doing."

Wyn shrugs. "Not really." Her skin is dotted with freckles. She's tall, but on closer inspection, she must be only thirteen or so.

I glance at Neel, who gives a brief nod. "Wow, okay. Thanks. We'll take the help." To Wyn, I say, "This is my cousin Neel. And I'm Riya."

"Almost like your name," Wyn says to her brother.

He rubs his hands together. "So, she's taken off, has she?" To Neel, he asks, "Something you said, then?"

Neel looks momentarily offended, insisting, "Not me" until he realizes Ryan is kidding.

We fill them in on where we've searched so far, ruling out the possibility that she might be back at the castle for now. Wyn whispers something to her brother, and he nods. "Yes, that. What about Holyrood? Been there yet? They've got a smart history tour. And lovely grounds."

We follow our tour guide.

Abby

I sit on a bench outside Holyrood Palace in the lush green shade of a tree. My tears attract more than a few alarmed glances from tourists. A man with a grandfatherly beard and jacket too warm for the day even stops, asking, "Can I help ya, lass?" but I just shake my head, and he smiles sympathetically and moves along.

When the tears finally subside, I call Dad, hoping he'll pick up my FaceTime. I'm eight hours ahead of him, so that makes it eight thirty a.m. in California. His workday has just started, and I worry he might be in a meeting he can't leave, but he picks up instantly. "Abby?"

"Hi."

His expression shifts from ease to worry at the sight of my tear-streaked face. "What is it?"

A breeze rustles the leaves of the trees around me. I stare at them, letting their green patterns mesmerize me. "Did you have to leave a meeting? It's eight thirty, right? At home. I'm eight hours ahead of you. Scotland is eight hours ahead. Can you believe I'm in Scotland? Too bad I can't fly back through time and get a do-over on these last few hours."

Now he looks even more concerned. "What happened?"

The fear in his voice snaps me back to the screen. "It's Riya." A last tear slides down my cheek. "She's not coming home."

"Has something happened to Riya?"

"She *graduated* from high school, Dad. She's moving to London in August. To be an actress. London, *England*!"

"I know where London is, Bee."

"She's not coming back to Yuba Ridge for senior year. We won't graduate together. We won't even be in the same time zone." I stare at a leaf on the ground in front of me.

Dad is silent for a moment, and then says, "But she's not hurt? No one has lost a limb? Gone missing?"

"No."

He sends a relieved sigh across the miles. "Okay, maybe lead with that next time?"

"Sorry." I pause. "Except, I am."

He frowns. "You're what?"

"Missing, I guess."

He frowns, confused. "Abigail, I'm going to need you to make just the slightest bit of sense right now, okay? You're being cryptic."

I fill him in on the high tea at the Queen Anne, on my flight from the table, on wandering the cobbled streets of the Royal Mile in a daze until I hit Holyrood Palace at the opposite end from the castle and decided to go in, even though I couldn't really focus on anything during the tour, couldn't retain any of the history facts about the opulent rooms. I wandered through it, blank.

Like I feel right now. "Is this what it's like to be an adult?" I ask Dad. "Because it seems like people just leave, change the plans. It seems like that is what mostly happens." I lean forward, my elbows on my knees, and I study his face for signs of evasion, that thing parents do with their eyes when they are about to dole out a euphemism. "Tell me the truth. Because if this is how it works, I would like to go back to being eleven if that's all right with the universe."

He smiles into the screen, the sweet smile he gets when I'm being amusing but he doesn't want to be patronizing so it just plays at the corners of his mouth. "I wish it worked like that. I wish we could have time machines to take us back to the good stuff." I know he does. If I'm honest, he has more to complain about on the adult front than I do right now. He clears his throat. "You need to text Riya and tell her where you are, okay?" When I shake my head, he presses. "You have every right to want to be alone or not see her or even come home. But you need to connect with her. She's probably worried sick."

"I know."

"Welcome to growing up."

"Thanks."

"It sucks sometimes."

I miss my dad. I miss my bed and our living room and the front yard where the old oak has grown and shed its leaves across the seasons of my childhood. I miss the narrow street where I learned to ride my bike and the trails by our house where we've taken a thousand walks with Henry. I miss Henry. I miss seeing the regular customers come in and out of the Blue Market, miss how the market slows on Friday nights and we waste time playing paper towel hockey with tubes of wrapping paper up and down the frozen foods aisle.

I don't want to be here anymore. "Dad?"

"Yeah?"

"I want to come home."

"What can I do?"

"Check flights, okay? And get back to me as soon as you know my options."

He promises. "Hold tight."

We hang up. My head foggy, I sit on the bench, staring at the tourists moving by me as they come and go from the palace, like a miserable teen guard dog.

Then, suddenly, I am eye level with our tour guide from the castle, who is squatting down in front of me. There is a girl standing next to him who looks like a younger, female version of him. With cuter shoes.

"Those are really cute boots," I say flatly to her.

"Oh, thanks." She glances down at them, then exchanges a concerned look with Ryan.

Ryan stands to wave at Neel and Riya, who are across the courtyard. I see them sprint toward us, Riya calling, "You found her!" and then she's sliding onto the bench next to me, her energy frantic, her arms around my neck. "Abby, I'm so sorry—" she starts.

"Just don't." I wriggle out of her grip. "Just don't say anything right now."

"Okay, but—"

I hold up a hand. "Please. Don't. Talk."

When I get back to the hotel, I open the curtains to let in the metallic light of Edinburgh. The bright day has grown overcast with oily evening clouds, and I take a moment to memorize my slim view of this old city. I like Edinburgh. Of all the cities so far, it might be my favorite – its size suits me, as does its history, its castle, its friendly people. When I go to college, maybe I'll apply somewhere that will let me study here for a semester. Maybe Future College Student Me won't be as distracted when I walk its cobbled streets.

Because time is supposed to do that to things. Heal them. That's what everyone keeps telling me.

I check my phone to see if Dad has located a flight for

me yet. No news. I toss my phone onto the plush amethyst-toned bedspread and turn back to my packing, taking everything out of my bag.

I spend the next twenty minutes refolding and sorting and picking through the items I've collected along the way. The fist-size gold-and-fuchsia mask I bought in Florence tumbles out onto the bed from where I had it rolled into Kate's yellow sundress for safekeeping. I pick it up, studying its empty eyes. Riya bought its match, and we'd giggled about hanging them in dorm rooms someday. Anger boils in me. She could have told me then. She could have said, *Oh, speaking of dorm rooms, mine will be in London!* But she didn't. She let me believe that her dorm room might even be the same one as mine someday. I guess, in hindsight, it fits that we were buying masks. Masks have long had a place in history, in myth, in theater. They are used to conceal. I wrap the mask in the Edinburgh sweatshirt I bought last night and jam it into a corner of my bag.

"So, you'll just leave, then?" I start at the sound of Neel's voice behind me. He comes in through the connecting door between our rooms and sinks into the brocade armchair near the window. "Is it me? Because I seem to have this effect on women." He tries to smile, but it doesn't reach his eyes.

"*You* didn't do anything wrong," I tell him, folding a pair of jeans.

"Well, that's hardly true."

I pause, the jeans a denim block held against my stomach. "Did you know? About London?"

"Yes."

"Perfect." I cram the jeans into my bag. "Speaking of your partner in crime, where is she?"

He runs his hands through his disheveled hair. "Downstairs. Talking to Aji in the restaurant. They're scheming about ways to convince you to stay. She's trying to give you some space. Thinks you might be too mad at her right now to really talk."

"She would be right about that." I swallow hard. "But I feel terrible that I ran out on your grandma at the tearoom. I just ... had to get out of there."

"She's not angry, Abby. Just sad. Sad that your tour might end this way."

I rummage through the pile of my things, searching for the black sweats I want to wear home on the plane. I find the glossy platter of gummies Will bought me in Zurich. Sighing, I tuck it between some T-shirts. "She should have just told me in the first place."

"She knows that now, doesn't she?" His eyes search my things strewn about the bed. "But maybe she had hoped to avoid this." He motions to the clothes and souvenirs.

I blink at him incredulously through the dim light; outside the sky has turned dark again, and I don't have any lights on in the room. "You're defending her?"

"That's not what I'm doing." He shakes his head, running his hand absently over the silvery brocade fabric on the arm of the chair. "I just wonder—" He hesitates.

"What?" I stare hard at him.

He ducks his head, as if expecting a punch. "How much of this is about Riya's news and how much of this is about your parents?"

"Oh, so you're a psychology major now?" He starts to answer, but I snap, "It's pretty ironic that you're taking Riya's side. You don't even like her!"

"I love my cousin," he insists, rubbing the pads of his fingers across his closed eyes. "Even if I don't always understand her." He drops his hand, watching me fold and sort, fold and sort, until he adds, "I thought perhaps we had that in common."

The main door clicks with the sound of the key and then swings open. Riya stands there, hovering in the doorway, her eyes wide. "Abby?" She has clearly given me as much space as she can stand.

I turn my back, picking up the pace of my packing. "I'm going home." Neel uses this as his cue to slip back through the connecting doors. On his way out, he tries to catch my eye, but I keep folding and refolding the same shirt and refuse to look at him.

Riya perches on the bed next to my bag, her eyes tracking my progress. She tries to help fold a pair of socks, but I grab them from her and stuff them into my hiking shoes. She licks her lips. "I'm sorry, Abby. I should have told you. I should have told you when I found out."

I let out an ugly snort. "You think?" It goes to show how angry I am and how freaked out she is that we don't comment on the snort.

"I was afraid if I told you, you wouldn't come." Her eyes brim, turning into glossy dark pools. "Please don't leave."

I slam my hiking shoes into the bag so hard that the force bounces several items onto the floor. "Why shouldn't I? Maybe I'm not interested in being a spectator in Riya's Awesome Future Life Tour anymore. A future life, by the way, that doesn't seem to include me at all."

"That's not true! You will always be in my life. Maybe not in the same way, but you will. I never meant for you to feel like my future didn't include our friendship." She leans to catch a travel blow-dryer that threatens to fall off the bed.

I snatch it from her, the cord whipping dangerously near my head. "It might not be what you meant, but it's what it feels like."

"I see how you could feel that way," she says diplomatically, smoothing her hand across the bedspread.

Her particular brand of diplomacy, though, comes off as placating. "Don't patronize me."

"I'm not!"

"Whatever." Anger surges through my limbs, a terrible

singed feeling in the layer right beneath my skin. Like reverse, fiery goose bumps. I head to the bathroom, stuffing my toiletries into my pyramid zipper bag. I point my toothbrush at her, telling her, "And for the record, today was definitely not wonderful. And you ruined the Harry Potter castle for me!"

I slam the door to the bathroom and sit on the edge of the white claw-foot tub, gulping at the stale hotel bathroom air, my heart hammering in my chest, my hands shaking. I study the forest-green wallpaper, the white sink with my toothbrush resting in the hotel glass, the plush white towels, until my breathing calms and I feel a bit better. I hate losing control; it just makes things worse. I need to go back out there, finish packing, and go home. I go to the sink, splash water on my face, and pat it dry with a hand towel before moving to open the door.

The doorknob spins in my hand.

You have got to be kidding me. I fiddle with the lock but it's frozen and won't turn. Seriously? This is not funny, universe. Not. Now.

I try turning it again, quietly, hoping Riya can't hear it rotating. Of all days to add Scotland Bathroom to my catalog of stuck places.

After a few minutes, Riya knocks lightly. "Please come out."

I hesitate. "I can't."

"Can't or won't, Abby?" she asks from the other side of the door. "You can't stay in there forever."

"Well, I might have to."

"What? No—" She rattles the doorknob. "Turn the lock."

"I did!"

She tries again, and I can hear her try to hide a giggle.

"Do not laugh at me. Not now."

"I'm not, I swear!"

I hear her walking away from the other side of the door, picking up the phone, calling the front desk. In a moment, she's back. "They're sending someone up."

I sit back down on the tub. Through the door, I hear my phone beep. "Is that my dad?"

"He can't get you a flight until tomorrow."

"Oh." I stare at my shoes. Somehow, this deflates the last of the surge moving through me. It's tough to storm off in anger when you have to wait around to do it while locked in a bathroom.

"He wants to know if he should book it." I can feel her waiting on the other side of the door. "Please come with me to Iceland. That's our next stop. Tomorrow."

My stomach flips. Iceland. When Riya and I were five years old, we built an elaborate fairyland in the yard to the side of her house out of sticks and river rock and moss, and named it Iceland. This was of course before we knew there was a country of the same name. Our Iceland was a land of magic and snow and elves where we ruled over the entire kingdom. There, we pretended to eat sweets all day and care for the majestic unicorns that lived in a nearby forest. Sometimes, they would let us weave ice flowers through their manes, but they mostly kept their distance and refused to let us ride them. Some of them could sprout gossamer, delicate wings and fly into the white sky. We had names for all of them. Chalk. Jasper. Lizzie. I especially loved one named Mirabelle who would not let us touch her no matter how hard we tried or how many carrots or apples we left out for her. We spent many childhood hours in our Iceland by the river.

Now she wants to take me for real.

"We were pretty mad at Iceland when we found out it was a real place," I mumble through the door.

But even with this barrier, she senses me softening. "We just have to agree it will only ever be second best to *our* Iceland."

I will probably never get another chance to take a trip like this again.

I hear Riya answering a knock at the hotel door, and a moment later, the doorknob gives a shudder, twists, and the door pops open. I grin sheepishly at the serviceman. "That probably happens all the time, right?" He shakes his head, gathering up a few tools at his feet.

Avoiding Riya's anxious eyes, I take my phone from her and move to the chair by the window.

I text Dad: i might stay?

Dad: Haven't booked flight yet. Stay. Once in a lifetime and all that.

Me: true.

Dad: Love you, Bee. For the record, I think you should stay.

Me: okay.

"I'm still mad at you," I say to Riya.

Silently, we get dressed for dinner and meet Neel and their grandma in the lobby. Everyone speaks in the fake, cheerful voices people use with children after they've thrown a fit, and I try not to feel ashamed of today.

"I'm glad you're staying," Neel says, opening the heavy door of the hotel for me.

"It's expensive to switch flights. It's better if I stay." I study the sidewalk dotted with rain, but none is falling.

"It is better for many reasons." Nani, wrapped in a pale blue pashmina, reaches out and rubs my arm. She turns to Riya. "Neel is going to take me out to dinner. I've made reservations for you both. Please, enjoy."

Riya and I walk to dinner past the Georgian buildings near our hotel without talking. I know how hard it must be for Riya to keep silent. Her unsaid words burn in the space between us. Finally, she stops in front of a wide glass window and checks her phone. "This is it. Nani says it's delicious. Modern Scottish." Inside, I take in the restaurant's dark walls and leather booths with rich brass detailing, glancing uncertainly at my plain black skirt and the jean shirt knotted at my waist. "I'm underdressed," I whisper to Riya, who shakes her head at me, and then smiles widely at the tall hostess, who's wearing a simple black dress with plaid details and glossy patent heels. Riya gives her name and the hostess nods, collecting two leather-bound menus and motioning for us to follow her to a raised booth in the window.

Riya slides into the seat across from me. "You look great. I love that shirt on you." Glamorous in her loose dress of dark teal and a cropped metallic leather jacket, Riya twists the chunky bracelet on her wrist as she studies the menu. "Mmmm, I've heard that bridie pies are yummy. I bet they're good here." Her voice is breezy, light.

For now, both of us are trying to avoid the glass shards of the last few days lodged in our skin.

"Mmmm," I echo, reading the description. A bridie seems like a Cornish pasty but without the potatoes. Of course, the potatoes are my favorite part, and I feel a stab of homesickness settle back in. Yuba Ridge was founded by Cornish miners during the gold rush, and one of the things that stuck was the handheld pies in their flaky crusts, stuffed with potatoes and chicken or beef or veggies. Since about sixth grade at Cornish Christmas downtown each year, Riya and I would order a pasty and then walk around to the vendor booths, munching our dinner and trying to find the lady who dresses up like a Christmas tree. I catch Riya watching me over her menu. "I was just thinking about the Christmas tree lady."

"I miss Cornish Christmas. It was the best!" She's trying too hard, and I'm glad when our waitress comes over and we order drinks, salads, and bridies.

Then, silence. Louder than on our walk over, the kind of silence that hisses *what now? what next?*

Riya sips her water and stares at the passing people on the street outside. I fiddle with my silverware, working up the nerve to ask her what I've been thinking for so much of this trip. "Do you think from now on, we'll only ever have the past in common?"

"Don't be silly."

I give her a hard look. "It's a legitimate question. Especially now."

She folds her napkin into her lap. "I thought history was the most important thing to you?"

"It used to be."

Her eyes plead with me. "But it's one of the most important parts! If we don't have history, we just spin into the future without any sense of connection."

Funny, that's exactly how I feel right now.

Our waitress drops off the food, and we eat in silence for a few minutes. The bridie is savory and delicious, its flaky crust perfectly baked.

"That's a cool painting." Riya points out a framed scene on the far wall of the restaurant: an indigo stretch of water with a glowing white horse emerging at its edge.

"The water horse," our waitress tells us, following our gaze as she refills our water glasses.

Riya squints through the amber light of the restaurant. "Is that horse a ghost?"

"A kelpie." The waitress smiles at our interest. "They are mystical creatures who live in the lochs, shape-shifting spirits. They can take human form, but mostly appear as horses. They pull people to them through their enchanting beauty, but then you can't let go and they drag you to your watery death." The waitress shifts a plate to make her load more balanced. "When I was a lass, my nanna warned me against straying near the water's edge for fear a kelpie would pull me under."

Riya and I have exchanged glances. Not sure whether the waitress still believes her nanna or not, I try to joke, "Fear. The cornerstone of any solid child-rearing platform."

The waitress shrugs. "Didn't drown, did I?"

We sleep in the next morning, dress quietly, and head out on our last planned outing in Scotland: Arthur's Seat, a peak in the nearby hills of Holyrood Park with a crumbling ruin and striking views of the city and castle. It's raining, just a drizzle, but I prefer it this way, not just because it matches my mood, but also because it makes the green-and-stone landscape of Scotland in front of us more mysterious and brooding.

At the top, with the wind moving the hair away from my face, I imagine the way the land looked hundreds of years ago when people lived in crude huts or stone castles and rode horses across the emerald expanse of Scotland. Mom always says I romanticize history too much. That life was hard in those times, most people just trying to find food and shelter. She's right, but I still think human dreams and hopes have fueled the forward motion of the world. Human nature builds history. That's what makes it relatable. Who knows, maybe some girl in the 1400s lost her best friend to a quest and her mom moved in with the village medicine man.

I walk to where Riya stands studying the landscape. "Do you think the future can be like a water horse?"

"Like the one in the painting?" She battles with the wind to tuck a lock of black hair behind her ear. "You're getting SPP. It's the view, right?" Riya started calling this pondering aloud of mine "School Paper Pensive" (SPP) on a camping trip when we were in eighth grade. It's when I start to overthink something or want to make a historical argument relevant to a current situation. She's got a point, and yes, it's probably the view inspiring this current SPP. But it's mostly her news. She chooses not to mention that part.

I study the soft lights glowing in the windows around the city stretching out below us. "I worry that walking toward beautiful, ghostly things because they have a promise of something grand and special might not be what's actually good for us – they'll just drag us into dark water."

She grows still next to me, letting the wind win the battle with her flyaway hair. "You think London is a kelpie?"

"Maybe."

She stuffs her hands in her pockets, her brow furrowing. "It's not." Riya's face has always been an open, shifting canvas, her thoughts and feelings moving across it like clouds. Right now, the clouds are stormy, defensive.

I rub my hands together. It's cold now that we're not walking anymore. "I'm just worried about you, that you're heading into a glittery idea that's built to hurt you. I'm sure you'll make a wonderful actress, but it's such a tough life, even with talent and connections." I stop, trying to bite down on these practical bits of me. I've already said more than she wants to hear.

She motions to the view in front of us. "Some people think this place where we're standing used to be Camelot. You could be standing on the exact spot where Guinevere's tears soaked the ground while she longed for Lancelot."

"Guinevere cried because she was taken unwillingly

from her home and forced to marry an older man she didn't love."

"But also Lancelot." She smiles faintly when I roll my eyes. "You can't help when you love something." When I shrug, she says, "Do you think something is true because you believe it, or do you believe it because it's true?" Surprise, surprise. Riya lays down some SPP of her own.

I shrug. "Chicken-egg, I guess."

The rain has stopped for now, leaving a lingering mist in the city. Small droplets collect in the waves of Riya's hair, and when she turns to me, they sparkle like diamond chips. "I think it's true because you believe it." She takes my hand, cold in hers. "I know you're worried, that it seems like a leap for me. Thank you for worrying. But I want to live in London and study to be an actress because I need to try it. No sense kicking in our own teeth before we've given it a go, as Neel would say."

"Neel said that?" Traitor. Even more annoying that he's probably right.

She nods. "I know you want me to come back to Yuba Ridge and fill out college applications and grumble about where we got in or where we didn't and walk across the field together in those horrible green gowns… I just can't, Abby. Not anymore. But it doesn't mean you can't do all those things. And it doesn't mean I can't support you in all those things."

"Especially now that you've made them sound so

appealing." I drop her hand, ducking my head so she can't see my lip quiver. I know we can't force our friends to want what we want. My head, at least, knows this is true. But I can't help feeling like she's on a full-speed rocket, shooting farther away from me each moment, and its trajectory keeps widening the ache in my chest.

She starts to bounce a little up and down beside me, trying to stay warm. "Can we go now? It's bloody freezing up here."

I groan. "Please tell me you're not going to end up with a fake accent because you moved to the UK. You're from Northern California." I remind her mostly to make a point, but also because it feels like she's forgetting.

the fifth Wonder

REYKJAVÍK, ICELAND

Riya

As the plane begins to descend into Reykjavík, Abby turns to me from the window, her hand circled lightly around her nearly empty orange juice cup. "Icelandic history tidbit. When the Vikings landed in the 800s, they called it Snow Land, not Iceland. So if that name had stuck, we'd have totally come up with an original name for our kingdom."

My stomach wobbles from a sudden dip of the plane, but also from her small peace offering. "Yeah, stupid Vikings. Thor stole our thunder." I try to get comfortable in the airplane seat, stretching out my legs, rolling my shoulders.

"You okay?" Abby asks. "You've been fidgeting the whole flight."

I massage the back of my neck. "I'm a little stiff. No big deal." She nods and turns back to the window. I keep waiting for the sense of relief I expected to feel once Abby knew about London, waiting for my body to feel lighter now that it has been unburdened of my secret.

But it doesn't.

"I'm so tired all of a sudden," I say aloud.

"Wait, you're human? Congratulations." She swirls the last of the ice in her cup and points at my half of the *kleina*, an Icelandic doughnut we ordered from the flight attendant and charged to Neel. "You going to eat that?" I shake my head as she bites into the pastry, and I can't help but giggle as it crumbles down her front. Chagrined, she shrugs, brushing at the crumbs. "You've got yourself one classy travel partner."

A surge of love for her rushes through me.

Even Abby doesn't know how many days during the last four or five years I would sit with my fect in the river near my house and dream myself out of Yuba Ridge into a faraway future. Sometimes, San Francisco or Seattle. Or farther: New York or Europe. It's an embarrassing cliché, but there were even times I'd imagined falling hopelessly in love with someone who loved me back in an I-would-follow-you-across-the-sea sort of way.

Watching Abby now, I feel like an idiot for not realizing that I already had that sort of love. It had been at first sight, actually. Day one of preschool, a spider crawled into the small kitchen where we ate our snack, and Abby picked it up with her bare hands and carried it outside. She told us his name was Sam and he was, she said quietly, "a little lost." I knew instantly we'd be friends. From that day forward, I spent years not feeling lost because behind every school year, every summer vacation, every television series or book I loved, every boy I crushed on, every doubt I had about my life, there stood dependable, practical Abby.

True love. The follow-you-across-the-sea kind.

I hope I haven't messed it up.

She's putting on a good face for now, but I know how much my decision hurts Abby. My life has taken a careening turn around a blind corner, and she must feel helpless watching me. In my theater classes, my teachers always talk about point of view, about looking through our characters' eyes from their vantage points. Sitting here, I try to imagine how Abby must see things now that she knows about London.

I probably seem like I've lost my mind.

I haven't, though. For years, even in the midst of summers by the river and camping in Tahoe and countless sleepovers, I've been missing a piece. The purpose piece. The bigger, driving piece. The one that snapped into place in Berlin, lit up my life in a way nothing ever has before. Well, nothing except Abby.

For the first time in months, doubt chokes me. "Abby?"

"Yeah?"

"You know I love you, right? No matter the geography." I put my hand over hers and squeeze, and she gives me a short, surprised smile and squeezes back.

Just after eleven p.m., we land at Keflavík Airport and

head toward customs, passing shops for juice, burgers, and coffee. Icelandic sweaters hang on racks. Abby points out tiny elves made of felt sitting in groups on blond wood shelves. After customs, Neel locates our driver in the arrivals hall, and he leads us outside to a small parking lot. I can't stop staring at the strange periwinkle light, my breath catching in the chilly air.

Neel sits up front with Karl, our driver, and we ride in the back, drowsy in the plush leather seats. During the drive to Reykjavík, I can't pull my eyes from the lush, flat green all around us, the roads lined with purple flowers. I study the crisp, neat houses with their angled roofs, boxy and clean, like Nordic wrapped packages. I slip deeper into my tired haze, and Abby, quiet next to me, seems to do the same.

"Sunset will be in a couple of hours," Karl announces, moving the car along the highway and through a town, the stoplights pale, glowing eyes in the elongated twilight. "But it won't get fully dark. Not this time of year." Finally, we pass a sheet of gray-blue water and Karl pulls the car into the parking lot of a hotel right off the highway. Leaving his door open, he hefts our bags out of the truck, wishes us well, and then drives away into the pale, endless light.

Abby slings her bag onto her shoulder and follows Neel inside. I sigh, hoping some of our famous Iceland magic will work its way into us while we're here.

Abby

It takes forever to check in, something weird with our reservation, so we don't get into our third-floor rooms until almost one a.m., but Riya has clearly gotten a second wind. She dumps her bags on the floor, saying, "Let's go explore – things stay open late because of the light." She brushes on some lip gloss, frowning when she turns to see I've already collapsed on my bed. Through the doorway of the adjoining room, we can just see Neel's feet splayed out on the end of his bed. Riya groans. "Oh, come on, you two! We're in *Iceland*. Look alive!"

"I'm game," Neel mumbles, but his feet remain motionless.

"I'll pass." I dig through my bag for my pajamas.

Riya's face falls. "You're still mad?"

"That's not it. I just need sleep."

She's not convinced, but doesn't press. "Neel?"

"Right, coming!"

A few minutes later, Neel and Riya leave to explore

Reykjavík. Basking in the quiet of the room, I brush my teeth and adjust the blackout curtains in the window, but no matter how hard I tug, they won't close properly. I climb into bed, wrapping a T-shirt around my eyes, only then I just feel smothered. I throw the T-shirt across the room at my bag, missing by at least three feet.

A half hour later, the light slanting across my face, I give up and call Mom, who has called twice and sent three texts since yesterday. Dad obviously told her about Riya's news and my subsequent disappearing act. Her last text simply read: CALL ME!

Kicking off the white duvet, I FaceTime her. She picks up instantly. "Abby?" Mom hates FaceTime, hates the awkward delay that sometimes happens, but for once, she doesn't complain about it when she answers. Instead, she asks, "Where are you?"

"Iceland. Riya said she sent you an itinerary." How does she not know where I am right now?

"Right, right. I don't have it on me." She is sweaty, her hair pulled into a ponytail. I must have caught her on a walk. "How are you holding up?"

Without warning, the tears start flowing. "I'm – I'm sorry," I gulp, embarrassed.

"It's okay – you just got some difficult news."

"I've had a lot of difficult news this year," I mumble.

She frowns. "I'm assuming that was a shot at me. Most of them are right now."

"Maybe you could try not to take this one personally."

Through the screen, Mom's brown eyes search my messy face. "Where's Riya?"

"She and Neel are out exploring Reykjavík."

"Why aren't you with them?"

I almost tell her about just wanting to get some sleep, about the odd late light here keeping me awake, but instead I tell her the truth. "Because I don't really want to be with Riya right now." All year long, I only wanted Riya to come home, longed to see her face in the halls at school, hear her yelling out the car window in the morning, her door already partly open before Dean even reached the curb to drop her off. But now I am avoiding her in an Icelandic Radisson. And, apparently, throwing myself a small pity party about it.

Mom pushes some wisps of hair from her face. "Honey, you can't let Riya's decision ruin your trip."

"I'm not—"

She overlaps my argument. "I've never been to Iceland. You're really lucky to have an opportunity like this one. Don't waste it sulking."

Annoyance bubbles up in my stomach, a tourniquet for my tears. "Wow, thanks, Mom, for that inspiring insight."

"Well, you don't have to be a snot."

Heat surges through me. "Let's look at why I'm being a snot, okay? Let's look at the timeline of my year. Last summer, my best friend told me she was moving to Berlin.

That's in Germany, remember? Then in January, my mother told our family that she doesn't love us anymore and moved in with our dentist. I pretty much spent the last five months going to school, working at the Blue Market, and taking care of Ghost Dad, while my only real friend was having major life epiphanies in Germany without me. Then, to top it off, my magical trip to Europe is a scam because the aforementioned best friend forgot to mention that she is moving to London to become an actress. So, you'll excuse me, but I think I'm inclined to be a bit of a snot right now. I think I've earned it." I stop, my chest heaving, the room suddenly as cold and empty as the light.

Mom doesn't say anything for almost a full minute. We just stare through a tiny screen at each other on two different sides of the world. "I never said I didn't love you anymore. That's ridiculous."

"It's an actions-louder-than-words thing, Mom. Actions louder than words." I click off the phone. My hand shaking, it drops into my lap. I've never in the history of my life hung up the phone on my mother. Come to think of it, I haven't done any of those clichéd teenage things. Never slammed the door in her face. Never screamed at her that I hated her. Not once. Even when she left, packed her things, stood outside our house, her arm across the open door of the Volvo, I never did something like this.

Maybe it's about time.

ϟ ✈ ♡

The next morning, I pile my plate with eggs and toast from the breakfast buffet, not feeling quite adventurous enough to try any of the various kinds of smoked fish in the row of glass pots. Across the room, Riya scowls at the make-your-own-waffle machine, muttering low insults at it as she investigates the stainless-steel block from all sides. "Maybe it doesn't respond to negative reinforcement?" I come up alongside her.

"It's not working!" She slaps its side, wincing, "Ow, hot!" before rattling off a louder string of colorful curses that raises the eyebrows of a white-haired couple who are sitting at a nearby table.

"Be nice to the waffle maker. Did you pour in the batter?" She nods, so I press the button that cooks the waffle once it has the batter, and a minute later, I slide a sugary golden-brown disc onto a clean plate for her. "There – see?"

"I tried that." She takes the plate, muttering, "It hates me." She smiles ruefully at the couple pretending they aren't eavesdropping.

We join Neel at a far table. Not taking his eyes from the article he's reading in the *Economist*, Neel says, "Thought that machine was going to have to bring assault charges against you."

Riya ignores him. I reach for a silver pitcher of milk, noticing that everything in the room reflects shades of white, silver, and glass, like we're having breakfast in a spaceship café. I'm also acutely aware that the energy at the table feels strange. I glance at the two of them. They are actively not making eye contact. Did something happen between them last night when they went out without me?

Apparently, we're all nursing stings we're not talking about this morning.

Neel checks his watch. "Our tour driver for the Golden Circle picks us up at nine. Meet downstairs with your bags packed in twenty minutes." He scoots his chair back crisply, tucking the magazine under his arm the way he has in so many other breakfast rooms on this trip.

I watch him cross the room before turning to Riya. "Trouble in Iceland?"

"Not really." She licks some syrup off her finger. "I mean, we sort of got into it last night, but it's fine."

I motion to his exit. "That didn't look fine."

"That looked like Neel." She stands. "Oh, and don't forget your phone on the side table by the bed. Did you see it this morning? Your mom called like five times."

I saw it. That's why I left it in the room.

A little after nine, Neel, Riya, and I wait outside the hotel near an enormous white van with bright blue lettering reading *Iceland Adventures!* Gunnar, our tour guide and driver, leans against the van, talking into his phone. Today he's taking us on an overnight tour of the Golden

Circle, a loop showcasing some of Southern Iceland's most famous features. Well over six feet, with a bushy white-blond beard, and built from bricks of muscle, Gunnar has a fitting name. In fact, all the Icelanders we've met so far seem to have won some sort of genetic lottery. His voice, though, surprises me: low and musical, full of soft syllables. Mom would call him a gentle giant. A stab of guilt hits me when I think of her. Up in the room, I didn't call back. I texted: busy, heading out on a tour! She hasn't text back.

"Look." Riya elbows me and nods in the direction of some other passengers coming through the hotel doors. We eavesdrop as they introduce themselves to Gunnar. A family from Spain: a mother, father, and two cute shaggy-haired teen boys who turn out to be twins. "Nice," Riya whispers to me when she hears this, "one for each of us." She gives them a sunny smile when they glance in our direction.

Next, a middle-aged couple joins the group. Rand and Suzie. They're from Vermont, stopping over in Iceland for three nights before continuing on to Paris. Rand nods at something Gunnar says and adjusts his faded gray baseball hat, which reads *Bennington College*. Next, a woman decked out in full hiking gear and a puffy down vest hurries out of the hotel. She has dyed black hair but appears to be in her late sixties or early seventies. "Sorry I'm late. I've been trying to wake my friend."

Gunnar looks alarmed. "Is she ill?"

"Just lazy," our new guest assures us, digging through a backpack that appears outfitted to save us on the off chance we end up lost in the Icelandic wilderness for the next month. Our last passenger, the hiking woman's friend, emerges from the hotel a few minutes later, clothes spilling out of her unzipped green duffel bag, her closely cropped white hair sticking up in places. "We almost left without you, Carol," Hiker Lady says, shaking her head. Gunnar assures her we did not.

"My alarm didn't go off, Maggie, don't make a federal case of it," Carol says sharply, trying to stuff the dangling arm of a shirt into her bag and smooth her hair down at the same time.

The Spanish family takes the long bench seat for four in the far back. Riya scurries to take the bench seat in front of them, and the other two couples settle into the seats near the front. Carol adjusts a mini blue backpack on her lap and stares straight ahead as we begin the drive out of Reykjavík. Maggie hands her something wrapped in a white napkin from the hotel. "Here, I made you a toast sandwich. You missed one heck of a breakfast spread."

"You're not supposed to steal the hotel napkins," Carol replies, but she nibbles the sandwich.

Neel nudges me, whispering, "That's you and Riya in fifty years." I fake a horrified expression, but Riya doesn't see it. She has turned in her seat to chat up the boys, Diego and Matías, who are from Barcelona. "I've always wanted to go to Barcelona," she's saying, her laugh silvery. I turn, too, listening to the conversation, nodding, smiling, but my eyes keep slipping outside to the stretch of wide, cloud-filled sky, the green of Iceland rolling out on either side of us as we move through the volcanic landscape toward Thingvellir National Park.

When we arrive, Gunnar parks the van next to several other tour vans and buses. In the dusty parking lot, he collects us into a half ring, giving us a brief history of the dramatic land around us. For the next hour or so, we will walk the Mid-Atlantic Ridge, where the North American and Eurasian tectonic plates are slowly splitting apart. "Do we have any history fans?" he asks, and I raise my hand. Actually, everyone raises their hands, but he smiles straight at me and says, "Thingvellir was the seat of the first Icelandic parliament in 930 AD, the Althing, and considered by many to be the oldest parliament in the world."

He motions for us to follow him to a trail, stopping when we come to a rocky outcropping overlooking a valley. Below, fingers of water spread out from a bright expanse of river. Gunnar points out the white Thingvellir Church on the other side of the river before explaining that where we're standing is a possible location for Lögberg, or Law Rock. Here, people would come forward and give important speeches to the gathered members. After answering some questions from Carol and Maggie, Gunnar continues along the trail, and I start to follow but notice Riya hanging back, standing at the railing overlooking the valley.

"Hey, we're going," I call to her, motioning to where the rest of our group makes their way up the hill.

"Gunnar said this is where they make important speeches in Iceland." She slips her hands out of the pockets of her red Patagonia vest. "I have an important speech to make." She holds her arms dramatically wide, like a queen would to her subjects. "I am here at the Lögberg."

My cheeks heat when several other tourists stop to watch her. "Riya, you don't have to do this—"

"Silence! I am orating." She clears her throat dramatically. "I would like it known that here on this clear day in the glorious month of July in the seat of the oldest parliament in the human world—"

"Good to specify. We wouldn't want to offend the aliens."

"Shh!" She holds up her hand. "Here on this great day, I want to apologize in front of all the land for not being honest with my best friend about my London plans. She didn't deserve to be left in the dark, and I, from herewitherforth—"

"Not a word." I try to hide a grin.

She raises her arms regally. "From herewitherforth,

I will talk to her, confer with her, and not keep secrets from her when it comes to issues that might affect her future, too."

Tears prick my eyes. "Seriously, cute Spanish boys. Getting away."

She doesn't move from the spot, even as another tour guide attempts to explain the role of the parliament to his gathered travelers. Riya stares at me, her eyes growing serious. "Does the aforementioned friend accept my apology?" When I hesitate, she bellows, "I demand an answer!"

"Okay, okay." I hurry to her side. "The aforementioned friend herewitherforth accepts your apology." She throws her arms around me, and I whisper into her hair, "But can we go? This is sort of embarrassing."

We head up the stairs to catch up with our tour. "Pretty impressive speech, though, right?"

"*Game of Thrones* will be calling for an audition for sure." We try to hurry, but Gunnar has already walked back down searching for us.

"The group stays together, ladies," he admonishes in his soft-edged voice.

Riya whispers, "Uh-oh, Thor's mad at us."

I hook my arm through hers. "Totally worth it."

After a short hike, we take the van to the rim of the Kerid Crater, a deep volcanic crater with an indigo lake at its center. We eat a picnic lunch and then snap some photos. Motioning to Neel, who stands several dozen feet from us, peering down into the blue water, Riya mumbles, "Wonder what Nani would say if she found out he ended up in the bottom of a volcanic crater?"

Before I can respond, Gunnar calls us, and we scramble back into the van to head to the Haukadalur geothermic area. The chill I noticed earlier between Riya and Neel has reached new levels, more appropriate for winter in Iceland than summer. Sitting between them, I'm my own mini Berlin Wall; both of them are plugged into their phones, staring in separate directions out the windows of the van. When Neel tugs his earbuds out, I see if I'll have better luck with him than I did with Riya at breakfast earlier. "What are you two fighting about? Blink if I come close. Moira? Travel? Whether or not Iceland should host a Winter Olympics?" Not blinking, or answering, he turns back to the window, but not before his pained expression cuts off any further questioning from me.

When we reach our destination, we park and cross the street to the trail that leads to the Strokkur geyser, Gunnar encouraging all of us to bring our rain jackets. In the last fifteen minutes, the sky has grown thick and gray with storm clouds. As we walk the trail lined with pools of steaming water that hiss and bubble, Maggie peers worriedly at the sky, wondering aloud when the rain will open up on us. The closer we get to the geyser, though, the harder it is to tell where the moisture stems from, the ground or the sky. Everything around us is steel gray, the smell of sulfur strong in the wet air.

As Gunnar gathers us into a group on the wet rock a hundred feet from the geyser, Riya makes sure we maneuver close to Diego and Matías. Gunnar waits until we're all quiet. "The word *geyser* that most of you know originates from this region. It comes from the Old Norse verb *geysa*, meaning 'to gush.'" Gunnar has the hood of his jacket cinched so low over his eyes that his exposed face is almost entirely yellow beard. We all follow his lead, battening down our own hatches, as the first raindrops pock the steaming surface of the geothermal pool. A crowd gathers to wait for Strokkur to erupt.

We hold our breath and wait, watching the changing light cast a blue glow across the wet patches of ground. Before anything happens, a group of tourists in matching crimson slickers moves like a swarm of red bees into the viewing space in front of us. "Oh, wait – what?" Riya glares at them. She clears her throat, but the dozen red-jacketed hoods don't budge. Her eyes search out a different space. "Look, no one is standing over there in that flat area. Let's go over there."

"I see okay," Matías tells her while his brother fiddles with his phone.

"Abby?" Riya asks me.

"Gunnar said to stay here." I glance at Neel, who nods in agreement.

"Ugh, maybe you two should just get married and get it over with!" Riya storms away to the bare patch of stone ground, where she stands with her back to us. What was that about? I'm turning to ask Neel when the ground explodes in a shooting stream of water. People cry out, delighted, their cameras poised, capturing the geyser's blast.

Thing about water that shoots high up into the sky? It has to land somewhere.

That somewhere is on Riya.

One moment, she's watching as it roars toward the sky, then, just as suddenly, she screams, vanishing into a white, drenching cloud. "Riya!" I start to run to her, but Neel grabs the back of my jacket. "Hold on, she's fine." Out of the wet cloud, I hear what at first sounds like crying, but realize is actually laughter. As the mist dissipates, Riya's form materializes. She is sopping wet, her hood knocked back, her hair hanging in dripping strands around her face, but yes, she is laughing.

Diego and Matías clutch their stomachs, doubling over with laughter. She takes slow, sodden steps back to us. Flipping some wet hair from her face, she beams at them. "I guess that's why no one stands over there."

Gunnar doesn't notice what happened. He's already quite far away, walking up the path with Carol and Maggie. Riya needs to change, but Gunnar has the keys to the van. "Gunnar!" I shout, the wind grabbing my words, carrying them away into the wet air. He can't hear me. He's so far away now, he's just a dot with a beard.

Riya, looking like she could give a seminar to drowned rats on how to appear more pathetic and miserable, chatters, "It's n-n-no problem. I'm f-f-fine." The wind has picked up, and even though her shower was a hot one, she shivers visibly. Matías offers to get the keys from Gunnar and trots off in the direction of where Gunnar disappeared behind a mound of volcanic hill.

"That could take a while." Neels sighs. "Let's at least get you something hot to drink."

Diego unzips his jacket, pulls off his sweatshirt, and hands it to her. She takes it gratefully.

We warm up across the street in the building that houses a cafeteria-style restaurant, restrooms, and a large gift shop. Riya sits by the window squeezing out her hair into paper napkins, leaving tiny pools of water on the floor around her. When there is no sign of Matías, Diego heads out to find him.

A few minutes later, Neel brings her a dry T-shirt and a pair of bright pink fleece pajama bottoms dotted with sheep to wear until she can get into her bag to change clothes. "Souvenirs. Who knows how long it will take to get into the van." Riya holds up the shirt. It reads: *If you don't like the weather in Iceland, wait five minutes.* "You'll get used to that in London, too," he tells her. She scoops up the new clothes and Diego's sweatshirt and hurries to the bathroom to change. Neel slides onto the bench next to me, his hip touching mine. The damp has turned his hair wild and curly.

I nudge him. "You have some crazy hair going on."

He tries to tamp it down but only manages to isolate certain chunks. Catching my eye, he says, "Don't laugh, curly. You should see your hair."

He's right. I'm like Frizzy the Wet Weather Clown, but I hold his gaze. "Oh, I'm not laughing. I like your hair like that."

"Do you now?"

"Yes." We're locked in one of those moments where neither of us wants to drop our eye contact, but keeping it builds an intensity we keep dancing around. Until now. "Was your fight with Riya about me?" I ask. He doesn't answer right away, just drums his fingers lightly on the table in front of us. I can't help constantly noticing small things like this about him, like how nice the blue of his jacket looks on him, or how adorable the creases at the edges of his eyes are when he laughs.

Those eyes now dart toward the bathrooms. "Who says we had a fight?" When I just stare at him, he clears his throat and sits back in his chair. "Yes. It was about you." He doesn't offer up any more information.

"Do you want to give me any specifics?"

Neel glances at the closed bathroom door again, but his eyes make their way back to me. He clears his throat.

"Riya is concerned that I am developing feelings for you."

My heart flips just once. "Feelings, like wow-that-Abby-girl-is-really-annoying-I-wish-she'd-go-back-to-California kind of feelings?"

A smile plays at his mouth. "Not exactly."

The heart flip develops into a full-blown cardiac gymnastic event. He's sitting so close, I'm sure he hears it, but I force myself to sound casual. "And you got into a fight because she was out of line and completely off base about the whole thing?"

Neel leans into me, his arm warm along my arm. "Actually, the fight had more to do with her accuracy."

"Wow." I place my hands flat on the table in front of me to keep them from shaking.

"Right, then. So, we may or may not have a problem." He covers my hands with his and pulls me gently toward him until we're facing each other. I clearly need to hold up my end of this surreal conversation I'm having in the middle of Iceland, but I've completely lost the use of my voice. Apparently, all the clichés are true. My voice is nowhere to be found.

He notices. "So, the problem, of course, is whether or not you feel the same." He places one long index finger beneath my chin, tipping it up to meet his gaze. "Do you?"

My neon-sign face always answers these sorts of questions for me, and it's working overtime now. "Yeah, we definitely have a problem." Then, surprising myself perhaps even more than I surprise him, I plant my hands on either side of his face and pull him in close to kiss me, his lips warm and tasting like the mint tea he's been drinking.

Now I know how Riya felt when that cascade of water hit her.

I hear Gullfoss before I see it.

On the drive here, and now, walking through the parking lot to see the famous waterfall, I can't stop my mind from spinning, from replaying the kiss with Neel. Somehow, Riya didn't catch us; she returned from the bathroom wondering if she should buy a pair of slippers shaped like goofy Icelandic horse heads and we'd been sitting there, blinking into the space between us. She has no idea that during her wardrobe change in the bathroom, my world tilted on its axis.

Turns out, secrets are harder to share when they're yours.

Now we all take a collective gasp as Iceland's most famous waterfall appears, wide, white-watered, with a ribbon of rainbow shimmering across it in the newly emerged sun. I try to focus on its two-tiered surging zigzag drop into a long, narrow canyon. Around us, the air is wet, with that damp green smell that permeates near a large body of water. We navigate our way carefully down the wooden stairs and find places near the cabled railing where we can stand eye level to the plunging falls. I've seen pictures, but nothing can truly capture how massive it feels to be standing this near to it. No wonder Gullfoss routinely ends up on top-ten lists for world waterfalls. A true natural wonder. The kind that reminds you it has been here a long, long time and will exist into a future you will never see. Dad calls these Nature Reality Checks.

I sort of need one right now.

"Abby! Come get a picture with me. Give Neel your phone." Riya wears the pink sheep pajama bottoms tucked into a pair of black boots she changed into in the van. She still wears Diego's sweatshirt. When Matías, Diego, and Gunnar found us in the cafeteria, Gunnar was spewing apologies, hadn't realized the girl drenched by the geyser had been part of his flock. "Happens all the time," he told her.

The waterfall rushes behind us, and I put my arm around her. She motions for Neel to take our picture. "Make sure you get the pants in the shot."

"Are you kidding?" Neel laughs. "This is going to be my new profile picture." When he hands my phone back, he lets his fingers trail across mine for a moment, and that rush from the waterfall has nothing on the one his touch sends through me.

Yep, we have a problem.

I hurry to join Riya near the trailhead. Gunnar leads us

down a narrow dirt path to a rocky ledge where we can stand next to the falls. The powerful spray spots my glasses, and Riya hangs back, wary of another shower. On the way back up, Gunnar pauses to show us a sign reading *Ástarsaga* that tells the legend of a shepherd boy in the seventeenth century who fell in love with a girl across the raging waters of the Hvítá River, and she with him. They pined for years, as the waters were thought impossible to cross. Finally, after years of making googly eyes at each other from afar, the boy found the shallowest possible crossing and made his way successfully across to her. They married and had many respected descendants in Iceland.

"I know what you'll say." Riya nudges me. "You don't hear about the after part. He probably never put away his shoes or took out the garbage." It does sound like something I'd say.

Rand comes up alongside me to study the sign, his hair curling under his cap from the waterfall spray. "Of course we don't hear about that part; that would deflate the power of the myth." At my surprised look, he grins. "Sorry, professional hazard. I'm a literature professor at Bennington, specializing in mythology."

"No, I agree with you," I say, squinting at the sign. "This is good stuff here. The contrast of his love with the pain and challenge that went into making his dream a reality."

He looks impressed. "Exactly. Examine almost any

myth, and at the center you find love driving it and something in its way. And not just romantic love. Sometimes, it's the love of wealth or power or self, but ultimately, everything is a love story." He stares out at Gullfoss, perhaps imagining that young Icelander attempting to cross it all those years ago. "The after part isn't the point."

At the end of a rural road, Gunnar parks the van next to a white farmhouse, the perimeter dotted with four white cabins. The clouds shift in layers of gray, blanketing the light and bringing out the lush green of the landscape. A woman in a flannel shirt with a thick blonde braid hanging over her shoulder emerges onto the front deck, a collie trotting behind her. Gunnar starts piling our bags next to the van.

"Hallo!" The woman motions for us to join her on the deck, where she begins passing out keys to our cabins. "I'm Sabrina and I'll be your host tonight." She smiles at Neel as he collects the key for number three. "Dinner buffet will be ready in a half hour," she tells us. "We meet here in the main house, so feel free to find your cabin and freshen up first." The dog licks my hand, and I look down into his sweet eyes, his black-and-white head like a patchwork quilt. "That's Ingi. Don't give him any cheese," Sabrina tells me, her ice-blue eyes serious. I immediately agree not to, even though it's not like I'm smuggling cheese in my pockets to hand out to random dogs.

"Sorry, Ingi." I scratch his shaggy head. "No cheese for you."

We cross the front yard to Cabin Three. To the side of the narrow porch, I notice a stack of rocks and a tiny wooden house. The other cabins have them, too. Sabrina wanders by with a stack of towels. "What is that?" I ask her, motioning to it.

"An *álfhól*." She peers at it affectionately. "For the elves."

"Right, okay." I remember reading something about Icelanders and their elves and trolls. Hidden elves in gardens. Troll faces frozen into various rock formations. Icelanders have a deep belief in magical hidden worlds. My kind of people.

Neel unlocks the door, and inside, we're met with the clean, Nordic orderliness I'm coming to expect in Iceland. White walls, blond wood floors, two single beds with crisp white duvets, each with a single pillow and a white towel and washcloth folded and waiting at the base. No frills. To the right of the bathroom, there is a separate bedroom with a double bed. Neel goes into it and closes the door.

I fall onto the bed nearest a sliding glass door that opens to a small deck, my limbs feeling like they've been weighted down with cement. I set my glasses on the bare table next to me and rub my eyes. After a few minutes,

I hear a door slide open and shut, and out of the corner of my eye I see a slightly blurry Neel outside, leaning on the railing, watching the light move across the hills beyond. He has changed for dinner into jeans and a light wool sweater the color of pumpkins. I study the long lines of his back. Does someone get even cuter after you've kissed him? Can the features morph? When I first met Neel, he didn't strike me as anything special. He's attractive in that nerdy way I tend to like, but he's not going to be posing on magazine covers anytime soon. But over the last couple of weeks, I can't seem to stop thinking about all the tiny details that make him Neel. The way he sits casually in a chair, his long legs splayed out, his feet just a little too large in his shoes. The way his soccer jersey stretched across his shoulders that night in Berlin when we watched the James Bond movie. Even how he always folds his magazines or newspapers in half and tucks them beneath his arm after reading at breakfast.

The bed shifts next to me, and Riya's face appears inches from my own. "I got mad at Neel."

I stare up at her. "I know."

"Did he tell you why?"

"Yes."

She looks surprised. "I feel like I'm not allowed to have a normal reaction to this news since you're still mad at me for the whole moving-to-London situation." She flattens a wrinkle on the black sweater dress she has changed into and crosses her legs, now clad in thick teal tights. She waits for my answer, elbows on knees.

I slip on my glasses, tugging at my pillow so I can sit up to face her. "You are allowed to have whatever reaction you want." Now would be the time to mention, *Oh, yeah, I kissed Neel.*

Riya sighs. "I want you to know I told him that under no circumstances is he to complicate things with us."

Did she mention what to do if *I* complicate them?

Neel opens the sliding door and steps into the room, hesitating when he sees us talking on the bed. "I thought it might be time for supper."

My stomach rumbles at the thought. "Perfect timing." I wiggle past Riya and grab my jacket. "I'm starving."

As I pass him, his eyes ask, *Did you tell her?* and I give the slightest shake of my head. *No.*

Inside the farmhouse, the massive buffet table takes up an entire wall of the high-ceilinged dining room. Different salads, meats, a silver tureen of creamy soup, fish, meats, a cheese plate, and four different loaves of bread for slicing on a wood cutting board. Sabrina stands next to the spread, beaming, reminding us to "leave room for dessert!" We fill our bowls and pile our plates and find seats around the community table.

Riya sits down next to me, holding a piece of bread up for me to inspect. "Are those walnuts or white raisins?"

She peers suspiciously at the bread, and then nibbles at it. "Walnuts," she declares.

"And one of the world's most vexing problems gets solved."

Riya ignores me, waving to Diego and Matías to sit with us. Diego takes the seat next to Riya, and Matías sits down next to me. Neel finds a seat at the end of the table by the twins' parents, Manuel and Josefa, and Rand and Suzie sit across from us. Carol and Maggie scoot into chairs next to Gunnar, and everyone starts eating. For several minutes, the only sound in the room is the scrape of forks against plates, water being sipped, the creak of a chair as someone shifts their weight in it.

It's the kind of silence that makes Riya nuts. "Okay, travelers!" she says to the group. "Shall we play a game of Stump the Nerd?"

I groan. "Let these people eat their meal in peace."

"What is Stump the Nerd?" Diego asks, his mouth full of salad.

Riya explains the game we haven't played since before she moved. My dad started it when we were ten to try to trip us up with Harry Potter trivia, but over the years it evolved into a random trivia dinner game.

Rand leans forward in his chair. "Can you ask anything? Or just our areas of interest?"

Riya and I glance at each other. We've never really had anyone take our game seriously before. "Um, I guess we usually give categories like the Seven Wonders of the Ancient World or *Doctor Who* or whatever the person who's playing is nerdy about." I eat a forkful of beet salad. "Like maybe for you, it would be Stump the Mythology Lit Professor."

"We would try to ask you a question about mythology you can't answer," Riya adds.

Suzie snorts. "Good luck."

"Or something else," Riya says, eyeing Suzie. "It doesn't have to be mythology."

Matías says, "For me, it would be Stump the Nerd for Football."

Diego nods. "Me too."

"Or Neel would be Stump the Economics Nerd." I glance down the table, but he's talking quietly with Manuel and doesn't hear me.

Rand pauses for a moment. "That sounds fun. Try it with me. Mythology."

"I have a question." Matías sets down his glass of water. "Volcanoes. Here in Iceland they have much volcanic devastation, and I think of Pompeii." Rand nods for him to go on. "How something can be, er, *aniquilado*" – he searches for the word in English – "wiped out. A city. A civilization."

"Like Atlantis?" I ask.

"Oh, one of his favorites," Suzie mutters.

"Not one of yours?" I take a small bite of fish.

She sips her wine, mulling my question. "It's not that," she says. "It's just, well, when you've been married to a professor of literature and mythology for twenty years, sometimes you just want some concrete answers. Yes and no. Black and white." She looks at Matías. "I'm sorry, what was your question?"

Matías considers. "I wonder how some stories, Pompeii" – he smiles sideways at me – "or Atlantis succeed, when others do not."

Riya frowns. "Usually in the game you just ask a question that can be directly answered, like 'Name one place rumored to be the former site of Atlantis?' and the Nerd would say—" She glances at me.

"Santorini, Greece," I supply.

Rand nudges his wife. "See, honey, there is a black-and-white answer in mythology. Name one place Atlantis might have existed? One place is Santorini." He winks at me. "Of course, some people argue that it was beneath Antarctica."

Suzie shakes her head, her lips pursed. "Here we go."

Matías's gaze slips between Rand and Suzie. "I think maybe I say the wrong question?"

"Not at all!" Rand butters a thick slice of bread. "I think it's an excellent question." Matías seems pleased, sitting back with his own slice of bread to listen to Rand's answer.

Maggie signals from down the table. "Speak up! Some

of us want to eavesdrop and don't hear like we used to."

It might be my imagination, but it seems like Suzie's face darkens as everyone turns attention to Rand. He colors a bit, repeating Matías's question for the benefit of the people at the other end of the table. "I'm off the clock for lecturing, so I'll try to keep it short. I guess my answer would be that Pompeii's legend perpetuates because of historical evidence. But Atlantis is one of the great myths because it has continued to be passed down despite such evidence, having perhaps its most famous voice in Plato in the Socratic dialogue in *Timaeus*. So his fame was a huge reason it persisted, though Plato used it, I think, as a philosophical parable, more than to prove its actual existence."

"So you don't think it's real?" Carol asks, her face aglow in the candles Sabrina has lit along the middle of the table runner.

Rand leans his forearms on the table. "My interest in mythology isn't about whether or not it's real. For me, the truth in mythology is that it taps into our human capacity to wonder and imagine things – no matter the time period." He digs into some roasted potatoes.

Josefa, who hasn't spoken much with us during the trip, clears her throat. "I love the myth of Atlantis. But my father told it to me as a little girl as the story of Iram."

"Iram of the Pillars," Rand adds. "The Atlantis of the Sands."

Matías and Diego catch each other's eyes over our heads. "Mama told us that story as boys," Diego explains.

Josefa nods. "The city was consumed by sand in a single night, in what is now Saudi Arabia." My skin tingles. Iram is a new one to me; I haven't read anything about it before. This is one of the reasons why mythology and history are so cool. You pull one thread and you suddenly dislodge all these other strands. Josefa continues, echoing my thoughts. "In all these separate cultures, before they had a chance to be connected, I have always found it fascinating that they told versions of the same stories, whether it was water or sand or ash."

"The connective power of myth!" Rand exclaims.

Maggie claps for him. "Excellent discussion; what fun!"

"Not when you've heard it a thousand times," Suzie mutters, getting up to inspect the dessert that Sabrina has been setting up while we've been talking. I raise my eyebrows at Riya as the others go back to smaller conversations, and she mirrors my look back at me. Rand stares after his wife, any earlier enthusiasm draining from his face.

Riya

Outside, after dessert, Diego and Matías kick a soccer ball back and forth on a patch of grass. Abby and I play around with them for a bit, kicking the ball, but soon, Abby grows bored and wanders over to a paddock where three Icelandic horses graze near a wooden fence. I toss the ball to Diego and trot over to where she stands watching them. "You found our unicorns." I reach out to pat the brown-and-white patterned nose of the closest one, but she gives an annoyed snort and moves away. "I guess this one's Mirabelle," I say to Abby, who tries to click and kiss the horse back to us. The mare answers with a quick swish of tail and turns her back.

Abby laughs. "Stubborn. Definitely Mirabelle."

Sabrina brings us some carrots to feed them. "That's Feima." She motions to the horse I tried to reach out to. "It means *the shy one*."

"She's beautiful." Abby tries to lure her with a carrot. Again, Feima swishes her tail, but she's thinking about it.

"When you're ready, we have chairs by the fire and some hot cider." Sabrina points to the chairs set up around a flickering fire pit. It's not too cold and the light is still strong, but the fire casts a warm glow.

"Let's get some cider." I tug at Abby's sleeve, but she won't give up on trying to coax Feima over for a treat.

She waves the carrot. "I'm stubborn, too."

"Where do you think Mirabelle got it from?" I tease, waiting, my arms draped over the wooden fence.

Finally, Feima creeps over, head down, plucks the carrot from Abby's hand, and trots away. "Yes!" Abby grins at me, brushing some hair from her face. We say good-bye to the other horses and head over to the dark green Adirondack-style chairs, where Sabrina gives us two steaming mugs. Settling into the chairs, we watch the twins kick their soccer ball back and forth, back and forth, their motions growing hypnotic.

Rand sits down in the seat next to me. "May I?"

"Sure." I try to study him without him noticing. He's a little older than my dad, maybe early fifties, and he stares sullenly into the fire. Stump the Nerd went sideways on us at dinner. We clearly managed to upset Suzie, and she seems to have disappeared into her cabin for the night. "Sorry if we made your wife mad at dinner," I tell him, watching the flame flicker and shift.

"It's just a silly game we play sometimes," Abby adds, sipping her cider.

He stuffs his free hand into the side pocket of his red North Face jacket. "Oh, don't worry about that. She was mad long before dinner. It's sort of her resting state right now. Constant mad."

Abby and I exchange glances. Neither of us seems to know what to say to this, so I do what people often do when someone overshares something uncomfortable. I change the subject. "You're heading to Paris next, right? I love Paris."

He frowns into the fire. "Paris isn't my favorite; too busy. But Suzie loves it, has that whole artistic attraction to Paris and its aesthetic, I guess. I chose Iceland; she chose Paris." He hesitates, thinking. "But then we're on to Italy for a couple of weeks. This is our let's-see-if-travel-can-help-fix-all-the-things-that-have-gone-wrong-in-the-last-twenty-years trip." He must notice my alarmed face, because he clears his throat. "Whoa, sorry, more information than you needed to hear."

"No big deal." I try to laugh. My acting teacher Niles says that we should soak in other people's stories when they give them to us because we can use them later for characters. Besides, I can't possibly judge Rand. I'm trying the same sort of strategy with a friendship right now.

Rand sets his mug on the flat arm of the chair and then leans forward, holding his hands out to the fire. "So you like Paris?"

"I've only been once. We went for Christmas last year." I tell him about our long weekend there, remembering the way the lights reflected in the watery streets, the dusting of snow on the branches of the trees along the Champs-Élysées, wandering the rooms in the Louvre. Maybe I'm like Suzie and love it for its aesthetic, for the *feel* of it. Both Berlin and London, too.

I don't notice at first when Abby leaves her chair, but then I see her, letting herself in through the front door of our cabin. Watching her, I decide to share something of my own with the total stranger sitting next to me. Maybe it's easier because I'll never see him again. "You know how you said you're trying to travel to see if you can fix things?"

He looks surprised I've brought it back up, but nods. "Yeah?"

"Me too." I motion in the direction of our cabin. "With Abby. We've been like sisters since we were three years old, but I moved away from our hometown last year and I've been screwing some things up with us."

Sitting back, he lifts his mug again. "What makes you think that?"

I study the closed door of our cabin. "It was hard being so far away. The new school, the time difference… I was just trying to figure things out in Berlin. But her parents split up last winter, and I could have been a better friend during it."

Rand stares in the direction of the cabin. "Have you told her that?"

"I've tried. But I kept some things from her. And I didn't reach out enough." I sip the cider that has gone lukewarm in my mug.

The fire glints in Rand's dark blue eyes. "I think with any long-term relationship, it's a two-way street. She could have reached out to you. None of us are mind readers."

"That's true." I glance at the closed cabin door. It's already eleven, even if it doesn't feel like it with the blue light, so I tell Rand, "I think I'm going to turn in."

He holds up his cup in a *cheers* motion. "Good luck."

I cross to the cabin and push open the door. As I walk through it, at first, I think I'm imagining things. But no, I've caught Neel and Abby in a deep kiss, standing by the half-open sliding glass door, Abby's arms around Neel's back, Neel's hands in her hair.

I freeze.

They hear the door shut behind me. "Oh—" They both stumble apart, avoiding my eyes, Abby fiddling with her glasses, Neel running his hands weirdly through his hair, adjusting his shirt. Anger bubbles up. He *promised* me.

"Riya—" he starts, taking a step toward me.

"Are you kidding me?!" I shout at him. "Did you not just make a promise to me barely a day ago that you wouldn't complicate things with Abby?"

"Things changed—" he starts again.

"I don't care! This is *our* trip. Mine and Abby's. You have no right to—"

"Just stop it!" Abby's voice rings out in the cabin, and it takes me a minute to recognize it as hers. "You don't get to tell him what he can and cannot do. He doesn't have to promise you anything."

I turn to her, feeling my face heat. "How could you let this happen? This trip was supposed to be about us, you and me. Not some messed-up triangle. That's not how I meant for this to go."

"Welcome to my year." Her voice has gone quiet again, the sound of it like ice.

I cross my arms snugly across my chest, mostly to control my shaking hands. "This is ridiculous. You wouldn't kiss Tavin but you'll kiss Neel? It's crazy."

Abby nods slowly. "Oh, I get it. You're mad I did something crazy you didn't plan. Because it's usually you doing the crazy stuff, right? And me following along. It's usually you kissing the boy you shouldn't." She ticks off her fingers. "Trey Christopher. Mark Sears. Greg Newman. And Alec Limm, who was my friend, too. And I took sides. I said I wouldn't and I did. Do you remember whose side I took with Alec?"

I swallow. "Mine."

"Right. I took yours. Always." Abby holds my gaze. "Whose side are you taking right now?"

Standing here, in the late blue light of the cabin, I don't know how to answer her. She's right about those boys. With each of them, she stood by me. Every time. But this is different. It's Neel. And this trip was supposed to be about our friendship. How could she do this? "It's completely different, and you know it," I tell her. "This trip was supposed to help us. How does this" – I motion at the two of them – "help *us*?"

She lets out a low laugh, one that holds notes of being hurt, disappointed, but also not completely surprised. It's the sound of this last bit that cuts me. Shaking her head, she moves by me to the door. "You're unbelievable." She turns to Neel. "Fire pit?" He slinks by me and follows her out of the cabin.

The next morning, Maggie and Carol keep up a constant chatter at breakfast. It helps make it seem like I'm not ignoring Abby and Neel. They stayed out by the fire pit until almost two last night, when I heard them creep quietly into the room. I kept still, pretending to be asleep, while they took turns brushing their teeth and then, after the snap of the bathroom light, Neel closed the door to his bedroom, and Abby crawled into the other twin bed near me. My eyes slits, I watched her settle next to me, the violet form of her slipping under the covers. She turned to face me in the shadows of the room. "Riya?" she whispered, waiting. I didn't answer.

Finally, she rolled over, her back to me, and soon I heard the steady purr of her breathing.

The morning passes as Gunnar drives us to visit volcanic, bubbling mud pools and an old lighthouse. Back in the van, he tells us about the terrible eruption of Eyjafjallajökull in 2010, how the ash caused trouble with air traffic for nearly a month. I only half listen, zoning out by the window, as we pass farmhouses and pastures, wide green fields dotted with sheep and, occasionally, those beautiful Icelandic horses. Abby's right. It's harder to care about the big problems when the personal ones are taking up all the space.

My phone buzzes with a text from Will: how's iceland?

I text back: volcanic.

His series of happy faces and flames brings the first smile of the day to my face.

I glance sideways at my cousin. He sits between Abby and me, but his body is angled away, leaning a little forward to listen to Gunnar. He motions at something out the window and Abby nods, grinning back at him. As she does, she catches my eye for a moment, but quickly looks away, her expression darkening.

Before heading back into Reykjavík, Gunnar takes us to the famous Blue Lagoon geothermic spa built into a lava field in Grindavik. Leaning against the edge of the pool, the alien, pearlescent blue water so opaque I can't see my own body in its depths, I study the white clouds swirling overhead and try to convince myself the trip hasn't been a complete bust.

Abby wades over to me. She holds two neon-orange juices from the swim-up bar. "Healthy beverage?" I take one, and she leans against the side of the pool with me. "This place is a trip." I nod, sipping the gingery carrot juice as she takes a long drink through her straw. "I like the name Grindavik," she says. "It sounds like a friendly, wise elf from *The Lord of the Rings*. The one who tells the travelers the right way to proceed."

I eye her. "We could use one of those now."

Abby points to the pool deck with her plastic cup. "Maybe we should just enjoy the view." The Spanish twins lounge in their swim trunks, their bodies gleaming from just coming out of the sauna.

"You don't have to do that."

"What?"

"Pretend you're interested in them because I thought they were cute."

"I'm not interested," Abby says, watching them. "But I'm not blind, either."

My gaze catches on something at the far end of the pool, and a giggle bubbles up. "Oh, wow. Carol and Maggie have found the silica mud." Across the blue expanse, the two women are slathering on the signature mud found in various containers around the pool, only their eyes visible through their white masks, like pale, muddy raccoons. "Supposedly, silica mud brings out the skin's inner glow. Try it. You'll look ten years younger when you take it off."

"Fabulous; I've always wanted to look seven again."

"I want to be seven again." I sigh. "Second grade seems like a million years ago. The worst thing that year was your fish that kept pretending to die. He traumatized us for, like, a month."

Abby almost spits juice into the water. "Patch McSpotty! That fish had one seriously dark sense of humor. What fish floats upside down like that? Weirdo. We made that thing at least five RIP rock headstones before we had to actually use one."

"RIP Patch McSpotty." We take a moment of silence for Patch, the dark-humored fish.

We quietly take in the activity around us for a few moments. People lounge in the ghostly water, chat at the swim-up bar, walk in white robes across the small bridges over narrow parts of the pool. "What are we going to do about all this?" Abby finally asks, setting her empty juice cup on the edge of the pool.

"I have absolutely no idea."

She brushes a stray lock of hair from her eyes, squinting in the slash of sun that has come out from behind a cloud. "I went for a hike with my dad before I met you in Florence, and he told me a little about what happened with him and my mom." She lowers her voice, so I edge closer to her in the water. "He said of all the things that did them in as a couple – that's the way he put it, *did them in* – anyway, of all the things, it was the score-keeping."

The tingling in my legs isn't from geothermic activity. "Scorekeeping?"

She nods, holding her hand to her forehead as a visor from the sun. "How they started keeping these mental scorecards against each other. Like, I cleaned the bath-room three times in a row. Or I did all the grocery shopping last month. Or you haven't taken Henry to the vet once in the last five years. He said it didn't start out that way. But instead of talking to each other about it in a real way, they started shooting these darts into each other. For years. And then it was like a habit they couldn't break." She blinks at me from under her hand. "I don't want it to be like that with us. Keeping score." And she doesn't even add the normal Abby joke at the end, like *because I'd win – ha!* She's serious about this.

"Me either."

She points to Carol and Maggie, who are now sitting on the edge of the far pool, slathering their arms and legs with white mud. "Okay, seriously, I'm thinking maybe a silica intervention might be necessary." There it is. The lightening of the atmosphere. It's something

I realize I've grown to need from her, even when maybe it's not fair to always expect it.

Later, Gunnar pulls into the Radisson parking lot, depositing our bags where he collected us thirty-three hours ago. Neel hangs back, talking to Gunnar; he's been giving us a wide berth today. We say good-bye to Carol and Maggie, and the Spanish family. When Manuel and Josefa disappear into the hotel, I give Matías and Diego each a big hug. Diego holds on to me a bit longer than usual. "Come to Barcelona someday," he says in my ear. "I can show you the city."

I pull away, smiling at his messy, coppery hair, his wide-set dark eyes. "I'll keep that in mind."

What I'm really keeping is his sweatshirt.

We wave to Rand and Suzie, but Suzie, who spent most of today hiding behind large black sunglasses, doesn't wave back. Abby walks over to where Rand unloads his luggage from the van. She returns with his card. "He said I should check out his college," she tells me, her voice sounding hopeful.

"You mythology nerds need to stick together."

We spend the early evening wandering around Reykjavík, checking out the jagged church, marveling at the massive boats in the harbor, eating yummy vegan bowls at stand-up tables in a brightly painted restaurant. We wander back to our hotel by eleven, since we have to be up at three to catch our shuttle to the airport tomorrow morning. While Neel is downstairs settling the bill and organizing a bag breakfast for our early departure, I hand Abby a white envelope.

"What's this?"

I sit next to where she's sorting her bag on the bed. "I've been going back and forth on whether to give it to you. I made it before we started our trip. It's a scavenger hunt I planned for London."

She inspects the bulky envelope. "I love scavenger hunts."

"I know – and I want you to go on it with Neel when we get there." When she looks like she might argue, I hurry to explain. "I have a student orientation I should probably attend tomorrow. For my new school. I wasn't going to go because, well, honestly, I hadn't planned on telling you about it until our last day, but in light of everything..." I trail off.

Abby pushes her bag out of the way and sits down next to me. "You want to go to the orientation?"

"I do, yeah."

She bites her lip, looking down at the envelope in her hand. "And you want me to do this with Neel? Really?"

I nod. "I think you would have fun, and he knows the city. He helped me with some of the details in the first place, and, well, maybe you two need some time to sort out that kiss?" I study her face. "It looked like it might have been a good one?"

She flushes, dropping her eyes. "There have been several good ones."

"What?!" I try not to visibly shudder. "Okay, officially – *ew.* He's—"

"Smart and adorkable and gets my nerdy self," she cuts in hopefully.

This time the shudder is visible. "If you say so."

the sixth Wonder

LONDON, ENGLAND

Abby

Neel holds open the glossy red door of his family's flat in Bloomsbury while Riya and I step inside, tired from the early-morning rise in Iceland, the flight to Heathrow, and the ride into London to the quiet, tree-lined street where Neel grew up.

"Just feel lucky Nani booked us a car," Riya says, walking into the living room. I follow her. The flat is quiet, the drapes drawn, and smells like cinnamon and clove.

"Are your parents here?" I ask Neel, depositing my bags in the cozy book-lined den Neel points out to us.

"They're in Berlin, actually," Riya answers for him. "Getting a few details squared away before we head back to California." She grabs her bag. "I'm going to go change for my orientation," she says, and disappears into the den, closing a sliding door behind her for privacy.

I scan the elegant flat, its rich carpets and deep-taupe walls. Neel opens the drapes, letting in a spill of late-morning light. He takes his bag into the room next to the den, and I catch a glimpse of soccer posters and a navy bedspread. "You've lived here your whole life?" I ask when he emerges.

"Most of it. We moved here when I was two."

Riya comes out of the den in the pink maxi dress she wore in Berlin, and her leather jacket. She's dabbed on some lip gloss and brushed her hair. She gives me a twirl. "Not bad, huh? After all that travel."

"You look great."

She checks her phone. "I have to scoot." Her eyes shift between us. "You two all set for your day?" We nod. As I walk with her to the door, she whirls around, giving me a fierce hug. "Text if you need anything, okay?" She pulls back, her eyes searching my face.

"Wow, just going out for the day, Rye. Not to the moon."

She skips down the steps, her whole body light and eager, and heads off in the direction of her new school. My chest tightens. Maybe this is what my parents felt when they watched me disappear inside my kindergarten classroom for the first time all those years ago. Funny how life has a few of these visible moments, where you can actually see someone turn a corner.

Iceland's entire population is roughly 325,000 people, with about two-thirds living in Reykjavík, making it the most sparsely populated country in Europe. London's population is over 8.6 million and climbing. The contrast between these stats hits me as Neel and I step out of the cab onto the sidewalk in front of Westminster Abbey at noon on this overcast Monday. Neel pays the driver, grumbling at the cost. He only agreed because I wanted to ride in one of London's famous black taxis. "They're so cute!" I protested when he said he almost never takes them. "They bloody well better be." But he'd agreed, telling me to enjoy the ride because from here on out we'd take the Tube.

The cacophony of busy London whirls around me, and I simmer with excitement. I can't believe I'm in London. Around me, taxis, cars, and buses zoom by; people in sharp business attire hurry past, shouting into their phones; tourists crowd the street, taking pictures. I take a minute to remind myself to breathe it all in, to let the whir of the city settle on my skin like rain. When it's clear I'm taking too long on the soaking-it-all-in front, Neel tugs me out of the direct sidewalk traffic and pulls me toward Westminster's wide walkway. "Clue Number One." He points up at the famous Abbey. "Your namesake."

"Except no *e* in my version." I unfold Riya's instructions, the title in purple ink:

Seven Wonders of
London Scavenger Hunt!

(so you can start to fall in love like I did)

In the letter, she explains that each of the seven smaller white envelopes inside are titled with one of the Seven Ancient Wonders and include a clue to link them to a London "point of historical awesomeness." I read the first clue again: "This place provides the resting Corner for the mind that told Tales: the Miller, the Wife of Bath, and the Knight alike." I glance up at Neel. "Chaucer."

He nods. "Right. He's buried in Poets' Corner. But what does that have to do with the Mausoleum at Halicarnassus?" He peers at the title Riya has given Clue #1.

"It held the ashes of Mausolus. And this place holds Chaucer – connections, Neel. Connections. That's history!" I head toward the entrance.

He trots to catch up with me. "Okay, but what exactly are we doing with these clues?"

I turn. "Drinking in the wonders! And taking a picture to prove it." I hold up Clue #1. "With Riya's suggested silly face."

"But why?" He stops, tucking his hands into his pants pockets. His face is expectant, curious, and he flashes a sheepish smile when I pause at his incessant questioning. In that moment, I realize how much I will miss him when I leave on Thursday. In a way that will feel like a missing tooth. It hits me that the next few days will be like wiggling that tooth until it comes out: exhilarating, and with a constant underscore of ache.

I take a few steps toward him. "Listen, if we're going to hang out, you have to understand that we never need a reason to take a suggested silly face picture. It's a reason in and of itself. It brings history alive." I show him the envelope. "Riya clearly understands this."

"Right." His grin sends a tingling rush through me. "I don't know what I was thinking even asking."

"You are forgiven."

An hour later, we have our picture in front of Poets' Corner (overly serious poet faces) and Clue #2, Big Ben, which I learned is the name of the actual bell itself and not the tower (wide, bell-worthy faces). Riya linked Big Ben to the Great Pyramid of Giza because it's a "recognizable landmark even if you're not a history nerd." For Clue #3, she included one-way tickets for a river cruise on the Thames and linked it to the Lighthouse of Alexandria. "Tower Bridge," Neel says, inspecting the tickets while waiting for the light to change so we can cross the street to Westminster Pier.

"Nice touch," I say, "since they both sit out on the edge of the water." We locate our boat and join the queue for the next available departure.

Aboard, Neel finds us seats on the top level and motions for me to take the one closest to the railing. As we wait for the rest of the passengers to find their seats, I study the gray rolling Thames, my eyes scanning the stone buildings along the London riverside. My brain is like a ticker tape. Shakespeare walked along this river. Winston Churchill walked along this river. Virginia Woolf walked along this river. I feel Neel watching me. "What?"

He tugs one of my braids. "Nothing. I'm having fun, actually."

"Don't hurt yourself." I let my hand fall next to his on the plastic seat, keeping my eyes on the water.

He twines his fingers through mine until we're holding hands, and there it is again. That happy ache of my wobbly tooth heart. "Always a possibility." The way he says it makes me think he might have the feeling, too, or some version of it.

The boat starts moving. Max, our river guide, is the canned sort of funny you get from the guides on Disneyland's Jungle Cruise. I love the guides on the Jungle Cruise, so this works out for me. Plus, he has a British accent, so double win. I laugh at all his jokes. All of them. And he reads me as a receptive audience (or maybe thinks I'm a bit of an idiot); either way, he starts to wink at me a lot during his talk. As we travel down the river, he points out the Houses of Parliament, the Abbey, and the London Eye, each paired with a joke that's even more fun because of his accent. We pass under Waterloo Bridge, known as the Ladies Bridge, because, as Max tells us, it was built entirely by a female workforce during World War II. It's the only bridge in London to come in under time and under budget. "Well done, London girls," Max drawls into his mic.

"Probably the twelfth time he's said that today," Neel whispers. "And he's playing up that accent, by the way." I shush him. Don't dis the British Jungle Cruise.

Max points out the Shard, the tall glass skyscraper, shooting like a blade into the sky. "The Tower of London has nothing on this Tower of Power and Riches. Don't look too closely, they might charge you." I laugh, but Neel lets out a bored groan.

"Jealous?" I tease.

"Annoyed."

I take his picture and text Riya, captioning it: neel's annoyed face.

She texts right back: tell him you will force him to go on the eye during high tourist time if he doesn't behave!

I show Neel. "Behave yourself. Or heights. Crowded ones." He disappears downstairs to get us some snacks.

While he's gone, Max points out Shakespeare's Globe and a pirate ship that was used in *Pirates of the Caribbean*. Neel returns and hands me a bag of potato chips. "Crisps?" he offers, just as Tower Bridge and the Tower of London come into view. I sit up, gaping at the Tower. I'm not always a gore girl. I mean, I like a good dungeon story as much as the next history nerd, but I don't usually saturate myself with all the gory history details. History = horrid bloodshed. Got it. Except sometimes the stories are just too interesting and political to pass up, and the Tower of

London fascinates me. Lots of historical blood soaking into that ground.

I munch my chips. "Worcester Sauce flavor?" I study the bag. "Surprisingly delicious."

"You should try the prawn cocktail crisps."

"Maybe next time." The Tower grows closer. "I know it had creepy torture stuff, but is it true that the Tower of London had a zoo?" I ask Neel.

"Not exactly a zoo. More a menagerie. Dating back to the thirteenth century. It was a sign of wealth and power for the kings." He frowns. "Sad, actually, though, for the animals. Some were made to fight."

I nudge him. "Well, hello, Tour Guide Neel."

"Took enough tours there as a lad." He brightens. "Oh, this is a – what do you and Riya call them. History bits?"

"History tidbits," I correct.

"Here's a history tidbit I remember from one of my tours. Also in the mid-thirteenth century, the King of Norway gave King Henry III a polar bear, which he called a 'white bear,' and it was tethered to a long lead and allowed to fish and swim in the Thames."

"No way. Poor bear."

"A polar bear in the Thames. Can you imagine?"

I watch the Tower grow closer. "Historically, men – and yes, mostly it's been men," I insist when he starts to interrupt, "have made brutal, stupid choices in the name of power. Take the Lighthouse of Alexandria. Mostly built with slave labor. Sometimes, studying history makes me ashamed to be a person."

Neel gives my hand a squeeze. "It's why we study it, right? To not repeat it."

"How's that working out for us?"

He considers this for a moment. "I like to think we're improving, even if it's in slow increments." Neel settles against the back of the bench seat we're sharing and puts his arm around me, starting into a story about the lions that were moved to the London zoo in the 1800s. I settle into his arm. It's a good story, but I'm not really listening. My ears are buzzing with the weight and heat of his arm, with his nearness, and I wish everything – history, the future – could simply disappear into the tumbling gray waters of the Thames.

It's late afternoon by the time we exit the Tube at Leicester Square Station. We're on Clue #5, having snapped our "Temple of Artemis" photo outside of St. Paul's for Clue #4 (reverent, angelic faces). During our too-quick tour of the Tower of London, Neel kept checking his watch as I lingered over the crown jewels or spent too long reading a plaque in the Armouries. "She's given you a whirlwind task today, I'm afraid," he said apologetically when I grumbled about having to leave. "We still have four more clues." Outside, he added, "I guess you'll have to come back for a proper visit next time."

I tried to play it cool in the wake of his invitation when I said, "I just might do that," but I'm pretty sure he saw the spark of hopeful smile I tried to hide from him.

Now we stroll toward Leicester Square Gardens to find the statue of Shakespeare. Our clue: "While not the King of the Gods, like our pal Zeus, this man is often considered the King of the English Stage, while we are 'merely players.' Find his statue in Leicester Square Gardens."

Up ahead, I see a leafy green area. "I think this is a cool tie-in: Shakespeare and the Zeus statue."

"How so?"

"The Olympics were first played at Zeus's temple. I think the tie-in is that the Olympics are a sort of spectacle, a show, like Shakespeare's plays."

Neel considers this, nodding. "I think it's brilliant how much you love the wonders."

I flush at his compliment. "Maybe, but it's not like I can control it. It's just what I love. You wouldn't be as impressed if I was hardwired to love collecting stuffed penguins."

"Don't be so sure about that. The penguin is a majestic creature." The sky above us shifts between gray clouds and patches of blue sky. It sends shadows drifting across his face as he walks.

I step out of the way of a man pushing a bicycle. "Don't forget we're also hardwired to dislike things."

"Name something you dislike."

"Mushrooms."

"No!" he cries, taking an exaggerated step away from me.

I tug him back by his sleeve. "Sorry, but they are disgusting, weedy little things, and I loathe them."

"Right. I guess it's just something we'll have to work through." He stops in the middle of the path and pulls me into him for a kiss, the press of his mouth turning my limbs light and fluttery. I've heard that everything disappears during a staggering kiss, but it's the opposite for me with Neel – everything intensifies, rendering the world sharp and clear. I'm acutely aware of the breeze on my neck, the filtered light through the trees, the splash of the fountain ahead of us, the shuffle of people walking past us.

I just don't care about any of it.

In the gardens, we find Shakespeare, stopping in front of the fountain with his stone likeness as its centerpiece. He appears slightly bored, leaning casually on a column, as if saying, *Yep, I write plays and stuff. Whatevs.* He's pointing to a stone sheet of paper that reads: *There is no darkness but ignorance.* "Riya wants a theatrical shot for this one." I point at the scroll the same way Shakespeare does. "Deep thoughts with Shakespeare!" Neel takes a picture, and then I wave him over. "Now one with both of us. Shakespeare selfie!" He leans in close to me for the shot.

While I check my phone to make sure the picture came out okay, Neel studies the splashing water. After a moment, he says, "For me, it started with numbers."

"What did?"

"Like you were saying earlier, about things we can't help loving. For me, it was maths. And that morphed into wondering about all the stuff we use as humans, all the resources and supplies that need calculating and figuring. So I'm studying economics, which, as it turns out, most people find terrifically boring."

"You're not boring to me." Maybe close proximity to fountains makes one prone to gushing?

I can't see a blush through his dark skin, but I can feel it, the heat from him at my words. He leans his shoulder into mine. "Thanks. I did not expect the trip to turn out this way."

"I know." My stomach twists. What am I doing?

When Riya said to go on a scavenger hunt so I can fall in love, I'm pretty sure she meant with London and not her cousin. Ugh. *Fall in love.* What a stupid expression. That's not what's happening. None of this feels like falling. It feels like panicking. Is there a difference? Maybe falling in love feels like room-closing-in-on-me panic? I wouldn't know. I've never felt like this before. Not with my other crushes. Probably because they never kissed me in London. Never talked to me about real things. Shakespeare lounges in front of us, leans so casually there with his fancy beard. Mr. Love himself. Parting is such sweet sorrow and all that.

Shut up, Shakespeare.

I turn abruptly, and it catches Neel off guard. "Well, I guess we should go find Clue Number Six. Hanging Gardens of Babylon. Must be a garden. Where's the nearest garden? I mean, other than this one. Let's read the clue." My hands shake as I open the envelope.

Neel narrows his eyes at my mood swing. "You okay?"

I swallow hard. How many times a day does someone ask this question and get a watered-down version or all-out lie for an answer? Are you okay? Yep. Sure. Fine. What if we answered someone honestly? What if right now I said, Actually, Neel, speaking of gardens, I seem to have grown some strange, messy feelings for you in the past couple of weeks that do not fit into my life right now, and you kissing me and being interested in what I care about isn't helping matters. This is confusing, not just geographically, but also because of my best friend, who happens to be your cousin, because she and I aren't in the best place right now. And even if she sent us out together today, she was pretty mad the other night when she caught us kissing. There was yelling. So, maybe this is actually a terrible idea. Except I really, really like the kissing.

What if I just said all that?

Instead, though, like legions of cowards before me, I say, "Totally fine," and read him the next clue.

Later, as we walk along the Serpentine, the water lit with a sudden emergence of sunlight, Neel explains that the bridge we're about to arrive at separates the Serpentine part of the lake in Hyde Park with what's known as the Long Water in Kensington Gardens, and Clue #6 links the Hanging Gardens of Babylon to Kensington Gardens. Eventually, we turn left and head into the heart of the gardens, with their rectangular dark-watered pools, potted plants, and meticulously manicured rows of flowers and shrubs. My heart stills. Something about a garden, the purposeful part of it, always relaxes me. No wonder they have been gifted to royalty and tended for centuries, these places crafted solely for beauty and contemplation.

"Did I say something wrong?" Neel looks concerned. "You've gone quiet all of a sudden."

Around us, people stroll through the park, sprawl on the grass, read on benches. I would actually live right here, in this park, like a hobbit, if they'd let me. "What does Tour Guide Neel know about Kensington Gardens?"

He knows I'm avoiding the question, but doesn't press. "Let's see. The Kensington Gardens were once private property of the palace—"

"Buckingham Palace?"

He shoots me an amused look. "Kensington Palace."

"You guys have a lot of palaces; it's hard to keep them all straight."

"Yes, are you going to be interrupting the tour this whole time, or shall I continue?" I give him my best listening face, and we wander in a loop, the light in the park dimming as the clouds roll back across the sky. Neel expounds on the Royal Parks and points out some of his favorite spots. I almost die of excitement because I swear I spot Daniel Radcliffe working out with a personal trainer, but Neel assures me it's just a guy who looks vaguely like shaggy-haired Daniel in the fourth Harry Potter movie, probably cross-training with a schoolmate, and not the famous movie star and a lucky trainer. We pass them up close and Neel's right. "He's about ten years too young, that lad." Neel chuckles at my disappointed look, and we wind back toward the Long Water, stopping to take our photo (dreamy garden faces) next to an especially vibrant, multicolored bank of flowers.

"Okay, Clue Number Seven." I open the envelope labeled "Colossus of Rhodes," but it's empty. I hold it out to Neel. "There's no clue."

He hesitates. "Right. About that."

"You don't want to dis Helios. He's the god of the sun. London's got enough cloud cover."

"Let's keep walking." As we continue along the lake, Neel explains to me that Riya removed the seventh clue back in Iceland. That clue was the one that would lead me to her new school. A statue in a niche of the building bears a resemblance to the Colossus of Rhodes's Helios.

"It's actually where she got the idea for the scavenger hunt in the first place."

I stop. "So, she was going to take me on this fun historical hunt all over London, butter me up, and then say, *Surprise, here's my new school?*"

Neel looks almost sick to his stomach now. "Yeah, I guess that was the basic plan."

Tears threaten my lashes. "Oh."

He takes a step toward me. "I'm sorry, Abby."

But he's misinterpreted the tears. I'm not sad or frustrated or mad. Riya knew it would be impossible to tell me this news, knew that no matter the packaging, it would be another blow in a year full of them. So she did the only thing she could think of: She created a day of history-geek fun tailored to me to ease the inevitable shock.

Friendship has a funny way of sneaking up on you.

"I'm fine," I insist when Neel moves in to hug me. And this time, I'm not lying.

Riya

The focus of our last two days in London must be *fun*.

History is Abby's great love, and theater is my new great love, so we need some of each. But mostly, after the way everything's gone down, I want to burn some fun memories into Abby's brain. So I organize two unbelievable days. Yesterday, we geeked out at the Harry Potter studio tour and then saw *Matilda* at the Cambridge Theatre. When we emerged into the glittering lights of the West End after the show last night, I couldn't help gushing to Abby about my orientation at school, about how excited I am to move here in less than two months. She curled her hand through mine and said, "I would be, too. Look at this place."

This morning, we soaked in some historical faces at the National Portrait Gallery, went shopping on Oxford Street, and finally, we find ourselves now gawking at the Rosetta Stone in the British Museum late on our last afternoon together. Abby is about to lose it in front of its massive historical splendor. She turns to me, her eyes bulging. "I mean, do you know what this thing did? Do you know its impact? I'm freaking out right now. I'm standing right in front of it! I could touch it. I mean, I wouldn't—" She glances nervously at the guard. "And it's behind glass, but I could, you know, because it's right here!"

The guard can't help but grin at her enthusiasm.

"Right. It's like Siri for hieroglyphics. Rosetta Stone," I pretend to ask the jagged block of rock inside the glass, "what is the hieroglyphic for 'Where is the nearest vintage shop?'"

Abby pinches her lips together so tight they turn white at the edges. Glancing apologetically at the guard, she unfolds the glossy British Museum map. "You're tormenting me on purpose."

I unwrap a piece of mint gum and pop it in my mouth. "I'm *teasing* you on purpose."

She fake reads the map. "Because I'm being overly dramatic about the Rosetta Stone?"

"Yes. And I have history overload and want to go find some cute shoes."

Snapping the map closed, she motions me to the next room, muttering, "You should be *more* excited about the Rosetta Stone," but her mouth twitches with a smile, giving her away. As a truce, I promise her that forever and ever I will be more excited about the Rosetta Stone. I will throw small dinner parties for it and make sure to serve its favorite kind of tea and biscuits, because it's been here a long time and has picked up all sorts of British habits. "I'm holding you to that," she tells me as we make our way into a room with carved stone panels. "And so is the Stone."

"Deal," I assure her. "But for the record, I'm a little disappointed it couldn't deliver on the shopping question."

That night, we pack our things, preparing for our trip to Heathrow tomorrow morning, where we'll meet my parents and head back to California. We sort through most of our bags, but finally need a packing break, so I take Abby up to the roof of the building to a wrought-iron bench overlooking the city. Lights glow through a low-hanging fog and the scent of rain hangs in the air. I spread out a towel along the damp bench and cover us with a soft cashmere blanket Neel said we could use.

"Wow," Abby breathes. "This is amazing. It's weird to think this is where Neel grew up, you know?"

I snuggle into the blanket, nudging Abby to do the same. "So tell me more about your day with Neel. I know you loved the scavenger hunt, but..."

"That was fantastic, Rye – I loved it. It was so *me*."

Warmth floods me. Even if things didn't work out the way I planned, I still think it would have been the best way to give her the news. But she knows that's not what I'm asking. When I pressed her for details the night they got back, she'd been evasive about Neel then, too, encased in full Abby Armor. But I push again anyway. "I meant with Neel."

She smiles awkwardly at me. "How much do you want to know? He's your cousin."

"He's a good guy," I tell her, meaning it. For all of our cousin stuff, I know Neel would never hurt Abby. "Was there more kissing?"

She hides under the blanket. "Yes."

"Will there be more kissing in the future?"

She peeks out from under the blanket. "I don't think so."

"What? Why not?"

She grows quiet, watching the fog curl over the buildings. "We just live too far away, Rye. It wouldn't work. It doesn't make sense to try to make anything out of it."

There she goes, tripping over her own practical self again. "Things don't have to make sense to work," I say. "Look at us. We don't make the most sense, either. We're so different. Always have been."

She considers this. "That's true."

I lean my head against her shoulder. "I think being with someone different, someone unexpected, lets you see the world with more than one set of eyes. That's the best part of it. But only if they love you for you. Not if they try to change you."

"Even if that person is super boring?" Abby's voice is 100 percent joke, though.

"You're only boring if you're bored. That was stupid of me to say. You could live in PJs and never leave the house. I'd still love you."

"Thanks, Rye." She sighs. "But I would definitely leave the house for this view. I mean, I know Neel has height issues, but his family must come up here all the time."

"Not exactly." I sit up and give her what I hope is a winning smile. "It technically belongs to their upstairs neighbors."

"Riya!"

"What? Neel said they're in Greece."

"So they're fine with his family using it while they're gone?"

"Not exactly."

"Great. I'm going to get arrested on my last night in London," she mumbles, looking around as if she expects the British Intelligence agents to bust through the roof door.

"Relax. You're not going to be arrested for sitting on someone's bench. Especially when they're in Greece. Just enjoy this, okay? Don't be such an Abby right now."

"This is the world through my eyes, babe. You're welcome." She tugs the blanket closer. Of course, a siren chooses this moment somewhere on the streets below to blare out.

I grab her arm. "Maybe that's MI6 coming to throw you in the Tower of London!" She gives me a playful shove but doesn't fully relax until the siren disappears into the night. Settling into the back of the bench, I inhale the wet air. Throughout our lives, Abby and I have sat together like this, curled on a couch in front of countless movies, on slabs of granite by our green river, on mountain trails, on weathered beach logs. No matter where we go, I know this will not be our last view.

Maybe she's reading my mind. "Seriously, though, this trip has been amazing. Riya, thank you. You've always been the one who can just sit with me like this and who I feel like I can say anything to." She pauses, chewing her lip. "I'm going to miss you in Yuba Ridge."

I take her hand beneath the blanket. "I need to tell you something." She looks at me sharply, and I hurry to explain. "It's not another bomb, I promise. I think you mostly know this already, but I'm not sure I've ever really said it." Abby's breathing stills as she waits for me to continue. "Okay, here it goes. I didn't just finish high school in Berlin because of the opportunity in London." I swallow over a hard lump in my throat. "Abby, I loved growing up in Yuba Ridge. But if I didn't get out of there, I was going to end up hating it. You were one of the only good things left for me there."

She stiffens. "How can you say that?"

I fidget on the bench, trying to get comfortable. "I felt like I was losing my mind there. It was always the same – the same school day, and then the weekends with the parties with the same people talking about the same things and judging each other over their clichéd red party cups."

"So don't go to those parties—" she interrupts.

"I *like* parties, ones where interesting people talk about things I care about and aren't just getting drunk and hooking up and trying to act cool. People think it makes them wild and edgy to do all that stuff, but speaking of boring, I was bored out of my head."

Abby frowns. "I don't think it makes them cool; I just don't care if they're doing it. I don't go. *They* probably don't think they're boring. Maybe they like their red cups."

"I know. You're better at that than I am. Always have been." She has never truly understood that even if I didn't like to hang out with certain people or go to their parties, I still had an underlying need to be a part of the place around me. Abby has always reveled in her distance from other people. "You took the good parts of Yuba Ridge and the rest didn't matter. I struggle with that. Always will."

Abby watches a plane blinking across the dark sky. "Remember sophomore year when we had to do that About Me project in English?"

I groan. Every year the sophomores at Yuba Ridge have to do a project where we take a bunch of personality tests and study careers that the tests generate for us. "My possible career list was so random I figured there must have been a system glitch or something."

Abby fiddles with the edge of the blanket. "Yeah, but yours showed that you're consistently good with people, that you're flexible and" – she hesitates – "what did they call it? Interpersonal?"

I roll my eyes. "That's the catchall personality for the person who talks too much in class." Secretly, though, I liked being dubbed flexible, good with people, able to adapt, even if it suggested I pursue a career in "human services," which sounds made up.

The fog shifts across the building tops, glowing purple at its edges. Abby takes a moment to watch it settle before she says, "Remember, though, it said you were an extrovert and I'm an introvert."

Now that she mentions it, I remember it really bothered Abby for a few days after we took those tests. "Introvert in a good way, not in a weird way," I remind her. "Just that you recharge alone and extroverts recharge with other people. It doesn't mean you want to live in your basement like a troll person and never come out."

She picks lint from the blanket and rolls it between her fingers. "Thing is, though, it's more socially acceptable to be an extrovert."

"Yeah, but you're an introvert, so you think those people are idiots."

Her eyes gloss with tears. "Last year, I just wanted the idiots to invite me to a few things. And no one did.

I haven't been very good at making friends this year. Or ever, really. I always had you for that."

I give her a nudge with my shoulder. "You can invite them, too. You think I sat around and waited for people to ask me to things? I asked them. I called them. You can't wait for other people to do things for you. Not if you want them to actually get done." Of course, even as I'm telling her this, I know that it was Kiara who invited me to that first meeting at the Collective. It was Kiara who made that happen for me. Why is it always easier to be brave on behalf of other people?

Abby frowns. "I think the biggest issue is that for years, I would just slip into whatever you were doing or I would do stuff by myself. And the last couple of years, I spent so much time working at the Blue Market that I could stay busy. And you always organized enough social stuff for me. It's like I didn't grow any of the muscles for that, which isn't your fault. I let you. But then last year, when I suddenly needed those muscles..."

"And then your parents—" I squeeze her hand. "I should have come home to be with you when it happened."

She squeezes back. "No, see – that's scorekeeping. And I don't want to do that anymore because I already wrecked one year doing that. I could have told you I needed you. I should have tried harder to find other people. You're living your own life. I have to learn how to not need you so much." Her words prick like needles along my body.

Before I can say anything, she drops her face into her hands. "I hate feeling like this. And people keep saying *it will get better.* Or *you have to be strong.* Or *time heals.* It's so irritating!"

I put my arm around her, knowing I've been guilty of a few of those statements. "Bumper sticker philosophy. Sounds great in theory. Rarely works on a deeper level. Sometimes, people, including me, don't know the right thing to say."

She starts to cry. "See – I needed you there to say stuff like that! I miss that! Ugh, I just want to stop being so sad about everything, stop feeling like I'm missing a limb because you're not five minutes away. Emo is not a good color on me."

I want Abby to need me, want her to know I'm her best friend, but I also know things are changing for us. We can't always be there for each other like we were as kids. It's not possible. But that doesn't have to be bad. "Here's a thought: Maybe right now, right here on this bench, we decide this change looks good on us."

"What?" She uses an edge of the blanket to wipe her face. "Sometimes, I think archaeologists need to find whatever Rosetta Stone works on translating you."

I try to sort my swirling thoughts. "Stay with me, I think I'm onto something here." The blanket falls away from my shoulders as I turn to her. "I know we won't ever have what we had before. It's not realistic, but it's not sad."

"It's not?"

"No. We've heard about some true tragedies on this trip – this isn't one of them. Because we have us. We're both going on with our lives, and we're going to do the things we're meant to do. But the *us* part? That stays. We love each other. That's never going to end. It just changes shape." Her comment about the Rosetta Stone triggers something. "It's like your wonders. What do archaeologists find when they know a building used to be somewhere?"

"The foundation."

"That's us."

A watery smile moves across her face. She's hearing me, even if she's not admitting it. "Ruins?"

I pretend to strangle her. "No! The foundation! The part that will always be there." The fog gets thicker, and soon we can't see the lights anymore, just a thick gray glow. Clever London fog getting all metaphorical on us. In acting class, Niles taught me to say yes to what the scene presents for me. Improvise, and say yes. Even when I can't see where something is heading, shine a light there. I can do that now, here, so I tell her, "Besides, not all of your wonders were lost, or ended up in ruins. The Great Pyramid is still standing, right?" She nods. "Then I'm your Giza Pyramid. You're stuck with me."

Abby

Riya sleeps on the air mattress next to me, snoring into her pillow, her hair its usual black tangle. I can't get comfortable, squinting into the dark of the den, too aware of an unseen ticking clock hiding somewhere. Butterflies for the flight tomorrow circle my insides like tiny vultures in training. Riya's coming home to Yuba Ridge before she moves to London, and I keep wondering if we'll have a temporary return to our former selves, or if the rest of the summer will be stained with her impending exit. I try to shake the worry from my head. She said we have to decide this change looks good on us. Like most things, it seems easier said than done. But I guess that's why growing up doesn't happen all at once. It's a practice. Like yoga. Or memorizing vocabulary words.

Or saying good-bye.

A light in the kitchen snaps on, and I slide out of bed in my T-shirt and sweats, throwing on the Edinburgh sweatshirt I plan to wear on the plane tomorrow.

I find Neel in his pajamas in the kitchen, dropping a tea bag into a blue ceramic mug. He starts when he notices me. "Oh, hey. Can't sleep?" I shake my head. "Tea?" The British solution to almost anything.

"That'd be great." I slide onto one of the black leather barstools at the kitchen island. He moves around the sand-toned kitchen, collecting another mug, another peppermint tea bag, checking the kettle. I allow myself one delusional moment of fantasy where I imagine this as our apartment, our life, and this night ritual is something we do on a regular basis. Then I toss the fantasy aside. Why torture myself?

"Thank you," I say to his back.

He waves me away. "I was already making some."

"Not just for the tea."

He turns from where he stands over the kettle, his face veiled. "Right. Should we, um, discuss, er—"

I motion to where the kettle starts to steam, and he hurries to catch it before the whistle wakes Riya. "Let's not try to figure this out, okay? Not tonight."

He pours hot water into our mugs, and the room fills with peppermint and steam. He sets one mug in front of me and runs his hands through his hair. "I'm just not sure—" he starts.

"Neel." I stop him. "Let's just leave it at a great trip. I live in California. You live in England." Stupid geography.

"Not logistically ideal," he agrees, blowing across the surface of his tea, and the motion strikes me as old and comfortable. Like a favorite pair of shoes. An adorable pair. That I want to make out with. Okay, get a grip. I take a tentative taste of my tea, a ribbon of pain shooting through me that has nothing to do with how hot it is.

Tonight's theme seems to be realism and embracing change, so I say to him, "It's okay. We had a great time."

"Yes, you could say that." He sets down his mug. "And you and Riya?"

"We're figuring it out." I sip my tea, adding, "I'm glad you turned out to be so much more than her annoying cousin." He smiles and I feel it across the island, like fingertips brushing my face.

Outside, it's raining, and it spots the windows with dark drops of water. Look at me: sitting in a Bloomsbury kitchen in London, composed, adult. Even if I might throw up at any moment, I secretly congratulate myself about how mature I'm being right now. Seriously, some adult organization that specializes in awarding moments of maturity should give me a medal because what I really want to do is fling my arms around his neck and beg him to move to California, screaming, *No fair, London! You don't get to have EVERYONE!* Which would be awkward. For both of us. So I put on my best accepting-my-lot-in-life face, peer over my tea mug, and ask, "We'll stay in touch, right?"

"Right, of course." He nods, his hair mussed, his charcoal LSE T-shirt frayed at the neck. "Yes, quite right. That's best, really." He keeps nodding harder until his whole body seems to be shaking, and his tea spills, scalding his hand. "Bollocks!" He clunks the mug down on the stone counter, turning to run his hand under the cool water of the tap. I scramble out of the chair, coming alongside him at the sink to check on it. He looks sideways at me, his dark eyes rueful. "Sorry."

I put my hand on his back, feeling the ridge of his spine beneath my fingers. Can you miss someone's spine? "What happened?"

He scowls at his hand, watching the water spill over it into the sink, his shoulders slumping, but he winds his other arm around my neck and pulls me close, kissing my forehead, my eyelids, the tips of my ears. "Bloody logistics happened," he says into my hair.

the seventh wonder

YUBA RIDGE, CALIFORNIA

Riya

"Do you want to take this? London can be freezing, even in the fall." Mom holds up the ancient orange Patagonia down jacket I've had since eighth grade. It's worn and covered in glossy spots where Dad patched holes so the feathers would stop poking out. It feels like wearing a favorite childhood blankie as a coat.

I hesitate. "It's pretty trashed. Might be time for a new one."

"Right." She holds it over a pile of tangled jeans, folded sweaters, sweatshirts, T-shirts, several pairs of shoes. "Salvation Army?"

"No – keep it. For when I'm home at Christmas."

She comes in to sit on the swivel chair, resting her arm on the almost empty desk. "I thought Abby was coming over?"

I fold a long black skirt into quarters. "She's working. Until seven."

Nodding, she picks up a framed photo of us as

kindergartners. It's Halloween, and I'm dressed as an exotic winter fairy with icy wings, a sparkly dress, and elaborate blue, white, and silver face paint. Abby wears a firefighter uniform. With a Viking hat. Even then, she always added a little history flair. I'm grinning straight at the camera. Abby's digging through her treat bag. I love that picture. Mom holds it out to me. "You should take this. You've always had a thing for costumes."

"Mom," I groan.

Smiling, she sets it back with all the others. I let my gaze trail over the other frames I've stared at a thousand times. Holidays. Vacations. Field trips. Eighth-grade graduation. A school dance photo Abby and I took freshman year together because our dates were being lame. My childhood, framed in eight neat photos. In the last few days, I've stripped the room bare, sending bags of clothes and toys to the Salvation Army and our local hospice, sorting photos and trinkets, carefully selecting the items that will make the trip with me to London. It's been obvious for weeks now, but somehow it suddenly hits me that I might never actually live in this room again. Might just be a visitor when I come for winter break, or for summers. Maybe just a week here and there. Swallowing thickly, I turn back to my open suitcase.

I try to hide a swift itch of tears, but I'm no match for Mom Radar. "The semester will go by in a flash, you'll see," she says to my back.

"I know."

I feel her hesitation before she asks, "Are you and Abby going to be okay?"

Now it's her turn to sense my hesitation, but I meet her concerned gaze. "We will be."

Over the river's rush, I hear Abby picking her way across the rocks behind me. She sits down next to me on our flat rock, wearing shorts and a pale blue polo shirt from her shift at the market. She hands me a white paper bag. "Twice-baked potatoes."

"What, seriously?" I peer into the bag. The Blue Market's deli has the best twice-baked potatoes I've ever eaten in my life. "But they only make these in the winter!"

"Dan made an exception."

I pull out two still-warm paper containers and hand one to Abby. "I've always liked that Dan."

"Yeah, you two are tight." She takes her container and the fork I hand her. Setting them down next to her, she kicks off her shoes, dipping her feet into the cool water at the far edge of the rock. "You all packed for tomorrow?"

"Pretty much." The twilight turns the river into an inky mirror, the horizon holding its last band of pale light. Above us, the sky grows dark, with only a few first winking stars. It is an ordinary summer night, one I've seen hundreds of times. Only tonight its beauty cuts invisible slivers into every inch of my skin. The last month here in Yuba Ridge has been filled with packing and planning, hanging out with Abby when she wasn't working, helping Mom get her garden back together. Each day, though, felt like air, a translucent placeholder until London. Now I'm leaving tomorrow. And it seems too abrupt.

"Are you excited?" Abby opens her container, mashing some of the potato with her fork before she takes a bite.

I nod, my untouched potato warming my lap. "And scared."

She looks at me across our rock. "It'll be incredible. How can it not be? *You'll* be there." She motions to my lap with her fork, her mouth full. "You should eat that before it gets cold. Cold twice-baked potatoes suck."

I watch her chewing hers for a moment, then dig into my own.

Dang, that's a good potato.

She watches me, sees something shadowy move across my face. "Don't worry," she says. "I hear London likes its potatoes."

Abby

It is nearly seven in London. In an hour, Riya will step onto a lit stage for the first performance of her college life. And I'll be missing it. In fact, I'll be sitting in AP English trying to make sense of *King Lear*. Fathers and daughters. Apparently, it's not a new theme. But for now, I can at least make sure Riya knows I'm thinking of her before she goes on. And she'll be especially pleased that I'm about to use a favorite page from her playbook. I slide out of my desk. Everyone around me in Economics works on the group projects we're about to present. Mr. Song sits at his desk, sorting rubrics, looking up only when I'm practically leaning over him.

"I left the poster in my car. Can I go get it?"

Mr. Song is a cool teacher – young, uses hair product, wears designer jeans and brightly colored New Balances. He must have about ten pairs. But he also hasn't been teaching long enough to loosen up on most of his rules. "What's the rule about using the pass on Fridays?"

"No passes on Fridays."

"Yep."

"But, Mr. Song, I left our group's poster in my car. I don't want them to be affected because I made a mistake. Can I take a lowered grade and go get it?" I even try Riya's earnest smile, the one that says, *See, I know how to do the right thing. Personal accountability matters.*

It works, and moments later I'm pushing through the hallway doors and out into the crisp light of early October, my phone to my ear. I find a spot behind the high wall of the cafeteria, near the loading dock. School security never seems to make the effort to check back here. It's been the best place for calls to Riya this semester.

She picks up instantly. "The flowers are gorgeous!" She's already hyped up on preshow jitters. "Thanks for remembering."

"Break a leg. You know, I looked up the origin of that expression – some historians think it had to do with performing on a table-like stage so enthusiastically that a leg would break. Drama history tidbit."

"Fascinating. I'll make sure to tell my theater history professor he should fold that into his next lecture. Aren't you supposed to be in Econ?"

"I told Mr. Song I'm getting the poster from my car."

"You don't have a car."

"He doesn't know that."

"So. Proud."

"I should let you go," I tell her. "And I should get back to class."

"Totally."

"Riya?" My voice catches.

She hears it. "I miss you, too."

The next morning, Dad taps on my door. "You up?" Without waiting for me to emerge from under my mound of covers, he comes into the room with Henry on his heels.

I sit up, rubbing my eyes. Henry leaps up next to me, curling alongside my legs, leaning in so I can pet his head. "What time is it?"

"Just after ten." Dad hovers in the doorway. He needs a haircut. I've reminded him twice this week. "How'd Riya's show go last night?"

Yesterday, she texted: amazing! amazing! amazing!

I motion for Dad to come see it. He grins. "So, it went okay?"

"I think it did."

He sits down on the bed next to Henry, giving him a scratch behind his ears. "Seems like she's loving it."

"She is."

He smiles sympathetically, knowing I still have to practice being brave about Riya's new life in London. He gets that I haven't quite found the tricky balance between staying in her life and moving on into our separate futures. I'm trying, though, even as fragments of jealousy remain like pieces of broken mirror inside me. A few weeks ago on a hike, I talked to Dad about them, and he confessed he knows the feeling, knows how we have to actively keep brushing those pieces away so they don't lodge themselves inside us.

Most days, I'm genuinely happy for Riya.

Dad crosses his arms, watching me settle back on the bed. "You working at the museum today?"

I nod. "Twelve to five." When school started, I cut back on my shifts at the Blue Market and started volunteering at one of our local museums, just two rooms in a downtown storefront, but the owner, Leslic, has an infectious passion for local history. I'm there Tuesdays after school and most Saturdays. Leslie even let me curate an exhibit this fall called "The Wonders of the Gold Rush" that got written up in a Sacramento tourist magazine. I bought two copies and sent one to Riya, who took a picture and reminded me to post it on my Instagram. I'm pretty sure I'm the only person on social media who seems to lose more followers than she gains in any sort of consistent way, but I've managed to attract 168 people who seem to like history as much as I do. And that's kind of fun. Okay, I love it. They post great stuff. And I'm back in touch with our friend Ian Campos, who is a bit of a history geek himself.

Even Neel got himself an Instagram.

Dad stands and walks back to the door. "You need a lunch? I'll pack you one."

"No thanks. Mom's taking me to brunch before the museum."

"Glad to hear it. Come on, Gimpy," he says to Henry. "Let's take our little walk." Dad waits for the dog to limp past, and then closes the door behind him, but not before I notice his smile fade. Each day, I see the effort he puts in, see him trying to emerge from the pain of losing her, of letting go of our former life, but it's in slow motion, the way someone moves through waist-level snow. It's this way for both of us. It helps that we're partners in the struggle, our new lives like drastic haircuts we can't quite get used to but might end up looking good on us when they grow out a bit. He's glad I take the time to see Mom each week. She and I are picking slowly over the rocks in our way. It takes work and it's not linear. Some days I feel more forgiving than others. Some days I cry. Today, at least, there will be peach pancakes at Helene's, my favorite brunch place. Mom's, too. I even said she could bring Dr. Spits-A-Lot. And I manage to not call him that to his face. Baby steps.

Each day, I practice my new life.

I flip the covers back, studying the familiar walls of my room: the posters and pictures of the Seven Wonders of the Ancient World, the dozens of photos of me and Riya, the newest an eight-by-ten Neel took of us standing near Gullfoss in Iceland, laughing as we get caught in a sudden burst of spray. He sent it a couple of weeks ago.

My eyes fall on a photo Dad must have tacked to my bulletin board in the last few days. He took it in front of the Legion of Honor in San Francisco last weekend. I'm with Lucy, a junior with wild red hair and an odd sense of humor who just started a History Club at our school. So far we're the only two members. I haven't once seen her wear a pair of socks that actually match, but she's funny, smart, and obsessed with the Civil War. The Legion of Honor was our first field trip, and she made T-shirts that said *#historygeek*. We wore them proudly and have another trip planned next month to see a private exhibit of Civil War letters in Sacramento. I can't wait.

As my eyes trail over the crowded, ever-evolving bulletin board, I'm aware of having my own archaeological site hanging right in front of me. And if my study of history has taught me anything, it's that the world is full of mysteries, most of which don't have a singular answer. If you dig enough, though, when you care enough about finding what's under the rubble, you can unearth treasures, and if you're lucky, you let these wonders light your way forward, no matter how uncertain the future may seem.

An Author's Wonders

The First Wonder: This book would not be what it is without the unwavering love and support of Tanya Egan Gibson. She knows why. The same is true for my incredible agent Melissa Sarver White. I am lucky to have you in my corner. In fact, every author should havc an agency like Folio in their corner – with a special thanks to Molly Jaffa for all things foreign rights related. Speaking of foreign rights: I am deeply grateful to Walker UK and Australia for their support and enthusiasm for Abby and Riya's journey, with special thanks to Emily McDonnell, Gill Evans, Chloé Tartinville, and Anna Robinette.

The Second Wonder: Scholastic, as a whole, is a true wonder. Countless people there support and love my books – I am so grateful. I want to especially thank my editor Jody Corbett for her enthusiasm for this novel. Thanks also to David Levithan, for his continuous support, and for chiming in early on to encourage this book. Thanks to Yaffa Jaskoll for her gorgeous design. Also,

Brooke Shearouse, Anna Swenson, Ann Marie Wong, and the entire Sales department.

The Third Wonder: I tend to be a big-picture, global kind of thinker. So when I decided to write a book with seven distinct locations, six of them European, in under a year, I became increasingly grateful for Ari Rampy and Marija Kopic for their Berlin research and input, and Michelle and Alex Ogaidi for all the help with Florence. I am also deeply grateful for Google and the wondrous Internet, which led me to the informative sites of National Geographic, History, and the Travel Channel. Any errors are my own.

The Fourth Wonder: I am truly grateful to be surrounded by such an incredible writing community. My writing group – Kirsten Casey, Ann Keeling, and Jaime Williams – has been meeting twice a month for over ten years (and I'm hoping for at least ten more, ladies!). Thank you to Michael Bodie, Sands Hall, Jessica Taylor, Josh Weil, Mark Wiederanders, and Gary Wright, who always seem to say exactly what I need to hear.

The Fifth Wonder: This is fundamentally a book about friendship, and I couldn't write without the encouragement of my friends and family. There are too many to name here, but I'm particularly grateful to Archna Sharma, for her insight and for loaning me her beautiful name, and to Erin Dixon for an early read of this manuscript (and constant support). My daughter has been blessed to grow up with so many incredible families; this book wouldn't exist without you and your amazing kids whose antics, dreams, challenges, and hilarity inspire me daily.

The Sixth Wonder: Over the years, I have received a treasure trove of letters, emails, and comments from readers – both young and not-as-young. I am genuinely honored when a reader takes the time to read one of my books (a wonder in and of itself!), so thank you to all my readers. And to the ones who write to cheer me on – an extra thank-you. You have no idea how much your kind words mean to me. I cherish your letters and emails and comments.

The Seventh Wonder: Peter and Anabella, you are my dearest wonders.

About the Author

Kim Culbertson is the author of *The Possibility of Now*; *Catch a Falling Star*; *Instructions for a Broken Heart*, a Northern California Book Award winner; and *Songs for a Teenage Nomad*. She lives in Northern California with her husband and daughter, her favorite travel companions. For more about Kim, visit www.kimculbertson.com.